Reluctantly, Josh picked up the mysterious skull and stared directly into its empty sockets. His teeth started chattering; he began to shiver involuntarily. He wanted to pull his gaze away from the skull, but he was incapable of movement. Strange sounds filled his head—a sharp gusting wind, leaves being torn from their branches, twigs snapping, and the soft crunch of *something* running.

Cold perspiration poured down his forehead, blurring his vision. He had never known anything like what he now felt. Another sound began, and it seemed to emanate from the jaws of the skull he was clutching.

It was the unholy howl of death . . . .

Quarrel With The Moon

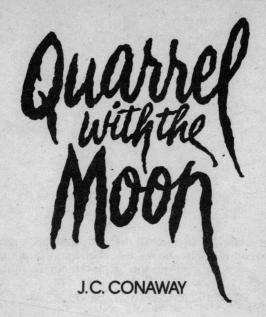

Quarrel with the Moon

J.C. CONAWAY

TOR

A TOM DOHERTY ASSOCIATES BOOK
Distributed by Pinnacle Books, New York

QUARREL WITH THE MOON

Copyright © 1982 by J. C. Conaway

A Tor Book

Published by Tom Doherty Associates
8-10 W. 36th St.
New York City, N.Y. 10018

First printing, April 1982

ISBN: 0-523-48033-4

Printed in the United States of America

Distributed by Pinnacle Books, 1430 Broadway,
New York, N.Y. 10018

*For Tom who does and for Megan who doesn't
and for Nick who has yet to find out.*

Quarrel with the Moon

"Like wolves, you undertake
A quarrel with the moon, and waste your anger."

—JAMES SHIRLEY

Prologue

November 9, 1949: The Appalachian Mountains of West Virginia

The moon at last made its appearance. Full and bloated, it drained the countryside of color, causing everything to turn a dull, tarnished silver. The rain which had swept through the mountains was over. In its wake the air smelled wet and rotten. It smelled of decay and dead things. The forest was quiet. No insect, bird or animal stirred. It was as if the entire world was holding its breath.

The silence was suddenly broken by an unearthly howl which sent animals scurrying through the wet undergrowth, and birds flying from their places of safety. A woman hurrying through the night responded to the cry and began to run faster. Her footfalls made soft, moist sounds, and the prints of her heavy shoes quickly filled up with water. The forest became dense as she reached an area known as "the Thicket." The trees lining the path grew close together, knitting themselves above it, ribbing the dark tunnel with their black boughs. The pathway, sodden with leaves, unwound before her like a wet ribbon.

A whitish fog came floating toward her, dampening both her clothes and skin. In the distance the lights of her daughter's cabin seemed to pulse. The terrible cry was repeated. It resounded throughout the mountains, then returned to its place of origin. Avarilla Chastain cursed herself for having left her daughter's side, but who knew that the baby would be three weeks early? She shouldn't have made the ten-mile trip to Jericho Falls. But what was she to do? It was her duty. Her brother's wife was due to be delivered. Avarilla, being the most trusted midwife in the entire country, certainly had to attend her sister-in-law in her time of need. It had been a tragic trip. Earlier that week Leoma had taken a fall. The baby became lodged in her side and had to be turned before it could be born. The poor woman suffered for a long time. It seemed like the baby wouldn't be born at all. And then when it finally came, it was dead. Not that Harley or Leoma held Avarilla responsible. They didn't. Still, it was the first time in her entire midwiving experience that she had lost a child.

Avarilla's face was creased with concern, not only for the child that had been born dead to her brother and sister-in-law, but now for her own daughter. It wasn't good for a woman to go into labor early. That always meant problems. And in Sissy's case there were other considerations. She was a frail young woman of seventeen who had the mentality of a twelve year old. Add to that the fact that Ben, her husband, had been dead for over a year. It was an enigma which troubled Avarilla. Sissy denied having intercourse with anyone but her husband and even refused to acknowledge her own pregnancy. But, as everyone said, Sissy was none too bright.

As she trudged forward, Avarilla turned the list of paternal suspects over in her mind. L.B. Cannon, Lester Brooks, Ketchy Addis. Not one of them would have shied away from marrying Sissy, for despite her strange, awkward ways, she was an oddly beautiful girl. A vapid, ephemeral being with preternaturally bright, empty, blue eyes and blond hair like spun meringue. Each of the men had denied being the father of Sissy's child and Avarilla believed them.

Avarilla Chastain was a muscular, handsome woman of thirty-eight years with a brisk, no-nonsense manner. Her face had a worn patina and her hair was prematurely gray. Her eyes, usually hard and uncompromising, were now full of anxiety. She stopped to catch her breath, leaned against a tree and clutched her heaving chest. If only the road hadn't been washed out, she wouldn't have had to take the long way around and would have been back in time. Upon arriving home Avarilla discovered a note pinned to her screen door. The note read: "Avvie, come quick to Sissy's place. Her water's broke an' she's went into labor—Jewell." At first Avarilla hadn't been worried. She knew that Jewell Runion had a nervous temperament and a tendency to overdramatize. But then she heard Sissy's piercing cry and she knew in her heart of hearts that the delivery was not going to be easy.

A bat, shrieking, flew by and spun away, silhouetted against the metallic sky like a tiny pterodactyl. Avarilla was jolted back to movement. When she reached the porch of Sissy's cabin she discovered Reuben hiding in the shadows. Reuben was twelve and Ben's younger brother. Since both parents were dead he had come to live with Ben and Sissy when they were married. And now that Ben was also dead, the boy, having no other place to go, stayed on.

"Reuben, what are you doin' there? You'll catch your death."

The boy screwed up his face. "Too noisy inside. I was thinkin' of takin' me an' Tooker," he indicated a small pup at his feet, "to the barn to bed down for the night."

Avarilla nodded in agreement. She never liked having children about when babies were being born. "Now that's a fine idea. You had your supper?" The boy nodded. "Bury yourself in the hay to keep warm. Then come back at dawn an' I'll make you a chompin' good breakfast."

Reuben lifted his plain face. His eyes were wet with unchecked tears. "That's not my brother's baby," he said in a broken voice. "I hope she dies." Then he bounded off the porch and ran toward the barn. The fat little pup followed. A sad sound escaped from Avarilla's lips before she went inside.

Two of the area's "granny women" were in attendance. Jewell Runion was a thin, dark-skinned woman, brittle and knobbly as a dead branch whose sap had run dry. In direct contrast was Faye Brooks, a small doughy woman with arms as fat as loaves of bread. Both looked up. Jewell spoke first in a high, staccato voice. "Thank heavens you're here, Avvie. Sissy's havin' a hard time of it. I took the precautionary of callin' in the preacher."

"She was like out of her mind with the pain," added Faye. "But we give her some sulphur an' wine of cordia. That'll work her female organs all together, an' the baby should be born without any trouble." Avarilla grunted. She did not hold with giving "concoctions" to expectant mothers. "We had to," Faye went on nervously. "She was just crazy." She bit down on her lip. "With the pain an' all."

"An' thrashin' about so much we had to tie her to the bed," said Jewell. "Not about to let her hurt the baby."

Avarilla tilted her head to one side and heard her daughter's soft but constant moans coming from the bedroom. "Where's the preacher?"

"Inside with Sissy," answered Jewell. "He's prayin' over her."

Avarilla pursed her lips and nodded. She shouldn't allow herself to become irritated with the granny women. They had come to her daughter's aid and had done what they believed was right. They had brought a laundry basket made of white oak splits for the baby and their bags containing scissors, thread, cloverine salve, "disinfect", clean white aprons and sheets. "When did her water break?" she asked in a softer voice.

" 'Bout eight tonight," said Faye. "You might as well have a nice cup of peppermint tea, Avvie. That baby ain't gonna come until midnight for sure."

"I'll look in first, then I'll join you," Avarilla replied.

Avarilla entered the bedroom. The air was stale with the sour smell of sweat, pain and frustration. Reverend Hooper, kneeling next to the four-poster bed, looked up. He smiled wearily and got to his feet. The preacher was a tall man in his middle years, broad shouldered and roughly handsome. His auburn hair lay about his head in soft, corrugated waves, and his eyes were as blue as cornflowers. His voice, usually gentle, sounded as if it had been strained through a coarse piece of material. "I was afeared you wouldn't make it back, Avvie. The roads an' all."

"I had to come the long way, Rev'rend. Bless you for comin'. How's Sissy?"

Without replying, the preacher stepped aside. Avarilla moved next to the bed.

Sissy's gauzy hair was as dank as the hair of a drowned woman and her skin, startlingly white and beaded with perspiration, looked artificial. Her stomach was swollen all out of proportion to her frail body. Strips of sheeting wound around her thin wrists and ankles were attached to the four posters of the bed and kept the girl immobile.

Avarilla touched her daughter's fevered forehead. "Sissy. Sissy, I'm here. Your ma's here." The young woman's lashes flickered open. Her eyes were glazed and shiny but when Avarilla bent to kiss her, Sissy managed an almost indiscernable smile. Avarilla loosened Sissy's restraints and brushed the matted hair from her face. Then she turned to the preacher and said, "Rev'rend, why don't you go an' have some tea? I'll keep watch."

"I'll do that, Avvie. Call if you need us."

Avarilla sat down next to the bed and held her daughter's bound hand.

Toward midnight the spasms were coming nearly every five minutes. Despite the drug, Sissy wailed in misery and helplessness. Avarilla untied Sissy's ankles. Then she and the other granny women held her knees so that Sissy couldn't kick her feet out. The baby began to appear. Sissy shrieked with agony as it made its entrance into the world. It was a boy but he wasn't breathing. Avarilla snatched him up and began to blow in his mouth. After several minutes, the infant's chest began heaving, and Avarilla knew he was all right. She cut the cord and tied it with a string. Meanwhile Jewell had scorched a piece of cloth by putting it on a shovel and holding it over the fire in the kitchen till the cloth was brown. Avarilla put that next to the baby's navel, cut a hole in it and pulled the navel cord through. The cloth was greased with mutton tallow and would remain on the child for five or six days till it disintegrated.

Sissy was still writhing in torment. The afterbirth had not yet come out. Avarilla laid the baby in the padded laundry basket and rushed to the foot of the bed. Sissy's body suddenly convulsed and a scream of terror rent the air. Another baby was being born. Sissy managed to tear one hand free and began clawing at her face. A froth of yellow spittle oozed from her lips.

"Make it come out!" Sissy begged. "Make it come out!"

The baby's head, covered with a mist of black hair, appeared. Avarilla's outstretched arms began shaking and she gave a start so violent that it seemed as if a hand with frozen fingers had squeezed her heart. "Lord God in Heaven!" she cried as the infant continued to emerge.

It was completely covered with the fine black hair and at the end of each of its grasping hands were thick, curved nails, now dripping with its own mother's blood. Jewell and Faye fell to their knees and began praying to fight the bile rising in their throat. Avarilla, her mind numbed with shock, nonetheless did what had to be done. Automatically she severed the umbilical cord and put the greased cloth into place. She stood holding the writhing infant, not knowing what to do with it.

Sissy raised her head and when she saw what had come out of her body she began banging her head against the wall and screaming anew. Something within her that had always been fragile had finally shattered. It was her sanity.

The preacher, aroused by the commotion, rushed into the bedroom. When he saw what Avarilla was holding in her hands, he gasped and drew back in horror and revulsion. Summoning all his strength, he denounced the child as "the spawn of Satan" and commanded that it had to be destroyed. Jewell and Faye nodded in silent agreement. He made the granny women swear before God never to reveal the circumstances of that blasphemous night and then he sent them home. They hurried away from the cabin with relief.

Avarilla tried to close her mind to the preacher's words which assailed her like hurrying nightmares. He coaxed, cajoled, and argued, until at last she spat out the terrible words . . . "No, no, I'll do it, Rev'rend. It's my . . . it's my own blood." Their eyes met briefly, flickered with terror, then were swiftly averted.

"I'll dig the grave," offered the preacher. "It has to be here, you know. It can't be buried in the churchyard." He took one last look at the male infant, shuddered and said, "Let God's will be done."

For a long time Avarilla held the strange child in her arms, trying to avoid its piercing yet inquiring eyes. When she heard the sound of the shovel striking the earth outside the house she was prompted to action. She carried it into the kitchen and laid it on the table. A bar of moonlight made a wavering silver band down the full length of its body.

Avarilla went to the cabinet drawer and withdrew a butcher knife. She held it high and looked
at it. Light from the hanging lantern glanced off
the blade and struck her eyes. A sudden pounding
filled the room. Then she realized it was the beating of her own heart. Scarcely daring to breathe,
she crossed to where the child lay waiting and
forced herself to look down.

The color drained from her face and the knife
clattered to the floor. She slammed her fist
against her mouth to keep from crying out. The
hair was fast disappearing from the infant's skin.
It was as if it was being pulled beneath the surface
from within. Blinking and unblinking, Avie stared
at the phenomenon which was taking place before
her eyes. The hair continued receding until the
child's flesh was soft and amorphous, like an
underexposed print. Even the nails had disappeared. The child looked normal, as normal as its twin
who lay in the laundry basket in the bedroom. Was
she hallucinating? She looked out the window and
saw the preacher silhouetted in the harsh light of
the moon. He was there and he was digging a
grave beneath the willow tree.

She fell to her knees and clawed at her own
cheeks, digging into them as if to tear them off,
pull them out by their very ligaments. She could
hear herself straining for air. Her tongue felt thick
and there was a bad taste in her mouth. It was the
coppery flavor of blood. She had bitten through
her lower lip. Oblivious to the blood flowing from
the corner of her mouth, she worked her lips in a
soundless prayer. A sign—she pleaded—something to guide her. She couldn't kill her own
grandson even though he was a creature of the
night. Slowly, as if by an act of will, Avarilla's eyes

rolled back in her head and she both saw and understood what she must do.

The moon had faded into a translucent disk. The preacher stood next to the small open grave, his boots and trousers covered with mud. He saw Avarilla approaching through the veil of limp branches and reached for his coat which he had hung over the handle of the shovel. She walked slowly toward him like a somnambulist clutching the blanket-wrapped bundle in her arms. He took it from her and felt the cloying warmth of the small body inside. He could not help but notice the stain of seeping blood like an opening flower. He knelt on the wet earth and placed the ghastly package in the grave. Then he righted himself and in a tremulous voice began an improvised prayer, a prayer he had never uttered before and never would utter again. As he intoned the words he glanced at Avarilla. She quickly bowed her head so that he couldn't see her face and perhaps know what she had done.

Part One

Behold, I send you forth as sheep in
the midst of wolves; be ye therefore
wise as serpents, and harmless as doves.

ST. MATTHEW, 10:16

1

August 23, 1982

The moon, full and orange as an overripe pumpkin, hovered over the city, threatening to fall from the skies. A breeze moved languidly through Central Park, barely rippling the surface of the artificial lake. It brought no relief to that sweltering summer night, and the parched grass seemed to sigh in resignation.

The two policemen glanced uneasily at one another. Their uniforms were damp and their faces glistened with beads of perspiration. They were both rookies and they were both nervous. One—Michael McCafferty, twenty-four, had been on the force two years to the month. The other, Leander Bullins, had been with New York's finest just short of six months. As they approached the edge of the lake, McCafferty cleared his throat in nervous tension and Officer Bullins blinked the sweat out of his eyes. The beams of their powerful flashlights crisscrossed the body which lay face down three feet from the water's edge.

"Jesus," muttered McCafferty. "Do you think he's been mugged?"

"Let's turn him over and find out," replied Bullins.

There was a sudden flapping sound. "Oh, my

God. What's that?" groaned McCafferty.

"Settle down, for Christ's sake. It's only the ducks."

Bullins knelt down and in a quick movement rolled the body over. The policeman leaned a little closer and the odor of alcohol struck him in the face like a fist. Bullins sighed with relief. "He's alive. Not mugged, not killed, just Goddamn drunk."

McCafferty ran the flashlight up and down the man's body. "Look, he's barefoot. Do you suppose somebody swiped his shoes?"

"That would be a new one." Bullins began shaking the man. "Come on, buddy, wake up. The party's over." The man didn't budge. Using his hands as cups, McCafferty carried some water from the lake and dumped it on the drunk's face. The man's eyes snapped open. They were light grey and flecked with gold, and at the moment completely uncomprehending. "Get up, buddy. You can't sleep it off here," growled Bullins and nudged the man's shoulder with his night stick.

The man groaned and sat up. The two policemen appraised him. He was about thirty-two years old and very handsome. Thick black hair, a ruddy complexion and an athletic physique gave him the appearance of someone in the peak of physical health. He rubbed his eyes with the back of his hands and stared at the uniformed men until they came into focus. Then he glanced at his surroundings and asked, in a tone which was apologetic and arrogant at the same time, "How the hell did I get here?"

"You better tell us," Bullins said softly. His voice had lost some of its strident quality. "Hell, you're lucky to be alive. Central Park at three A.M.

Hey, have you got your wallet?"

The young man slapped his hand against his chest, felt the familiar outline and withdrew a slender leather billfold. "Credit cards O.K. And what money I didn't spend is here."

"Let me see that," Bullins held out a broad and somewhat battered hand. He quickly checked the identification. "You're Joshua Allen Holman? 200 West Seventy-Seventh Street?"

"What's left of him," the man replied dully.

"What's your line of work, Mr. Holman?"

"Anthropology. I work at the New York Institute of Anthropology."

"How did you get here?"

Josh closed his eyes and winced. His recollections were embarrassing. "I had a fight with my girlfriend. We were at the Krypton Klub. I left her there and—well, hit a couple of bars."

"Why did you end up in Central Park?"

"I like to run," he replied matter-of-factly. "I run here every morning."

"Do you always run barefoot?"

Josh shook his head and was immediately sorry. A jolting pain caused him to wince. "No, of course not. I have several pairs of running shoes."

"Well, you either removed your shoes yourself or some bum came along and removed them for you. I opt for the first. If somebody took your shoes, they probably would have taken a good deal more than that."

Josh stared forlornly at his bare feet. This was a new low—even for him. Why did he have blackouts when he drank? Why could he not remember his actions? And how long would it be before it happened again?

The cops discussed Josh as if he weren't there.

"What do you think we ought to do with him?" asked McCafferty.

Bullins dug a thick finger beneath the collar of his uniform and ran it around the full circumference of his neck. Wiping the perspiration on his trouser leg, he replied, "He's harmless enough. No point in taking the poor son of a bitch to the station house. Come on, we'll drive him home."

They pulled Josh unceremoniously to his feet. "I really appreciate this," Josh grunted. "I'm going to be in enough trouble at home."

"You and your lady friend live together?" asked Bullins. Josh nodded. "Then I don't envy you. My old lady would be waiting with her mouth open and her legs closed. You understand that we're going to have to take you right to your door?" Josh looked sharply at the officer. "Regulations, Mr. Holman. We got to make sure that you're really who you and your wallet say you are."

"But I don't want Cresta to see me arriving with a police escort."

"Sorry, Mr. Holman. We can't bend the rules that far. We should be taking you down to the station house."

Josh's eyes flashed with anger, but he said nothing.

The policemen walked on either side of Josh in case they were needed for support. But the young man seemed to regain his sobriety with each step. A serpentine path led them through the maze which was called "the Rambles." The air became filled with the sickening sweet smell of honeysuckle. A half-dozen lightly clad figures who had been leaning against a railing began to move with purpose toward the exit.

"Goddamn fags," muttered McCafferty.

The air was heavy and oppressive, as if a damp blanket had been dropped over the entire city. A rolling bank of storm clouds obliterated the moon and chased away the stars. A roar of thunder rose and fell and lightning bounded across the horizon, filling the atmosphere with a sulphurous aroma which was almost tangible. Josh stared at the swirling sky as if it somehow held the answer to his dilemma.

As they walked up the dimly lit path toward Central Park West and Seventy-Seventh Street, they heard a rustling in the undergrowth. The bushes suddenly parted and an indistinct form rushed at them. McCafferty instinctively stepped in front of Josh to protect him; Bullins raised his revolver. The amorphous form of Maggie Meehan, a robust bag lady and denizen of Central Park, materialized under the street light. Both cops relaxed and holstered their revolvers. Maggie was harmless. Brandishing an umbrella like a sword, Maggie danced around the group, making thrusting parries with her weapon.

"Sons o' bitchin' cops! Why haven't you found my cart? They took my cart an' you ain't even looked for it." She scrutinized Josh with rheumy eyes set in a grotesquely made-up face. "Oh *no!* You're too busy gatherin' nuts to find my cart."

"Now, Maggie," said Bullins affectionately, as if speaking to a child, "you know that we've looked for your cart. We've looked and we've looked, but it's nowhere to be found. Perhaps you should go back to the A&P and get yourself another one."

"They been lockin' 'em up at night, the sons o' bitches," the old woman grunted.

"Have they now?" Bullins continued. "Well, I don't think they do over at the Big Apple."

"The Big Apple," the old woman rolled the words around in her mouth like a piece of hard candy. "Didn't think of the Big Apple!"

"I hear their carts are better anyway," grinned McCafferty.

The bag lady smiled broadly, revealing a profusion of teeth which resembled burnt tree stumps. Then she opened her umbrella. It was torn, its ribs showing, but that didn't seem to matter to her. As proudly as a drum majorette leading a parade, Maggie marched ahead of the trio until they reached the sidewalk. Then, with a flourish, she bent over, wiggled her buttocks at the passing cars and farted. Then, shrieking like a banshee, she disappeared into the night.

Josh glanced at the two policemen. "You seem to have your hands full tonight. I'm sorry to add to your problems."

"Hell, Mr. Holman," said Bullins. "Our night's just beginning. I'm sure you're the least of them."

The fast-traveling clouds, black and blue and roaring gray, broke apart. The rain cascaded down in silver sheets, scattering the hustlers, homosexuals, drug addicts, and winos from the shadows of the park to the safety of doorways and awnings. Cursing, the policemen hurried Josh to their patrol car.

A short time later the police pulled up in front of 200 West Seventy-Seventh Street. The building was 18 stories high and occupied one-quarter of a block. It had a shabby grandeur and had only survived because it had been proclaimed a landmark (albeit minor) by the City of New York. A pair of winged gargoyles stood sentinel at the entranceway. Perhaps they were guarding the aged doorman who slept inside on a once-elegant, rococo chaise.

For once Josh was pleased that the doorman was not alert and fulfilling his duties. He continued sleeping soundly as his tenant, escorted by the two policemen, walked across the marble tiles to the elevators beyond. They stepped inside and the gilded birdcage of an elevator noisily began its ascent. Josh glanced nervously at the policemen, hoping that would change their minds about escorting him to the door, but they ignored his silent entreaties.

The elevator jolted to a stop and the men stepped off. There were two apartments on the penthouse floor, and the hallway was in much better condition than the lobby of the building. Josh and the other penthouse occupant had chipped in to have the walls repainted and the floor recarpeted. They had purchased Victorian brass ceiling fixtures and mirrors in ornate frames for decoration. As Josh was fumbling with the three different keys which it took to gain access to the apartment, the door opened.

The police, startled, took a step backwards. Cresta Farraday was an astonishing-looking young woman. A model by profession and a very successful one, she was five feet, ten inches tall. Her bright hair hung around her face like a hood of silver-gold cloth. Her eyes were huge and a brilliant green, but smoldering rather than cold, like emeralds on fire. Her nose was narrow and had an insouciant tilt at the tip. In contrast, her mouth was broad and her lips full and sensuous. Perhaps her skin was her most arresting feature. It was golden and made her appear as if her veins ran with honey.

Cresta was dressed in a white satin gown cut on

the bias which she had obviously worn for the evening, for now it was wrinkled. Her face showed anger, worry and something else. Perhaps weariness of a situation which had occurred before.

Cresta flashed her eyes, first at Josh, then at the policemen. "Josh, what's this? What have you done?"

Bullins was the first to regain his composure. Officer McCafferty, his mouth hanging open like an unclosed drawer, continued to gape. "Ma'am, is this Joshua Allen Holman, and does he live here at 200 West Seventy-Seventh Street?"

"Well, yes," she replied, her voice rising. "What has he done?"

"Nothing, ma'am. He just . . . lost his way."

"And his shoes," McCafferty added with a grin.

Cresta looked down at her lover's feet. "Were you robbed, Josh?"

Josh uncomfortably shifted his weight and replied in a barely audible voice. "I was running in the park."

"Running in the park!" Cresta exploded. "For Christ's sake, now I've heard it all!"

Embarrassed, the cops took another step backwards. "Well, ma'am, we have to go now. We just wanted to see him home safe."

"Thanks, officers," Cresta replied vaguely. Then Josh stepped inside and she slammed the door.

While they were waiting for the elevator, Officer McCafferty remarked, "I don't know why he'd want to go running with something like that waiting at home, do you?"

Bullins shook his head. "Well now, Mike, I've never claimed to understand people and their relationships."

Inside the apartment, Josh made his way down

the long hall and turned to the kitchen. He threw off his jacket and went to the refrigerator. His mouth was dry and he wanted a beer. He opened one and was drinking it when Cresta entered.

"Haven't you had enough alcohol for one night?" she asked with a sharp edge to her voice.

He swung around. "Why don't you just go to bed, Cresta?"

"No. No, I'm not going to bed. I want to fight!" She ran at him and began beating her fists against his chest. "Damn you! Damn you to hell!" Josh pushed her away, and her pent-up tears burst forth. "I've been up half the night sick with worry. I've got a sitting in the morning, and I'm going to look like a piece of shit. Where did you go this time? Do you remember? I think that's just an excuse anyway. Were you out getting another stray piece?"

"Cresta," his eyes were pleading, "that only happened once."

"Once. You mean I only found out once. Why the hell don't you go West and become a Mormon? There you wouldn't have to keep up the pretense of being monogamous."

"Cresta, I swear to you it only happened once."

"How can you say that for sure, Josh? Really for sure? You don't remember what happens during these 'dark times.'"

"Why do you have to put a trendy label on everything? *Dark times.* It sounds like a power failure."

"Well, isn't that what it is, a blackout? What else would you call it? Christ, Josh, how can I help you if you won't help yourself?"

He finished his beer and took out another one. "I don't drink that often."

"No, you don't. But . . . ."

"I only get drunk about once a month. God, Cresta, you're acting like I was an alcoholic."

Cresta sighed. "Well, aren't you, Josh? Dr. Benjamin said that you don't have to drink often to be an alcoholic."

"Stuff Dr. Benjamin! I don't give a shit what your fancy Park Avenue psychiatrist has to say about me. Let him take care of *your* head."

"It's not just his opinion. It's fact."

"So what do you want me to do? Go to an AA meeting? Stand up among all those stumblebums and confess my wrongdoings? I haven't *done* any thing wrong, for God's sake!"

"You're doing wrong to yourself. One of these nights you're going to get yourself killed. Or worse."

Josh began laughing. "*Or worse?* What can be worse than getting killed?"

Cresta began laughing too. "Goddamn it, you know what I mean." Josh reached out for Cresta, but she backed away. "No, no, not this time." She was half-laughing, half-sobbing. "I want what I want, Josh."

"What do you want, Cresta?" he exploded and slammed the beer can down on the counter.

Her voice was tight, brittle, and controlled. "I want you to do something—see a psychiatrist, go to AA, join *est . . . anything! Just do something!*" She clenched and unclenched her hands as tears streamed down her face. "Jesus, I'm going to be a wreck in the morning. My eyes will be as puffy as poached eggs." She grabbed a paper napkin, wiped her eyes and nose and stared at Josh.

His straight black hair fell over his forehead like spilt paint, shadowing his haunting gray eyes. He returned her gaze with a pathetic little-boy look, a look she knew and loved. Cresta, at twenty, was not inexperienced in affairs of the heart. She had had two other lovers, but neither of them, neither, excited her like Josh Holman. Perhaps it was because he never catered to her; he hadn't even pursued her, for that matter. And once they were together, he accepted her with a casual affection which she found refreshing after so many overanxious men and tiresome compliments. She also loved him because he was intelligent, kind, and possessed a good sense of humor. But there was that other side to him. He was often moody, sometimes sharp, withdrawn and even cruel.

Cresta shook her head in consternation. "Josh, if you love me, then fight for me. Aren't I worth it? I love you with all my heart. I want to marry you. I want to have your children. But . . . ," she began crying again, "not the way things are. Please, *please* I—I can't—help you if you won't help yourself."

He touched her arm. "I'll try, love. I'll really try."

She managed a smile. "That's all I wanted to hear. Now, I'm going to sleep in the guest room tonight. When you drink, you snore, and I have precious few hours left to get my beauty sleep."

"Cresta, please."

"Josh, I have to. I'm doing close-up work tomorrow. It's that lipstick commercial. I can't go in without any sleep at all. Rudy will probably have a devil of a time making me up anyway." She kissed him lightly on the cheek and hurried out of the kitchen.

Josh finished his beer, then viciously crushed the can in his hands. She was punishing him. No matter what she said, she was not free of anger or doubt concerning his intentions. He knew that she had a right to be both angry and pessimistic. They had been through it all before. She had made the same entreaties and he had made the same promises.

Josh knew that he would break them again, and that knowledge saddened him more than anything.

2

The alarm went off at eight. Josh groaned, reached out to turn it off, and knocked it on the floor. "Cresta," he mumbled, "I knocked the God-damn clock on the floor." Suddenly he became aware that the only warmth in the bed was emanating from his own body. He raised his head. His brains felt scrambled. Leaning against the brass headboard, he tried to wish the throbbing away. He recalled having three more beers after Cresta had gone to bed. That had raised his alcohol level to such a point that he was able to sleep. Josh kicked off the light cover and looked down at his body. His feet were dirty and cut in several places. It came back to him in a rush. Central Park . . . running . . . the cops. Then he remembered that he didn't remember all of it.

He did remember the disco. The Krypton Klub was the "in" discotheque for all the beautiful, with-it people. It was the last place in New York City that Josh had wanted to be. But because Cresta was a top model, she was invited to attend every screwy affair in town. It was an opening night party for a rock musical which he had also had to endure—a pretentious piece of junk about a mass murderer.

As usual, Josh had acquiesced to Cresta's wishes; he would attend the show and later the party. The musical put him in a foul mood. And Josh knew on entering the Krypton Klub that only alcohol would allow him to deal with the deafening music, the flashing lights, and the shrill crowd.

Josh and Cresta were crammed at a miniscule table with five of Cresta's "dearest friends." The fat homosexual wearing giant pink glasses was a successful dress designer and fancied himself "out*rage*ous." Josh found him merely loud and obnoxious. There were two models who worked at the same agency as Cresta. Both were vapid and pretty, and both glittered in punk rock gear. And their dates: a blandly handsome actor in a soap who experimented with kinky sex and was more than happy to tell you about it, and an advertising executive who was fighting his age. His sunlamp tan, capped teeth and dyed hair only added to the artificiality of his life. The ad exec kept all of them (except for Cresta and Josh) supplied in "the best snow in town." As the rest of the table not-so-discreetly sniffed cocaine, Josh concentrated on drinking while Cresta glared at him. An hour later she coerced him onto the dance floor, and there they had a fight. Josh didn't remember what about. The play? Probably. Her friends? Most likely. The disco? Most assuredly.

After that everything was a blank except . . . *except* . . . .

Josh staggered into the bathroom, peered at himself in the mirror and decided that he didn't look as bad as he should have. He looked in the guest room. Cresta was already off to her modeling assignment. The campaign bed was neatly made. When Josh entered the kitchen he expected to find a note from Cresta. It was a habit of hers. A note asking him to pick up something from the market or reminding him of a social engagement, or simply a reaffirmation of her love. The note was noticeably absent.

He looked around the kitchen. Well, at least she had made the coffee. Josh poured himself a mug. While he was waiting for it to cool, he dissolved two Alka Seltzers in a glass of beer, drank it down and emitted a healthy belch. He wanted to call Cresta just to measure her mood, but he couldn't remember where she had said she would be shooting that morning. He knew that he could check with Famous, Inc., the model agency that handled her, but she didn't like to have her work interrupted unless it was an emergency. And since when was a hangover an emergency?

Josh closed his eyes and savored the aroma of the coffee. Suddenly the odor became mixed with something else. A dry summer night, stagnant water and hot, fetid air. A blurred image of vegetation, rocks, and undergrowth rushed past his mind's eye like an unfinished watercolor. He was running, running faster than he ever had. Running as if he were being pursued . . . or was he the pursuer? The predator or the prey?

Running in Central Park. Josh grunted, shaking off the disturbing images. It just . . . *didn't* make any sense.

After finishing his coffee, Josh went into the bathroom and turned on the shower. He glanced at himself in the fogging mirror, flexed his muscles, and smiled at his reflection. He was fully aware of his sensual good looks, his impressive physique, and he savored them, knowing that he looked nearly a decade younger than his actual thirty-two years. His shoulders, if not overly broad, were solid, and corded with muscle. His sharply defined pectorals were high and covered with a light spray of black hair which trailed down to his deeply set navel and exploded around his formidable genitals. He turned and examined his back. His spine was sharply defined and a soft circle of black hair grew just above the crevice of his buttocks which were deeply indented on either side. The outline of his bathing suit was still evident. Josh's skin seemed to drink up the rays from summer weekends and winter vacations and retained them the year round. Once again he examined his feet. They were not badly torn up. The soles were hard from years of going barefoot at every chance.

While the needles of water stung his flesh, Josh contemplated how he was going to deal with Cresta. Perhaps he would pick up tickets to that rock concert she wanted to see. Or else take a stroll through Bloomingdale's and select an expensive little nothing which might please her fancy.

He knew it would take more than that. Hell, Cresta would much rather he stopped drinking. But, damn it, socializing made that impossible. Besides, he didn't always drink too much, and he didn't always have blackouts. *Not always.* After briskly drying with a towel, Josh went into the bedroom to get dressed.

Even though the other members of the New York Institute of Anthropology, did not approve his mode of dress, Josh wore what he pleased to work. As he was pulling on a blue knit shirt, the running scene flashed across his mind once again. The blur of images puzzled him. He seemed to be seeing them from a speeding car.

"Maybe I run faster when I drink," he mused.

Josh put on a pair of worn jeans, sandals, and threw a faded madras jacket in shades of red and blue over his shoulder. He took one last look in the mirror and hurried down the hall of the apartment. He nearly tripped over the guitar, which was propped up next to the closet. "Goddamn it, Cresta!" He picked it up and jammed it into the closet. "Why does she keep it lying around? She's never going to learn to play."

Sometime during the night the rain had stopped. New York looked washed, battered, wrung out to dry. Ruffled gray clouds, rimmed in the west with pink, looked pinned against the sheet of startlingly blue sky. It seemed that the heat wave had passed and the people's spirits were high and their faces split by smiles. Like a gift from the gods, the clement weather had seduced the city into a false sense of security.

Josh reached Central Park West and, preferring the closer contact with nature, crossed over to walk on the park side. Sunlight streamed through the branches of the trees overhead and scattered across the sidewalk like golden coins. A whey-faced nun in her drab, modern-day garb ushered a wavering line of unruly boys into the park. They were indistinguishable from one another, wearing the same school uniforms, bandaged knees and sly smirks. Several of them gawked admiringly at Josh, momentarily making him the object of their "I want to be like that when I grow up" fantasies. As he passed the bus stop a young woman waiting for the uptown express turned to openly admire Josh. He managed a self-conscious look and stifled a desire to tell her that he appreciated her appreciation of him. Josh knew that he was thought handsome by most women—Cresta had mentioned it often enough. He turned and favored her with a dazzling smile. She burst into self-conscious giggles.

On the corner there was a newstand where Josh picked up his morning newspaper. While he was waiting for change, his eyes scanned the magazines hanging by clothespins from wires. Cresta was on the cover of that month's *Charisma*, a leading fashion magazine. Josh was immediately struck by feelings of guilt, not only for the previous night and other nights in the past, but because of his playful game with the girl at the bus stop. He was, as always, incredulous that he was involved with somebody who was in some circles a celebrity. Josh touched the magazine cover with his fingertips. Cresta was wearing a designer's version of a farmgirl outfit and was posed against a background of straw. She was looking at the camera (and the viewer) with what one fashion wag had called "a million-dollar come-'n'-get-it look." Josh had seen that expression many times before. She unconsciously employed it when she was interested in having sex. The glossy cover shimmered in the sunlight, and Cresta the farmgirl was transformed into Cresta the beguiling bride. He recalled their meeting two years earlier in the spring of 1980.

It had been a green-gold morning softened by a vaporous mist. The sun was a bright, yellow knot and Josh felt that he could reach up and pull it down from the sky. He had been up since before dawn and had already run two miles. He was about to leave Central Park by the Seventy-Second

Street entrance when he was drawn to a small
group of people gathered around the wisteria
arbor just inside the park. At first Josh reacted
like any native New Yorker and assumed that
there had been some sort of trouble—an early
morning mugging perhaps. Then as he came closer
he noticed the lights, the reflectors and the
camera. Apparently someone was shooting a
photograph.

Curious, Josh edged his way to the periphery of
the busy circle of people. No one paid any attention to him. They were all involved in a magazine
advertisement shoot. Everyone—photographer,
art director, makeup man, wardrobe mistress, and
a handful of assistants—had their attention
focused on the entrance to the arbor.

The rustic log arbor was a structure left over
from the Victorian age. It formed a tunnel of sorts
over and around which the grapevines grew. The
spring rains had been particularly abundant that
year and the arbor was replete with lush vines and
leaves. A perfect spot for a lovers' meeting.

It was then that he saw Cresta for the first time.
She emerged from the dark green shadows into
the filtered sunlight. She was wearing a dazzling
white wedding gown, a frothy confection of
organdy and lace. She smiled in Josh's direction
and, although he didn't think she actually saw
him, he felt as if she had favored him in particular.

Then a short dumpy woman stepped forward
brandishing a wedding veil and began to arrange it
on Cresta's head. A man wearing an impatient
scowl, oversized sunglasses, and a pair of brown
trousers which fit him like the skin of a baked
potato, walked over to Josh. His voice was high
but authoritative. "Where have you been? We've

been waiting to shoot for twenty minutes." He quickly surveyed Josh's face and physique with appreciation and added sharply, "Is that what Minnie told you to wear? Not very chic."

Josh stepped back and stared at the man as if he were insane. "I don't know what you're talking about."

"You're the model from Macho, aren't you?" the man snapped. "Six feet, ruggedly handsome, dark hair, running clothes. Now, come on, we've been waiting for you."

"You've made a mistake," said Josh. "I was running through the park and just stopped to see what was going on."

Cresta, looking slightly vexed, joined the two-some. Without acknowledging Josh she spoke directly to the photographer. "Simon, aren't we ready? I don't like to complain, but this organdy itches like a son of a bitch."

The photographer's reserve evaporated. "Well, you see, Cresta, this gentleman claims he's not the model we've been waiting for."

Cresta turned to face Josh. "Are you sure?"

Josh grinned. "I'm sorry I'm not. Not the model, that is."

Cresta loked first at the photographer and then at Josh. "Simon, I've got another shoot at nine-thirty and it involves an elaborate hair style. I mean, wouldn't he do? He's perfect. Beautiful legs." She smiled at Josh. "You should be a model anyway. Why aren't you?"

Josh began backing away. "Really, I don't think I . . . They wouldn't like it where I work . . . I've never . . . ."

The photographer interceded. "Look, you wouldn't even be recognized. You'd just be a blur running past Cresta here." He glowered at his assistant. "Find out what happened to that fag from Macho. He'll never work for *Charisma* again." Then back to Josh. "Look, I'll pay you the full fee, even though you're not a professional model. We've got to get this done. Like I said, not even your own mother will recognize you."

"Please do it," murmured Cresta. "I can't be late for my next booking without really screwing things up."

The photographer persisted, "All you have to do is sign a release, then run past that arbor where Cresta will be standing."

"You must," pleaded Cresta. "My career depends upon you."

Josh smiled self-consciously. "Well, if you're sure I'll just be a blur. Is there some way I could check the photographs after they're taken and before they're printed? What's this for anyway?"

The photographer slapped his head. "Oh boy, now we've got an amateur who wants photo approval for a spread in *Charisma*. You probably don't know, but it's a women's magazine." He went on "patiently" explaining. "You see, this is a bridal shot. See the bridal dress that Cresta's wearing? Instead of hailing a cab, she's going to be hailing a bridegroom. Get it? You, the runner. Very tongue-in-cheek and all that."

Josh did not like the photographer's condescending attitude but couldn't resist the hopeful look on Cresta's face. "All right," he said finally, "I'll do it if it doesn't take too long and if you promise I won't be recognized."

"Just a blur," sighed the photographer. "Now, come on, let's see what we can do with you."

Cresta squeezed Josh's hand. "You're wonderful

for doing this. I'd give you a kiss but Rudy's just spent forty-five minutes on my makeup." Nevertheless she brushed her lips against his cheek and hurried back to her position.

For the next fifteen minutes Josh endured attacks from all sides. He was wrapped in an oversized towel while his green shorts and white tank top were quickly pressed by one of the flunkies. His face and body were dusted with a shiny orange powder and glycerine was dribbled over his temples and arms to simulate perspiration (his had long since evaporated). His hair was teased and sprayed until it was "perfectly unruly." And a piece of bright green fabric had been found to use as a headband. The photographer examined Josh with a critical eye and pronounced, "Christ, you look gorgeous. Can you really run?" Josh opened his mouth to answer. "No matter, we've got to get on with it."

Josh spent the next half-hour streaking across the pathway directly in front of the arbor which framed Cresta. The young model was humorously posed clutching an oversized bouquet of white lilacs and green grapes, and, using two fingers in the mouth, whistling after the handsome runner. A message was implicit: today's young woman— the *Charisma* woman—was calling the shots.

As soon as the shooting was over, Cresta dashed into the portable dressing room and changed into her working model's uniform—tight, frayed jeans, a halter top made of two red bandannas, and giant sunglasses. She carried a portfolio and a shoulder bag the size of a tire. Josh was signing the release papers when she rushed over to him, kissed him warmly on the side of the head and said, "Sorry, handsome, I've got to run. No time for even a

Bloody Mary. I'll give you a call. Really, I will. I want to thank you in person." With that she had dashed toward Central Park West in search of a cab.

Josh had been sure that that was the last he would ever see of her.

3

"Hey, mister, you wanna buy that mag'zine or not?"

Cresta the bride faded away, and Cresta the farmgirl came back into focus. Josh shook off his reverie, pulled the magazine from its clothespin holder and paid the grumpy newsman. As he continued his walk, he leafed through the September issue of *Charisma* and was surprised to find that Cresta graced many of its glossy pages. The world of high fashion was alien to Josh. It always surprised him that his lover was one of New York's ten top models. He accepted Cresta for what she was to their relationship and did not become a member of her audience. He would make a point of reading the magazine over coffee, and then he would be able to discuss Cresta's work with her. Josh knew that would please her more than anything he could do.

The New York Institute of Anthropology was a sprawling brick and granite building. Constructed in 1892, it was considered one of New York's great monuments. Complete with rifle ports and graceful towers, the building evoked memories of long-forgotten operettas. The architectural integrity of the building had been preserved and the stained

glass windows, designed by Lewis Comfort
Tiffany, remained intact, despite constant at-
tempts at vandalism.

For decades the building had housed an
immense collection of books, artifacts and ex-
hibits on the evolution of man in the civilized
world. These treasures were available to the
public three afternoons a week and on weekends.

Josh bounded up the staircase leading to the
giant double oak doors inset with intricate brass-
work. The guard, a relic of respectability, wearing
an impeccably tailored uniform trimmed with
gold braid epaulets and buttons, touched his cap
as Josh entered. The young man was well aware
that the guard's aloof attitude toward him was
typical of the rest of the staff. Josh was the
youngest professor and newest member of the
professional staff of thirty-seven, not including
those of lesser standing—security guards,
janitors, and maintenance personnel.

"Good morning, Muldoon," Josh called out
affably. "Beautiful day, isn't it? How's the wife
and kids? Sure hope it doesn't rain."

Josh was considered an upstart despite his impressive credentials, the articles he had written
for many publications (including *Natural History*,
Smithsonian and *National Geographic*), and the
series of trade paperback books he edited, entitled
Plain Living. Despite all this, his position at the
institute remained the same as if he were a newly
arrived professor at a University. He would have
to wait out his apprenticeship, and he resented it,
although he was careful not to let it show.

The institute was, as usual, as quiet and proper
as a Boston library. Josh wended his way down
the corridor past a series of tiny, gerrymandered

office cubicles toward his own slightly larger office. He nodded brightly toward the various secretaries and study assistants. He filled a styrofoam container with dreadful coffee from the communal urn and went into his office.

A buxom woman with Teutonic features was standing by his desk arranging the mail. Her name was Elsa Krupp; she was the secretary Josh shared with several other members of the institute.

"Good morning, Elsa," Josh said without enthusiasm.

Miss Krupp adjusted the large coil of blond hair wrapped loosely around her head; it resembled a slipped halo. As usual, she eyed Josh suspiciously. She instinctively distrusted good-looking young men. "I've arranged your mail, Mr. Holman," she said unnecessarily. "I'm going to be busy today typing that report on Tibetan herdsmen for Professor Seymour." As she lumbered by, Josh was struck once again by her body scent. It reminded him of stale pretzels. "That's all right, Elsa. I can manage my own typing." Actually, Josh preferred typing his own letters. Miss Krupp had a tendency to edit and formalize everything he wrote.

His office had been part of a much larger room before the conversion to smaller compartments in 1948. At the far end two tall, mullioned windows offered testimony to the building's history. The other three walls, save for the door, were covered with modern bookshelves which had been painted white, as was the rest of the room. The shelves were haphazardly jammed with reference books, magazines, files, and personal odds and ends. Dominating the cluttered desk was a bronze reproduction of the famous sculpture which depicted

Romulus and Remus, the founders of Rome, being suckled by a she-wolf.

Josh sat down, sipped his coffee and quickly leafed through the copy of *Charisma* again, then irritably pushed the magazine aside. He hated to be reminded that Cresta earned more money than he did. Perhaps five times as much. *Charisma* and Cresta were quickly forgotten.

Employing a dangerous-looking letter opener, Josh began opening his mail. Most of the correspondence was concerned with his specialty—wolves. After doing undergraduate work at West Virginia University, Josh got his M.A. in Anthropology at Princeton. Somewhat tired of the study of man, he took his Ph.D. in Zoology at Cambridge, England, specializing in the study of *Canis Lupus* —wolves—and their behavior patterns. He had been drawn to that particular branch of the animal kingdom for a number of reasons. Throughout recorded history man and wolf had been antagonists and rivals, and like man wolves were a symbol of savagery, ferocity and courage. And man's legends surrounding the wolf were the stuff of outrageous fiction—Red Riding Hood and The Big Bad Wolf, for example. Not to mention the fascinating study of lycanthropy—the werewolf.

But there were deeper reasons.

As a child in Jericho Falls, a small town in central West Virginia, Josh had lived at the base of the Appalachian Mountains, his family's home surrounded on the other three sides by an expanse of unspoiled forest. The small Josh had often been awakened during the night by the howls of wolves prowling near the house. Instead of being frightened, Josh found their predatory cries comforting and usually was lulled back to sleep by their mournful lullabies. Later, when he was a bit older, Josh investigated the nearby forests which had long captured his imagination.

He learned to identify animals by their tracks, birds by their calls, and herbs and berries by their scent. The little boy was an explorer by nature, and his plain, hardworking parents, who were determined that Josh should have everything he wanted, encouraged his pursuits.

One afternoon Josh ventured up the mountainside for the first time, a new excitement coursing through his veins. He felt like a young Columbus about to discover a new world. On a small plateau, he knelt to drink from a cool mountain stream fairly bursting at its banks. There he discovered fresh tracks. Wolf tracks. He followed them. He knew that wolves were fast disappearing from that part of the country. He had overheard adults speak of killing the wolves, bragging as if they were riding the countryside of a pestilence. It had never seemed that way to him, although he didn't fully understand why.

Here the forest became sparse. The trees, which had been deformed by the high winds, jutted out at odd angles from the mountainside. Josh climbed over a ruined splitrail fence, a relic of the early nineteenth century. He lost the wolves' trail but continued on. The stream appeared once again, and nearby he discovered something else. The center of a large laurel thicket had been cut away, and there a still had been built. Of course, Josh had no idea what the furnace, still, barrels, and troughs were used for, but his instincts told him that it was not a place to loiter. At the edge of the thicket he picked up the trail of the wolves once again. His heart pounding in his ears like a jackhammer, he raced on. And then he saw them.

Lying comfortably in a "loafing spot" near the entrance to her den was a she-wolf suckling her four cubs. The cubs were about two and a half months old and had gray woolly coats. Josh crept closer. The she-wolf lifted her head and sniffed the air. Then slowly, the she-wolf fixed her gaze in Josh's direction and held it. Josh stepped out into the clearing.

The she-wolf did not move. Josh inched himself closer. The cubs stopped suckling and began playing with one another. Like puppies they were ungainly creatures, their feet ludicrously big for their bodies. They bit at one another and tumbled about in the fallen leaves. Josh sat down on a rock about twelve feet away and watched with complete fascination. He longed to play with the cubs. But he knew that the she-wolf would not permit that. He had remained, transfixed, for nearly half an hour when the she-wolf's mate appeared. He was a magnificent-looking animal with long legs, a thick and lustrous coat and a mobile face. He glanced at Josh briefly, almost with disinterest, and then greeted his mate. After wagging their tails, they placed their forepaws on each other's necks, reared on their hind legs, and kissed and licked one another. Then they bounded into play, chasing one another in a joyous game of tag. Embarrassed by a scene of such intimacy, Josh slipped away and hurried back down the mountainside.

He did not mention his experience to his parents; it seemed too private. But he made many more trips up the mountainside, and watched the wolf cubs grow into adulthood. That fall the family moved north to Morgantown, West Virginia. The change was prompted by his father's work. Mr. Holman had taken a job as a mine foreman. The move from Jericho Falls and the wolves broke Josh's ten-year-old heart.

Had wolves existed in Ancient Egypt? Josh was in the process of answering the letter of inquiry when the intercom sounded. It was Dr. Raymond Phelps, the director of the institute. His usually taciturn manner was charged with an unusual degree of excitement. "Josh, are you in? Of course, you're in, otherwise you wouldn't be answering, would you? Look, Josh, I want you to drop whatever you're doing and meet me in 'D' laboratory immediately. I have something astounding to show you."

"I'll be there right away, Dr. Phelps."

Josh was intrigued. Nothing, *absolutely nothing*, caused Dr. Phelps' carefully modulated voice to rise above a somnolent monotone.

The laboratories in the basement of the building were outfitted with every available scientific device for testing and authenticating anthropological "finds." Here the exact age of a Mayan mummy was fixed, the cause of death of an Assyrian sailor was determined, and human remains found in England were correctly placed in time according to the development of man.

Using his pass card, Josh unlocked the door to "D" laboratory. Dr. Phelps, who had been leaning over a lab table, swung around. Phelps was a gentle and undramatic man in his late sixties. Slight in build, he seemed to compensate for his lack of stature by wearing his unruly white hair in an explosive mass of disarrayed curls. His usually bland, pinched face was red with fervor, and, for the first time that Josh could remember, he was perspiring.

"Josh, you won't believe what I've got here. You simply won't believe it!" Josh started for the lab table, but Phelps stopped him, wanting to begin with an explanation.

"What is it, Dr. Phelps? What's happened?"

The professor shook his head. His hair bobbed up and down like caps on a raging sea. "Josh, as you know, Harry Evers is in the field."

Josh grinned. He and Harry were old friends, drinking companions and confidants. Together they railed against what they called the "tight-assed orthodoxy of the institute." "Yes, I know. Indian digs in the Appalachians."

"Delaware Indian digs," corrected Dr. Phelps. "Well, Harry and his assistants discovered something besides arrowheads." The professor was almost panting now. "You just won't believe what he sent back. The package arrived just this morning."

Josh waited patiently for Phelps to reveal the source of his agitation, but the professor rambled on. "That area is your neck of the woods, isn't it, Josh?" He smiled crookedly at his own poor joke.

"Yes, I was born in Jericho Falls. It's about ten miles away from the digs."

"Do you ever think of returning, Josh?"

The young man shrugged his shoulders. "There's no reason to. Both my parents are dead. I have an aunt who lives up in the mountains around there. We keep in touch with Christmas cards, but we haven't seen each other in years."

Phelps solemnly led Josh to the table. He placed his hand on a small wooden crate and said, "You must keep this in confidence, Josh. Do I have your word on it?''

"Of course."

Phelps opened the crate and carefully removed a skull and some bones from their resting place among the excelsior.

"Indian?" Josh ventured.

"Look closer, Josh." He held the skull under a strong arc light and turned it around so that it was facing the young man. Josh frowned and sucked in his breath. The professor thrust the skull at Josh. The young man dropped his hands to his sides and took a step backwards. "It can't be," he muttered. "It simply can't be."

The skull was shaped like that of a wolf, but much broader in the head, more like a man's. Josh tentatively approached the skull. "This can't be authentic," he said. And yet in his heart he knew that it was. Without taking it from the professor, he studied the comparative lengths of the muzzle and the brain case. "The muzzle is shorter and the brain case larger than that of a normal wolf. And look at the tooth arrangement. The grasp of the jaws is essentially right, and yet the line of the teeth is more, excluding the large canines, is more uniform, more like . . . ."

"A man's," supplied Phelps. "Take a look at the bones. Harry believes they came from the same body."

"Where did he find them?" asked Josh, anxious to leave the skull.

"At the mouth of a cave near the banks of the Cheat River. Harry thinks that the . . . animal, or whatever you choose to call it, went there to die."

"Die?"

"You'll note that section of rib bones, Josh. They appear to have been damaged by bullets."

Josh scrutinized the rib section. "The construction's finer than that of a man's. There's more of a crest." He pressed his finger to the indentations in the ribs. "Shotgun."

"That's what I thought. Now take a look at that foot or . . . paw."

"It's larger than it should be. Wolves walk on the digits, Dr. Phelps, and not on the soles of the feet. There are four toes, the fifth digit retained as a dewclaw. This enables the animal to dig in on the true foot or to slow down its progress on slippery surfaces such as ice or mud. But, Jesus, look at the Goddamn size of the thing! It's enormous. A man's size 10, 10½." Josh looked seriously at Phelps. "I hope this is some kind of an elaborate hoax."

"I don't think it is, Josh. But that's why I called on you. I want you to help me run the tests. If you have any appointments, cancel them. I'll send out for lunch. We can't act upon this until we're sure that the bones are authentic."

They spent the rest of the morning running tests. It was a slow and tedious process, but by two P.M. both men were satisfied that the bones were, indeed, authentic, and that in all probability the creature had died of shotgun wounds. They were also able to reckon its age. By man's standards it would have been in its late twenties; by a wolf's, three to four years old. The year of its death was almost certainly 1950.

Throughout the morning the men had worked without once daring to speak of the significance of the discovery. Now, at the end of their scrutiny, they faced one another and the inevitable.

"This is incredible," Josh said at last. A chill slid down his spine like an errant caterpillar. "It's the stuff of legends, the theme of nightmares. This creature is half-man, half-wolf.''

A note of hysteria crept into the professor's voice, grave and elated at the same time. ''For centuries the existence of such a species—half-man, half-beast—has persisted, and now we have positive proof that it does. Josh, I want you to go down there and investigate.'' His protruding eyes resembled those of a man in shock. ''It could be that there are . . . others.''

Phelps' proposal was unexpected, and Josh asked, ''Why me, Dr. Phelps?''

''The answer is obvious, Josh. You know that part of the country, you're from there. And you're considered an expert on *Canis Lupus*. I read the monograph you wrote while at Cambridge. I felt it was most impressive.''

Josh could not help grinning. ''This is like something out of a 1940's horror movie.''

Phelps scowled. A sense of humor had never invaded his scholarly personality, and he did not approve of it in others, particularly if their levity were applied to anything connected to the institute.

''I don't fly, Dr. Phelps. It's a . . . quirk of mine.''

The professor frowned again. He did not approve of people's phobias, either. ''There are other modes of travel, Joshua.''

Josh reappraised the situation. Dr. Phelps never called him Joshua unless he was irritated. And it wouldn't do to have the director of the institute upset with him. Besides, the way things were between him and Cresta, a temporary separation might do them both good, particularly after last night's ugly scene. Josh ventured, ''Would the institute cover all expenses?''

Phelps made an impatient gesture. ''Of course.

Don't we always?''

"I suppose I could rent a camper," Josh was slow to suggest. "I could be there in twelve to fourteen hours."

The professor nodded his head happily.

"If I do this, Dr. Phelps, I want no time limit put on my investigation. And I must insist that I be given credit for all data collected. Granted, Harry made the initial discovery and together we authenticated it. But if I follow it up, I want proper credit for everything I do above and beyond the institute."

Phelps didn't like the conditions, but he knew Josh was immovable once he had made up his mind. And he obviously had. "Agreed," he said briskly. The older man gathered up his notes. "I will leave you now, Josh, to make your arrangements. I'll have Eleanor draw up the check for you to cover expenses. Please put . . . everything . . . away and lock the lab."

"Yes, yes, of course. Is there any way I can let Harry know I'm coming?"

"I don't see how. He's miles from a telephone. But no matter. I'm sure he'll welcome your help on this venture. Tell Harry to drop the Indian project. Just keep it as a front for this . . ." he glanced uneasily at the skull and bones, "this surprise." With that, Dr. Phelps left.

Slowly, reluctantly, Josh turned to face the skull. Fascinated and repelled at the same time, he forced himself to pick it up and stared directly into its empty sockets. He suddenly felt so cold that his teeth started chattering and he began to shiver involuntarily. He wanted to pull his gaze away from the skull, to pack it away out of sight, but he was incapable of movement. He had never known the condition which was called "terror" before. He had never experienced it even as a child. It was a feeling which went far beyond fear because it was so unreasoning. Strange sounds filled his head—a sharp gusting wind, leaves being torn from their branches, twigs snapping, and the soft crunch of *something* running.

Cold rivulets of perspiration poured down his forehead, blurring his vision. He had never known anything like what he now felt. Sheer, mind-bending terror. Another sound began, and it seemed to emanate from the jaws of the skull he was clutching. It was the unholy howl of death.

Josh willed his eyes to close. That slight movement broke the hold of the overpowering sensation which had gripped him. The skull fell from his hand onto the tabletop. Josh took several tentative steps backward, not daring to look at it. Then some of the fear slipped away. His body temperature and breathing returned to normal. He might have remained in that half-hypnotized state for five minutes or fifty. At last he was able to open his eyes.

Josh told himself that the sudden sickness (what else could he call it?) which had overcome him was a result of the heavy drinking he had done the night before. That part of his mind which had nothing to do with reasoning accepted the explanation. It had to. But he really didn't believe it.

4

Josh left work early in order to go to the bank. After waiting an interminable amount of time in line for cash and traveler's checks, he then hurried back to his apartment to pack. He had rented a sixteen-foot-long camper by phone and arranged to pick it up at the garage on Eleventh Avenue by six o'clock.

He had only one problem. How was he going to break the news of his departure to Cresta? Every time he had made a business trip to a convention or for purposes of research, Cresta had whined, complained and acted like a little girl suddenly abandoned by her parents. Josh realized that Cresta depended upon him a great deal for support. Despite her beauty, her success and her friends, Cresta was a very insecure person.

They needed a little breathing space, and time to reassess their relationship. Besides, it was good for couples, married and otherwise, to get away from one another. Josh remembered those times when Cresta was off on location shoots, such as last winter's junket to the Virgin Islands. He had enjoyed being alone, having the apartment to himself. Even though he had missed her, he had been happy to have no one to answer to. Images of that time came back—himself cruising about a series of bars—music blaring, lights flashing, women inviting—invaded his mind. His freedom from commitment had been fun, and he hadn't had a black-out . . . had he?

Josh was packing when he heard Cresta's keys undoing the series of locks which, hopefully, kept them safe from burglars. Damn, he had forgotten to get her a present. Well, perhaps going away would be the best present he could give her.

"Josh, are you home?" she called out. Her cheerful voice held no indication of their quarrel.

"I'm in here, Cresta," Josh responded.

He heard her drop her packages in the kitchen and make her way down the hall toward the master bedroom. "I thought we'd eat in tonight, Josh. I picked up some things at the market. We'll start with a cold soup with sour cream and caviar, finish with fresh peaches, and for the main course I'm going to prepare a watercress salad and a mushroom quiche. You know, it can be fun cooking for a vegetarian." She stopped short at the bedroom door. "Josh, what are you doing?"

Josh looked up from his packing. He realized from Cresta's tone that she assumed he was leaving her for good. "Just a research trip, love. The institute is sending me back to West-by-God-Virginia."

"But, but when did all this take place?"

"Today. Sorry I couldn't give you any notice, but it's sort of an emergency trip."

"How long will you be gone?" Cresta stammered.

Josh shrugged his shoulders. "I don't know, love." She looked close to tears. "Probably just a couple of weeks, no more. Harry Evers is down there with a couple of assistants. They've set up camp on the Cheat River, just on the other side of the mountain where I was born. He needs some help and . . . ." Josh walked over to Cresta and put his hands on her shoulders. "Look, we've been getting on each other's nerves. It will be a good thing for us to be apart for a while. Don't you agree?"

Cresta backed away, tears flooded her eyes, making them sparkle even more. "You want to go, don't you? You want to get away from me. Your running away to West-by-God-Virginia won't solve anything, Josh." Cresta looked at him miserably. "Don't you care for me any more, Josh?"

Josh looked away. "Of course I still care for you, Cresta."

"You've got a fine way of showing it. If I didn't know how much you hated to travel, I'd think you'd arranged this trip on purpose. How are you getting there, anyway . . . Trailway Bus? Surely you're not flying."

In spite of the situation, Josh laughed. "No buses, no planes, no trains. I'm going first class. I've rented a Scamper."

"What's that?"

"One of those trendy new campers. You don't think I'm going to rough it down there among the hillbillies, do you? It comes complete with kitchen, bed and bath."

"Those things must be a block long."

"It's only sixteen feet. Don't you remember me telling you that in high school I worked summers driving a coal truck for the company where my old man worked?"

"No, I don't," Cresta replied bitterly. She wiped her tears away with the back of her hand and stuck out her chin in determination. "Josh, I'm going with you." He started to answer, but she stopped him. "No, no, I want to. It would be good for us. I know it would."

"But your work . . . . "

"Screw my work! I've worked like a Goddamn dog all summer doing the fall lines, with practically back-to-back bookings, five, six and seven days a week. You know that. Besides, there's a lull now. I don't have that much lined up for the next few weeks. I know I could fix it. And if Jason gives me any trouble, I'll just tell him my psychiatrist says I need a rest. Josh, I've never been to that part of the country. I'd like to see where you came from."

"It's pretty rustic, love."

"But we'll have the camper, darling. It'll be so perfect—all that mountain air, natural living . . . making love beneath the stars."

"We'll still be taking our problems with us."

"Oh, Josh, we'll work them out, I know we will. Part of it is just living in this Goddamn city—the terrible heat, the crime, all the lines you have to stand in."

Josh was not convinced. As casually as possible he asked, "But won't you miss the night life, the theater, the discos," he ground his teeth together, "your fabulous friends?"

Cresta came to him and brushed her lips against his. "I won't miss anybody or anything, darling, as long as I have you."

Josh kissed her in return, but he was frowning. "My business there, Cresta—it's confidential."

She made an elaborate show of crossing her heart. "I promise I won't ask you a thing about it. Goodness, Indian relics are probably the last thing

I'm interested in anyhow. Besides, I've been told I look awfully cute in denim. Check the *Charisma* cover."

"I know," Josh grinned, "I bought it on my way to work."

Cresta smiled with pleasure. "You did? Then you have to admit I look pretty sexy in a haymow." She kissed the tip of his nose. "Come on, Josh, what do you say?"

Josh smiled warmly at Cresta. "I'd love to have you come with me." He held up his hand. "But you've got to pack fast. I want to leave New York by six."

"It won't take me any time, and I'll finish yours, too! Oh, Josh, you've made me so happy."

"I'm glad. Now you get the packing done and call Jason. I'm going to pick up the camper."

"I promise I'll be ready at six." Josh kissed each of Cresta's tear-stained cheeks. "By the way, Josh, have you seen my guitar?"

"Your guitar?" he asked warily.

"Yes, I thought I'd bring it with me. A perfect time to brush up on my chords."

Josh began laughing. "She only knows one song, and what do you think it is?" He began singing in a wavering baritone. " 'I'm leaving on a jet plane.' " Before he closed the door he shouted, "It's against my better judgment, but it's in the hall closet."

Cresta forced herself to stop laughing, sat down on the bed and dialed Jason Gold, the owner of Famous, Inc. Modeling Agency. She braced herself for the inevitable loud arguments from her mentor. "Jason, it's Cresta. I've got a small problem. Jason, I *have* to get away, now, tomorrow. I want to take off a couple of weeks . . . yes, I know I've got bookings. But there aren't that many.

Jason, I'm really tired. Even the makeup man was complaining about the bags under my eyes this morning . . . Goddamn it, Jason, I've worked my ass off all summer, booking after Goddamn booking. I. Am. Tired. I'm standing on my nerve ends. My psychiatrist told me I need a rest. Look, Jason, you can scream all you like. Dr. Benjamin will write a letter if necessary . . . . Don't threaten me, Jason. You know as well as I do that a letter from a psychiatrist will stand up in any court." She held the receiver away from her ear while Jason cursed loudly at the other end. "Are you finished? . . . What kind of a deal? . . . Oh, no, you're not going to blackmail me. I will not spend the winter in Europe shooting the spring collections. No, I won't do it. Jason, you know I'm involved with Josh. No, I wouldn't consider it and that's final." She sighed and waited out another tirade. "Jason, I'm going, and *that's* final . . . . Two weeks, maybe three at the most . . . . To the mountains of West Virginia, that's where. Look, why don't you give that new girl, Cassie McLaughlin, some of my bookings? . . . All right, all right, you make the decisions." Her voice softened. "Jason, I really do appreciate this. I'll bring you back a jug of moonshine. Love you too. See you in three weeks."

Cresta put the receiver back on the cradle and pursed her lips in a soundless whistle. It had been easier than she had thought it would be. Then she quickly called her lawyer, who handled her business affairs, and her answering service, to make sure they would pick up all phone calls while she was gone. She thought briefly of phoning her parents, but changed her mind. They had never approved of her lifestyle, much less her relationship with Josh, and in turn Cresta had little to do with them. She wrote a note for Esther, the twice-a-week maid, and left her three weeks' salary in advance. Then she dashed back into the bedroom to complete Josh's packing and her own. Because of her work, Cresta kept her closet very organized, arranged according to season and mode of dress. Her shoes were lined up in colors as were her blouses, sweaters and lingerie. She managed to keep Josh's wardrobe and chest of drawers in similar order. She finished the packing with time to spare, treated herself to a quick shower, and, after drying off, began packing her toilet articles in a large straw hamper. She started to reach for her bottle of Valiums, hesitated for a minute and dropped them into the hamper. Humming to herself, Cresta carefully made up her face. She parted her bright red lips and sang with gusto, "'I'm leaving on a jet plane, don't know when I'll be back again.'"

At the rental agency, Josh signed his name to the forms and handed the clerk his American Express card. Since Cresta was coming on the trip, he had rented a much larger Scamper. This one had a complete kitchen, twice as much closet space, and what was called a bedroom. He glanced at his wristwatch, a thin sliver of gold which Cresta had given him the previous Christmas. It was five thirty-five. He was making good time.

Josh was in an exuberant mood as he drove toward the apartment. He had been caught up by Cresta's enthusiasm and, upon reflection, now believed that sharing the trip could only deepen their relationship. He handled the camper with ease, moving steadily through the thinning traffic.

At the corner of Amsterdam Avenue and Eighty-Sixth Street, a blinking neon sign caught his eye.

"LIQUOR—LIQUOR—LIQUOR."

Josh quickly pulled over, double-parked and went inside. After all, it was a holiday of sorts. He would just buy a few bottles of wine . . . and perhaps some vodka.

It was ten after six when Josh arrived back at the apartment. Cresta, sitting on a stack of suitcases in the hall, gave him a huge smile. Josh felt a sudden surge of tenderness for her. He knelt in front of her and buried his face in her lap. "It's going to be good, love. I promise you that. It's going to be so good."

Cresta was completely enchanted with the camper. She walked all the way around it, pausing to stroke the glossy white paint and trace her fingers over the intricate design—a stenciled band of curlicues—which ran the full circumference of the trailer somewhat like a belt. He took her inside.

"I can't believe it!" she exclaimed. "It's like a miniature house on wheels. We should give up the apartment, Josh. It would be much cheaper to rent a parking space."

Josh laughed. "We'd probably get hijacked by some freaky terrorist group."

"A shower, a stove, a john—everything really works?"

Josh nodded. "I tried everything, except, of course, the bed." He pushed open a sliding door leading to the tiny bedroom. "A wall-to-wall mattress. Just the thing for kissing and making up."

Cresta became serious. "Josh, we're not going to fight on this trip. I promise you. No more bitch."

"No more bastard." They embraced and held each other tightly. Cresta felt Josh become aroused. "Josh," she admonished, "we can't. Not here on the street."

"I know, damn it, we're double-parked. We'd better get going. We'll stop somewhere in Jersey at a supermarket and pick up some supplies. If you've noticed, the camper comes equipped with dishes, flatware, pots and pans and so forth."

"Wonderful. I thought we were going to have to live off of paper plates." Cresta flipped open a cabinet door and saw the collection of liquor and wine bottles. She bit her lip to keep from saying anything, and when she turned to Josh he was already climbing into the cab.

"Come on, love. At this rate, we'll never make it to Jersey."

Cresta glanced back at the cabinet. They would be lucky if they made it at all.

5

A burial mound is an artificial hill of earth built over the remains of the dead. They were characteristic of Indian cultures of Eastern North America from 1000 B.C. to A.D. 700. The mound on the Cheat River was approximately twenty-two feet high and one hundred and ten feet in diameter at the base. It enclosed several tomb chambers or vaults. Numerous relics had been discovered from two of the burial chambers, and Harry Evers and his assistants were in the process of excavating the third.

The camp was situated about thirty feet from a palm-shaped cove in the Cheat River. About a hundred and fifty yards to the right was the Indian mound, and beyond that the green curtain of forest.

The moon was full. Flat and white, it resembled a round piece of paper pasted against the indigo sky. Fast-moving clouds glided across the moon, making it disappear, reappear, and disappear once again like a magician's illusion. The shifting light infused the darkness with a certain life. Shadows moved within shadows, and the silhouettes of trees constantly rearranged themselves into different shapes. It was a setting full of surrealistic images.

The campfire hissed and sputtered as if protesting the ambiguous night. The trio—Harry Evers and his two assistants, Ted Dwyer and Amy Parrish—gathered closer to the glowing embers, but not for reasons of warmth. It was balmy, and under any other circumstances the three would have found pleasure in the comfort of the tepid air, the rushing sound of the nearby river, the scent of coffee brewed over an open flame. But they were troubled by things that they had left unspoken.

They glanced uneasily at the dream-haunted sky, then at one another. Suddenly they broke into shamefaced grins.

"How about a ghost story?" offered Ted Dwyer, a slender, bespectacled young man of twenty-three. Ted wore his black hair shoulder length and sported a full beard and mustache. From his left ear a feathered earring dangled like a bird wing.

"Ted! That's not funny," groaned Amy Parrish, his lover, a quietly pretty, serious young woman, also twenty-three. Amy's face was covered with freckles, but no makeup. Her curly red hair, parted in the middle, sprang from either side of her head at a forty-five degree angle, giving her the appearance of a hippie sphinx.

"All right," persisted Ted, "if not a ghost story, how about a love story?" He grinned and looked to Harry Evers.

Harry, a bulky man of forty-six years, with ginger-colored hair and watery blue eyes, smiled in the affirmative. He was a bit weary of the world, but *never* of the antics of young lovers.

Ted stood up and launched into a verbal valentine to Amy. "The young man and woman in this story had what the playwrights call a 'cute meet.'

The scene—Berkeley campus, the time—the first day of registration. He and she keep running into each other, since they're both signing up for the same courses." Ted's baritone raised and lowered at the appropriate dramatic spots as he told the tale with all the fervor of a snake-oil salesman. "Now being persons of a friendly nature, they introduce themselves, and bam! A couple of days later, they find themselves sharing the same frog in Biology I." Harry laughed gruffly and Amy, delighted at being the center of attention, clapped her hands together. "Now I ask you, was that or was that not a 'cute meet'?"

He started to sit back down but Amy protested, "Go on, Ted. Go on with the story."

Ted lowered his voice. "In addition to their *intense* physical attraction for one another, they have other things in common. They find that they care for the environment, worry about the preservation of wildlife and enjoy sleeping—together—in the same sleeping bag. They are kindred spirits of the heart, mind and . . . ," Ted bent over and kissed Amy quickly on the forehead, "body."

"And then they go to New York," prompted Amy.

Harry supplied the ending. "Where they come to work at the New York Institute of Anthropology. And after tight-ass Phelps gets a look at them, he promptly hands them over to Harry Evers." He regarded them affectionately. "Who is eternally grateful to the old son of a bitch."

Harry Evers' deep, throaty voice wrapped around the couple like a warm embrace. For the moment he dispelled the subtle undercurrent of fear which had pervaded their existence since the discovery of the strange skull and bones. Harry's self-assurance was perhaps not genuine, but he was stalwart to a fault and, as such, believed in "nipping trouble in the bud." Hadn't he single-handedly done as much in the past? He had convinced Javanese priests that his excavations would not bring down the wrath of their gods, persuaded angry workers at Luxor to return to the diggings after an insurrection, successfully traded trinkets for shrunken heads in Brazil and managed to keep his own at its original size.

Harry spread his stubby fingers and held his hands closer to the fire. The heat seemed to infuse him with more confidence. "So we found some remains of an animal we can't identify. Perhaps it's a hoax, kiddos, perhaps not." He paused for effect. "I think it's merely a fluke of nature." He smiled broadly and that smile effectively colored his voice. "On the other hand, kiddos, maybe everything *has* changed. This just might be the biggest Goddamn scientific discovery of the century. Hah! We'll all be in *People*. More coffee?" Ted and Amy held out their mugs. Harry filled them with steaming black liquid and then replenished his own. "I'll just sweeten mine up a bit," he said lightly and produced a bottle from his back pocket. "White lightning." He filled the mug to the brim, stirred the concoction with his finger, and took a hearty swallow.

Ted cleared his throat. "How do you explain that cache of human bones we found buried beneath the floor of the cave?"

Harry scowled. "I don't explain it. This is mountain country, kiddos. The mountains are populated with plain people who have volatile emotions. They live by their own creed . . . mountain justice. If a mountain man finds his wife in the hayloft with somebody else, then look out! Mountain justice is swift, fast, final."

"Oh, come on, Harry. What about the law?"

"They abide by their own laws, Amy. You've heard of the Hatfields and the McCoys, of course. For what it's worth, I figure those bones earned their resting place."

"You don't think . . ." Amy began.

"We're not found any evidence that it had any . . . descendants." He stood up and stretched. Despite his burly appearance, Harry was not an insensitive man. He had noticed the furtive looks that Ted and Amy had been giving one another. If memory served him, their expressions were unmistakable. "Nothing has changed except that I'm going to stand watch on the mound tonight." Ted started to protest, but Amy squeezed his thigh to stop him. Harry grinned. "I thought you might agree."

"I—we—really appreciate it, Harry," said Ted.

"Hell, kiddos, I was young myself—once." Amy jumped up, hugged Harry tightly and kissed him on the cheek. Harry pulled away, ashamed that he felt the faint stirrings of sexual arousal. "I'll just take my bottle and we'll go keep them dead Indians company."

The Scamper left the turnpike at Cherry Hill, New Jersey. Josh checked his watch. It was nearly nine o'clock. "We'll have to find an all-night supermarket. There ought to be one near the center of town."

"I've been making a list, Josh. No convenience foods, and nothing with sugar or preservatives."

"Don't forget to strike anything with nitrates

and artificial colors and flavors."

"My God, will there be anything left to buy? How am I going to get through the trip without my 'fillers'?"

Josh grinned. "I'll give you 'fillers'."

Cresta playfully hit him. "I've been thinking of giving up meat and becoming a vegetarian like you."

"Seriously, love, you'll have a lot more energy. Besides, once we get into the mountains we'll do some fishing and catch our own dinner."

"But we didn't bring any sticks and worms."

Josh laughed. "I'll buy a couple of poles and lines from the locals. And worms are definitely out. It's dough balls, love. That's what catches the biggest fish."

"What's a dough ball?"

"Sort of a sticky cornmeal concoction."

"Now you're even pushing vegetarianism on the fish."

The supermarket was not crowded. The cashiers, drained of color by the phosphorescent lights, leaned against their cash registers like a line of poor-quality mannequins. Josh and Cresta hurried down the aisles selecting condiments, paper products and other necessities. They kept their groceries to a minimum. Josh explained that they could buy fresh vegetables and homemade canned goods from the "hillbillies." They passed a haggard woman pushing a baby in a cart. When they passed Cresta said, "Did you see that poor kid? How could she keep it up so late? It's past his bedtime."

"Maybe she works and hasn't any other choice."

"I would never let that happen to my child. Ours, I mean."

Josh silently concentrated on the cantaloupes.

After loading the goods into the camper, they headed back to the turnpike. Josh's stomach began growling. Cresta asked, "Are you hungry?"

"Starved. I was tied up with Phelps in the laboratory all day. We meant to send out for lunch, but neither of us remembered it." A familiar yellow arch loomed up ahead. "Let's have one last pigout." Josh pulled the camper into the parking lot of a McDonald's.

"I'll get the stuff," volunteered Cresta. "What do you want?"

"Fish sandwich, french fries, and a couple of coffees. We've got a long drive ahead of us."

Cresta pushed open the door. "I feel like a condemned woman ordering her last meal. One Big Mac, please . . . to go!"

The river gurgled with what sounded like happiness. Ted and Amy, naked except for towels draped around their shoulders, hurried to the water's edge. Ted set the strong camper's lamp on a log and adjusted its position to illuminate their "bathtub." The cove was only moderately deep and retained the warmth of the afternoon sun. Moored nearby were the three canoes which had transported the trio and their equipment to the digs. Amy spread her towel out on a carpet of moss and, soap in hand, gingerly tested the water with her narrow foot. "Ohhh," she shuddered. "It's colder than yesterday."

"Coward," laughed Ted as he dropped his towel beside hers.

They joined hands and together waded to the edge of the drop, then took deep breaths and jumped in. They came up sputtering and squealing and held onto one another. They were both slim in build. In fact, to a stranger they would have looked like brother and sister.

Beneath the water Ted ran his hand between Amy's legs, but she pulled away. She wanted to talk. "Do *you* think it's all a hoax, Ted?"

Ted, quickly losing his erection, shook his head. "No. I don't believe it's a hoax and neither does Harry. That thing really lived."

Amy shivered. Perhaps it was the water. "It *hasn't* been the same since we made the discovery. Things have changed. The karma isn't right up here any more. Can't you feel it?"

Ted's erection returned in full force. He slid his penis between her legs and said in a mocking tone, "Can't *you* feel it?"

Amy did not respond. She looked first across the river, then toward the mountain slope, then back to Ted. "I feel like we're being watched," she whispered.

Ted laughed. "That's just old Harry getting his jollies."

"No, no," she protested. "He can't see us clearly from the mound. And even if he could, that wouldn't bother me. No, it's something else." Once again she looked toward the mountainside. A cool wind rushing down the slope whistled through the pines and came upon them like a sudden cold breath. "There's somebody up there. I can feel it. I can feel their eyes on us."

Ted shrugged his shoulders. "Maybe it's some of the locals spying on us. Perhaps it's that goofy Reuben who sells Harry his 'white lightning.'"

"Eeuuuwww! He gives me the creeps." She snuggled closer to him, pressing her small breasts against his chest and tightening her thighs around his hard column of flesh.

Ted crooned, "Isn't it something how our bodies fit? I mean they *just* fit."

The diversion worked. Amy began moving her pelvis back and forth against Ted's slim hips. "Yessss," she whispered. Hurriedly they soaped one another's bodies, dove beneath the surface to rinse off and then, back on the soft green bathmat of moss, grabbed their towels and dried each other off.

They ran back to the tent. Amy crawled in first and unzipped the huge sleeping bag they shared. Ted entered the tent and placed the lamp on the floor so that its beam was against the canvas, filling the entire tent with a rosy glow. He lay down beside Amy and began kissing her about the face and fondling her small, but well formed breasts. They turned to face one another. Amy slipped her hand between their tingling bodies, wrapped her fingers around Ted's swollen penis and rubbed the tip of it against the opening of her vagina. She started to guide him inside her.

A howl tore the night air. It traveled down the mountainside and rushed through the encampment like a messenger from Hell. The piercing cry silenced every nocturnal sound until nothing remained but an ominous hush which hovered about the tent like a questing beast. The howl was repeated, only this time it was joined by another, and then another, until there was a chorus of cries, each in a different key.

"Oh, my God," gasped Amy. "What's that?"

"It's wild dogs," Ted said soothingly. "Just wild dogs."

"Where do they come from?"

"City people drop off their unwanted pups up

here, damn 'em. They think the locals got nothing better to do than care for their strays."

"That's terrible! There are too many unwanted animals in the world as it is."

"Tell you what. If we can find one of the pups, we'll adopt him and take him back to New York City with us."

Amy began to relax. The howls stopped, and once again she reached for his still erect penis and guided him to her entrance. He entered her, and they were joined together as man and woman.

The oncoming headlights were as sharp and bright as the eyes of a giant animal but Josh didn't seem to see them. Cresta grabbed the steering wheel and spun it away from the approaching car. "Jesus, Je-sus! Wake up, Josh! *Josh!*" Josh opened his eyes and shook his head. He took the steering wheel and steadied the camper as it bumped over the shoulder and into a field of tall grass.

"What, what happened?"

"You fell asleep, damnit! Look, Josh, you're too tired to go on. You didn't get much sleep last night and apparently the coffee didn't help. Now be sensible and let's find someplace to park this thing. You'll get some sleep and when you're rested we'll continue on."

"I wanted to get there by morning, love," Josh growled.

"I want to get there in one piece."

Josh looked at Cresta. Her face was drained of color and her hands were shaking. He took them in his and steadied them. "You're right, Cresta. Let's see if I can get this thing back on the road and we'll find a place to park. Check the map, will you? Where are we?"

"The exit up ahead is Frederick, Maryland."

"That should do." Josh pulled the camper off Route 70 and parked behind a large sign advertising Seagram's Seven. He looked at Cresta. "Well? I expected you to say that's sure as hell appropriate."

"I wasn't going to say anything, Josh." She looked out the window. "This is cozy. That's a super big maple tree."

"That's an elm." Josh turned off the lights and climbed back into the camper. "I'm going to have a vodka," he said evenly. "The hair of the dog and all that."

"You'll get no argument from me. After that ride I'm going to join you. I'll have a glass of wine."

They had their drinks; then Cresta went in to take a shower. Josh poured himself another vodka and noticed that his hands were trembling. The incident had left him more shaken than he cared to admit. He downed the drink in one swallow and closed his eyes. Mentally he calculated how long it would take to get to Jericho Falls. If they started by eight in the morning, they should get there by one or two. Going back after so long a time made him feel depressed and elated at the same time. He wondered if his parents' former house still stood at the foot of the mountains, or whether it too had become a casualty of progress. It was probably a shopping mall, he mused.

What would he find on Chestnut Ridge? Would his Aunt Avvie still remember him? Was she even still alive? Josh closed his eyes and tried to remember her. She had made regular-as-clockwork appearances on holidays with gifts of homemade candies and jams. He recalled her as a sturdy, unadorned mountain woman who always regarded him with a certain strange sadness. As much as Josh had enjoyed her presents, he had always been relieved when she returned to the Ridge. Perhaps it had been that expression of sadness (or had it been pity?) which had made him uncomfortable. Everyone else had looked upon him with admiration or envy. Had the old woman seen a flaw in him that nobody else saw?

He glanced down at his glass. It was empty and he didn't remember finishing it. He quickly poured another and downed it. The vodka lifted his flagging spirits. He attributed his mood to the near accident, but he knew that was not really the source of his anxiety.

Josh stripped out of his clothes, opened the door to the small shower, and stepped inside. Cresta beamed with pleasure and moved back, allowing him room. "I thought you were tired."

"Only most of me. Not all of me," replied Josh. Cresta looked down. "I see what you mean."

From atop the mound, Harry lifted his head and listened to the dying howls as they reverberated around the mountains. Goddamn dogs. He wondered why he'd had no word from the institute. Perhaps he'd drive over to Jericho Falls in the morning and place a call. Surely they had received his package by now. Harry hoped that they would send Josh down to continue the investigation of this odd phenomenon. Harry liked Josh, liked his sense of humor and his easygoing manner. And he respected Josh's expertise. So what if Josh wasn't the world's most reliable drinker? Of course, he had always wondered why Josh spent so much of his spare time out drinking. He sure as hell wouldn't, not with a dish like that Cresta waiting at home.

Harry looked over his left shoulder at the tent and sighed wistfully. It glowed from within, making it resemble a giant wedge of pink cheese. He tried not to think of what was going on inside that wedge. But the simple act of two young people making love triggered a memory he couldn't resist.

Gracie Ferguson was the eternal party girl. If there was no party to be found she made her own. Harry and Gracie had dated on and off for more than fourteen years. It was a stormy affair full of good times, hangovers and hot loving whenever Harry was in town, between assignments from the institute. He had often asked Gracie to accompany him on his trips, but she had always turned him down: "No thanks, kiddo. I'm an indoor girl who dislikes sunburns, insect bites and fresh air." Had it not been for that difference and the long stretches of time Harry was gone, perhaps they might have married.

Years of hard living had caught up with Gracie. The last time Harry had seen her she was beginning to show the strain of her lifestyle. Her skin was as pale as skimmed milk and her hair was dull, dry, and lusterless. She had begun to lose weight. She was no longer the voluptuous, well-rounded Southern belle who, after thirty years in New York, hung onto her accent as tenaciously as a drink. Still they had a good time together.

The next time, when Harry returned from a long stay in Mexico, he found that Gracie had died during his long absence. Her liver had fallen apart like so many of her booze-soaked dreams. Sometimes when Harry was out in the field, he would suddenly think, "When this stint's over, I'm going to go back to New York, look up Gracie and marry her. But wait, I forgot, Gracie's dead." Funny how the mind worked to block out the pain of those things you couldn't face.

Harry lifted the bottle and took several long, hard swallows. The drink caused memories to buzz in his head. He closed his eyes and smiled. It was 1972, New York City. O'Lunney's Bar and Grill. Gracie had just played her favorite song on the jukebox and she was waving to him, urging him to come and dance with her. The stray tune tickled his memory. He moved his lips and tried to find the words to fit it. He found the words he was searching for and began singing to himself. "After . . . you've . . . gone . . . ." His eyes filled with tears which rolled down his dusty cheeks, leaving trails like transparent ribbons. "And . . . left . . . me . . . cryin' . . . ." A stray breeze picked up Harry's words and carried them across the treetops, then cast them upon the waters of the river.

6

From their vantage point on the mountainside they watched. They lifted their heads to sniff the air. It was pungent with the smell of the humans. They milled about, shifting their weight, touching and drawing strength from one another. It would be needed later. They began to grow anxious and lightly snapped at the air.

A short time later their dark forms moved with stealth down the mountainside, stopping at the edge of the clearing, across from the campsite. The human scent was stronger now, and they savored the sweet warmth of it. Saliva rose in their mouths and dripped from their tongues. They watched the tent and the shifting silhouettes. In the distance, outlined against the furtive moon, another human dozed, his legs drawn up under his chin.

Their leader, his ears pricked forward, detached himself from the confusion of the shadows. There was no sound except the river and the wind. Suddenly the tent went dark and the leader gave the awaited signal. He lowered himself to the ground and the others followed. They began moving forward. Slowly at first, and then with more urgency.

Ted had fallen asleep first. Amy cradled his head against her breast and listened to the night. Only after a moment she realized there wasn't anything to listen to. No serenading crickets, no rustling leaves, no tiny animals scurrying around the tent.

Amy was suddenly frightened. She tried to conquer her wild excess of imagination, but she could not. The ominous silence covered her like a cold sweat. "Ted," she whispered sharply.

"Mmmm," he answered in his sleep.

Amy stretched out her arm and turned up the dim camping light. Shadows skittered about the interior of the tent like dark and illusive imps. As the light grew stronger, the shadows scampered away. The bright glare made Ted groan. Shielding his face with the back of his hand, he turned over.

"This is silly," Amy told herself and turned off the lamp. "I'll just try to think of something pleasant." She closed her eyes and, despite the pounding of her heart, forced herself to lie back on the sleeping bag and pretend sleep. Perhaps if she did that it would eventually come to her.

A sound as soft and insinuating as a malicious rumor disturbed her manufactured dreams. Amy sucked in her breath, lifted her head and listened. Nothing. It was just her fertile, as Ted called it, imagination. Still, she held her breath. There was another sound, then another, and another. Breathing? Footfalls? She shook Ted violently. "Ted, for God's sake, wake up!"

Dark forms suddenly filled the tent. Amy screamed, not only with the horror of surprise, but with disbelief in what she was seeing. Strange humped shapes, their outlines undefined, amorphous like an underdeveloped print. An odor as pungent as decay permeated the interior of the tent. Amy struggled to get out of the sleeping bag, but the zipper jammed. Ted, unsure whether or not what was happening was real or the remnants of a nightmare, began flailing around.

They were caught, caught like two butterflies in a cocoon.

Amy lifted herself to her elbows. She felt something brush against her bare shoulder. It was furry and stank of the alluvial earth. She twisted her head and shrieked with mortal dread. The tent was swarming with *things!*

Ted balled his hands into fists and raised them. "Amy," he rasped. "The zipper! Work on the zipper!"

Mouths snarling, they sidled closer to the terrified couple. The zipper sprang free and Ted and Amy started to crawl out of the sleeping bag. But they were too late. The leader sprang at Ted, plunging his teeth into the young man's wrist and snapping it like a twig. The pain was crushing; Ted fell to his side, struggling to free his arm. To the left another dark shadow sprang. Amy shrieked as great jaws yawned in front of her face. Sharp fangs tore away her nose and part of her cheek. Another dark mouth closed on the top of her head and ripped off her scalp.

Ted had managed to wiggle out of the sleeping bag as far as his knees, but then they were all over him. He heard his ribs cracking apart. Then his stomach was opened up, and his entrails were pulled from their resting place. Ted was dying when another attacked his throat, crushing his larynx, taking his life.

Amy was still alive, but barely. She was wrapped in paralyzing agony. Her small breasts had been torn from her and carried away. The younger ones licked her body with long, wet lavings of their tongues. Amy's consciousness faded, and with it her life.

The tent became filled with the sound of bones being crushed and flesh rent as the predators devoured their prey.

Harry Evers was dead to the world.

The empty bottle lay next to his foot. His snores were loud and uneven and punctuated the night air like a faulty motor. A chilling gust of wind attacked him from the left. Harry rolled over, and his foot nudged the bottle. It went skitting down over the crest of the burial mound and fell onto a pile of rocks below.

He pulled himself to his feet and looked over the edge of the mound. The glinting shards of the glass on the rock pile told him what had happened. He grunted, then strained his eyes toward the tent. The light was out. He could imagine Ted and Amy snuggled together in the arms of sweet Morpheus. That's one thing he had liked so much about Gracie. It wasn't just the sex, it was the cuddling. When they had slept together they slept close, almost as one. He hoisted an imaginary glass in the air. "Here's to you, kiddo, wherever you are."

The moon was swallowed by a bank of clouds. The wind shifted and brought with it a scent so wretched that Harry gagged. It was an odor he recognized instantly. He had been in Korea. It was the overpowering stench of death. Despite the alcohol, he was suddenly alert. He turned in a three-hundred-and-sixty-degree angle, his eyes wide and staring at the blanket of darkness which surrounded him. He picked up his lamp and a pickaxe and carefully made his way across the boards which served as walkways over the dome of the mound, heading for the rickety wooden ladder which Ted had made from tree branches.

As he descended, Harry cursed the ladder's hurried construction. Halfway down it began to shudder and Harry jumped. He landed on his heels and fell on his buttocks with a grunt. The lantern flew out of his hand, its wavering beam highlighting a set of strange prints at the base of the mound. There were four toe prints and the form of a large, soft pad. But they were too large to belong to a dog, or even to a wolf. The hairs stood on the back of his neck.

Harry scrambled to his feet, grabbed the light and looked for more prints. He found them. They were fresh. No doubt about it. And they were circling the mound. He felt a clammy, wet fear crawl across his skin. His head was buzzing and he was having trouble keeping his eyes in focus, and he was completely unaware that he was whimpering.

Gripping the pickaxe, Harry began following the prints around the mound. Each step was like an eternity, and the only sound he heard was his own ragged breathing. He was halfway around when he thought he heard a movement in the nearby underbrush. He flashed the light against a clump of rhododendron. The leaves were shivering. Was it the wind, or something else? Harry stood there transfixed, trying to see between the graceful waxen leaves. Suddenly he swung around. He hadn't been thinking. What if the . . . animal . . . had circled all the way around the mound and was behind him? He took several steps backward, flashing the light wildly from left to right. He saw nothing but his own footprints. And the others.

He continued following the path dictated by the prints. Within minutes he had completely circled the mound. The prints continued on from where they had started. Was he stalking it, or was it stalking him?

Harry grabbed the makeshift ladder and steadied it, then quickly climbed back up onto the mound. At least there he could see if something were coming after him. Some parts of the mound had been weakened by the digging. On the edge of the mound, flanking the forest, there was a deep wedge cut into the structure where he and Ted had been working to gain access to the third vault. Harry gingerly made his way across the board back to the center and stood there staring at the ladder, knees trembling, sweat trickling down his arms.

The moon reappeared and lent a sinister light to the semi-darkness. The tips of the ladder were trembling. The way they did beneath someone's or something's weight. He turned his face to the indigo sky and squeezed his eyes shut. "Oh, God, please, please."

The figure sprang into full view. Harry gulped and nearly swallowed his tongue. It threw back its head and howled, then hurtled forward across the boards. Others, clawing away the dirt at the sides of the mound, found footage. Harry saw them materialize over the edge of the dome. He was surrounded.

Growling and snarling, they advanced. Harry was only aware of teeth and slathering open mouths. One crept closer than the rest and bit deep into Harry's thigh. He screamed, yanked himself free and rushed across the mound toward an open space. The dirt gave way beneath his feet, and Harry felt himself falling into the wedge-shaped hole. The dirt poured in around him, filling his eyes and nostrils and choking his throat. He almost smiled when he realized that they weren't going to get him after all. He was going to be buried alive. The fine earth, burned dry by the hot August sun, rained over him in powdery brown rivulets. Harry looked up and saw that the beasts were pawing the earth, helping to cover him up. Just before the dirt filled his nostrils, Harry muttered, "I've got news for you, Gracie. Dying is no big deal, kiddo."

When the hole had been filled in, the males urinated on the earth, marking their ground. At some later date, when the human had begun to decay and they were hungry, they would return.

7

Josh stood staring for a long time, not wanting to stay and yet not willing to leave. The house he had lived in as a child was in shambles. Part of the roof had caved in, and the rest was practically barren of shingles. The paint had long since peeled away and the boards had weathered to a dull brownish-gray—the color of a dead sparrow's wing. The front porch had completely collapsed. All that was left of it was a single wooden post and a broken-down swing seat, testifying to what it once had been. Weeds as high as his waist grew in profusion around the stone foundation, and in some places tufts of greenery sprouted from the house itself. The windows sagged, only a few jagged shards of glass remained. Josh lowered his head and stifled his urge to cry.

Cresta came up behind him and touched his shoulder, and without looking at her Josh said, "It was such a good house. Why didn't somebody live in it and care for it?"

"Josh, don't."

He pulled away from Cresta. "I want to go inside."

Cresta sighed and watched him cross the front yard. Suddenly she called out, "Josh, be careful.

Don't fall through the floor." Then she went back
to the camper to wait.

The front door was grown over with morning
glory vines. The hinges creaked loudly as Josh
forced it open. The hall had become a nesting
place for birds and sprouting flowers. The main
part of the floor remained, stubbornly refusing to
give way to the encroaching vines. The narrow
stairway, once leading to the attic, rose to nowhere. Its banisters were covered with greenery,
as if decorated for a party. The wallpaper, faded
and yellowed, hung in strips from the wall like
loose bandages. A group of fieldmice scurried to
safety. The sudden movement across the floor sent
balls of dust scattering.

He turned right and walked into the parlor,
where he found the remnants of several fires built
in the middle of the floor, probably by hobos.
Nearby lay the bleached bones of several dead animals: squirrels, rabbits, or groundhogs. Josh turned right again and entered his parents' bedroom.
It was completely empty except for a lazy black
snake sunning himself on the window sill. The
black snake lifted his head and, sensing that there
was no danger, went back to sleep. Josh stared at
the wall above the space once occupied by his parents' four-poster bed. A bleached pattern as distinct as if it had been painted there testified to the
past presence of a cross. Josh pressed his cheek
against the wall and traced the outline with his
finger. His father had carved the cross from a
piece of hickory and had presented it to his
mother at a Christmas long ago. The memory of
those almost-forgotten times caused him to weep.

Next, Josh revisited his own bedroom, which
was laced with extravagant cobwebs. It was

smaller, but now it seemed larger because it was empty. He glanced at the doorframe and smiled in fond remembrance. Nicks had been carved into the wood denoting his height for each year of his life. Josh estimated that he must have been four foot, ten or eleven inches tall when they moved from Jericho Falls. He squatted next to the window as he had often done as a child and stared up at the mountainside. It seemed much closer than he'd remembered. Perhaps it was. Soil washed down by the heavy rains must have brought the mountain closer and closer. In time, if the house lasted, the mountain would completely consume it. Perhaps that's why the house remained empty.

Squaring his shoulders, Josh headed back toward the front door. He had finished with his past. He would not allow sentiment, an unwelcome companion, to remain by his side any longer.

"Are you ready?" Cresta asked with forced brightness as he climbed back into the cab.

"Yes, I'm ready. We're going to have to stop somewhere for gas, and to refresh my memory on how to get to Chestnut Ridge."

Cresta kissed his cheek. "Josh, I'm sorry. It can't be easy. Returning to the place where you were born and finding it in such a dreadful state."

"I'm all right," Josh said more sharply than he had meant to. He started up the motor and Cresta flipped on the radio. Country music filled the airwaves. "You can sure tell we're in West Virginia," commented Cresta, eying the looming mountain range. "Are you sure we can make it up there, Josh? I mean, when you were driving coal trucks, did you ever drive one up there?"

"Nope. I was never up there. Don't know why,

but my parents never took me. And none of them came to visit except Aunt Avvie. That's funny. I don't recall any of them ever coming down. Of course, mountain people are like that. They don't like to mix except with their own kind."

Cresta laughed. "I don't know if it's the air or what, Josh, but your accent has suddenly returned."

A short time later they pulled into a dilapidated gas station which appeared to be constructed of advertising signs. Some probably dated back to the nineteen twenties—Mail Pouch Tobacco, Nehi Orange and Dr. Pepper. Standing forlornly in front of the station was a single gas pump. Josh blew the horn and the patched screen door opened. A wizened old man wearing overalls and clenching a corncob pipe between his gums emerged from the building. He slowly walked around the entire camper, spat a couple of times in begrudging admiration, then ambled up to the driver's window.

"What can I do ye fer?" he asked in a nasal twang.

"Fill the tank to the brim," said Josh. "I also have a couple of cans I want filled."

The old man appeared at the window. "Dollar thirty a gallon. I don't take none of 'em plastic cards."

"Will you write me a receipt?" asked Josh.

"Ye write it, I'll sign it." The old man looked oddly at Josh. "Where ye thinkin' of goin'?"

"Chestnut Ridge. I wonder if you can direct us there."

The old man spat and pronounced. "Never gonna git that big buggy up them moun-tains."

"Gonna try," replied Josh and then to Cresta,

"You want a cold soda?"

"A Tab if they have one and something to nosh."

While the gas tank was being filled, Josh went into the gas station. The interior was crowded with dusty automobile parts and an untidy assortment of foodstuffs. Josh helped himself to the bottles of soda resting around a block of ice in an old-fashioned cooler. There were no Tabs, so he settled for two Dr. Peppers. He looked over the counter at the old man's selection of confections and his face lit up.

He joined Cresta in the cab. "No Tabs, just Dr. Pepper, but you won't believe what I found to snack on."

Cresta eyed the square waxed-paper packages with suspicion. "What are they?"

"Moon Pies. I haven't had one since I was a kid."

"But what are they?"

Josh laughed. "A couple of cardboardy cookies filled with gummy marshmallow, then the whole thing is dumped into imitation chocolate." Cresta made a face. "Come on, try it, you'll like it. They're so bad they're good."

"I thought we'd given up junk food." She took a small bite of the Moon Pie and began to chew it. The expression on her face changed from disgust to delight. "Say, this is really good."

A mile down the road Cresta was still laughing. "I can't—wait until you—present *that* receipt to the institute for reimbursement!" She was referring to the receipt Josh had laboriously made out. The old man had signed it with a shaky X.

They reached the turnoff for Chestnut Ridge. A dilapidated sign pointed to a washboard road, narrow and dusty, which disappeared into a clump of chestnut trees. Cresta and Josh got out of the camper and looked up the mountain range. The road wound upwards. It looked like a dull, yellow ribbon randomly laced over the crown of a green bonnet.

"Josh, you must be kidding. This is a camper, a home on wheels, not a mountain goat."

"Not to worry. I'll get us there," Josh grinned. "That is, if we don't meet someone on the way down."

"How did Harry and party manage to make it?"

"The river's between those two mountains up there. They took canoes and paddled upriver."

"Then how do we get to the digs?"

"We'll park our camper on the ridge and back-pack down to Harry."

Cresta refrained from commenting. After all, she had asked to come along.

Low-hanging branches scraped the roof of the camper and berry bushes on either side of the road scratched the paint. The usually lush vegetation was showing signs of thirst, and the leaves drooped like the eyelids of senile old women. To avoid the dust Josh and Cresta rolled up the windows and turned on the air conditioner. A short time later the camper began its journey. Josh shifted into first gear. The road was bumpy, and the camper was brutally jolted. Several pots and pans fell from their places; Cresta climbed into the back to set things right. When she returned she asked cautiously, "How much longer is it?"

"Don't know." Josh was struggling with the steering wheel. "I guess we'll know when we get there."

"I feel like I'm leaving Kansas forever."

The road suddenly dipped into a gully dense with dying vegetation. An ancient log bridge crossed a dried-up creek. Cresta gasped. "Josh, that doesn't look strong enough to hold a shopping cart."

Josh parked, got out and examined the logs. They were split cypress and looked rotted. Even with his running shoes, Josh could kick away the outer layers. Still, the center seemed solid. He arranged his face into a smile and returned to Cresta. "They're just fine," he said cheerfully and pressed down on the accelerator. Cresta closed her eyes as they shot across the bridge. On the other side Josh said, "You can look now. We made it. I'm going to give the camper a rest. Let's get out and stretch."

For the first time since starting their ascent, Cresta and Josh took the time to drink in the breath taking vista. They stood beneath a palisade of fir trees on the southern side of the mountain. In the distance, rolling farmlands were crisscrossed by streams glinting in the sunlight like bands of crystal. The streams emptied into a lake —a sparkling mirror of blue glass. Moored boats fringed the lake and appeared as toys which had somehow escaped from their bottles. Moving patches of shade caused by the fast-traveling clouds constantly changed the pattern of the countryside. Behind them, the mountain rose like a great, verdant cone decorated with steep evergreen forests.

"Just smell the air, Cresta."

Cresta breathed deeply. "God, that's good. No soot, no pollution, no garbage. It's the difference between Perrier and Kool Aid." Then she noticed a colony of ants feeding on a dead squirrel. "Ugh! I spoke too soon." She got back in the camper.

The road shot upwards again at a forty-five-degree angle. The camper climbed steadily for more than an hour; then they reached a plateau, a narrow shelf set in the south side of the mountain. After a quarter of a mile, the road began winding higher toward the clouds. Suddenly there was a loud rumble like the sound of thunder. Josh looked up. A cloud of fast-moving dust was descending. "It's a landslide! Jesus H. Christ!"

He pressed his foot all the way to the floor and the camper zoomed forward. Cresta covered her ears and prayed as rocks and dirt bounced off the top of the vehicle. Josh stopped the camper when they were out of the way of the landslide. He got out. A great jumbled pile of rocks, dirt and up-rooted bushes now covered the road not twenty feet behind them. When the yellow mist cleared away, he saw that the road was blocked by the landslide. The rubble was as high as six feet in some places.

"It looks like we aren't going back," Cresta said carefully.

"Not for a while, anyway. I'll tell the people up at the Ridge. They must have some facility for clearing the road when this happens."

"I certainly hope so. I told Jason I'd be gone three weeks, not three months."

As they climbed, the road ceased to be dusty and the air was cooler. They turned off the air conditioner and rolled down the windows. The scent of pine was so strong that it seemed all the Christmas trees in the world were growing on that mountain.

"Can't be much farther," worried Cresta. "I mean, we're practically at the mountain top." They passed through a pocket of fog, and when they emerged the country village of Chestnut

Ridge was spread out before them. A dozen or so houses were visible between the trees; as they neared, the landscape became dotted with people.

"I can't believe it," exclaimed Cresta. "It's a backwoods version of Shangri-La."

Josh glanced up at the sun. "It took longer to get up here than I thought. Don't know if we'll make it to the campsite tonight." Josh took Cresta's hand. "Come on, let's drive down Main Street."

"Oh, Josh, give me a moment to freshen up first. I don't want to look travelworn."

"Cresta, this isn't an opening night."

"I know, but I want to make a good impression."

Josh knew better than to argue. He pulled over, made himself a drink, and sat down to wait for her to get ready.

Cresta shut the bathroom door behind her and pressed her head against the mirror over the miniature sink. Rarely had she experienced nervousness when meeting people, but the prospect of being confronted by Josh's aunt and perhaps other relatives unraveled her. She wanted them to like her. She opened the medicine cabinet and withdrew a plastic vial. After struggling with the childguard cap, she placed a Valium on her tongue and swallowed it dry. She closed the cabinet door and promised her reflection, "Just this once."

8

The camper made its way onto the one and only throughfare—an unpaved street lined with one-story houses. People appeared in doorways and windows and on their porches, squinting at the approaching sight with unabashed interest. A pack of hounds ran after the vehicle, snapping at the rear tires and announcing its arrival.

Josh pulled to a stop in front of a building, and the couple got out. The structure was identified as "Sophie's General Merchandise Store." It was constructed of split logs, and a long, narrow porch running the full length of the front of the building was littered with sacks of feed, barrels of apples, piles of cordwood and strolling chickens.

"Why, it's a regular Bloomingdale's," whispered Cresta.

The townspeople remained at a comfortable distance, but they were staring.

"Why are they staring at us?" Cresta asked out of the side of her mouth.

"Not us, *you*," Josh replied. "You look like you're outfitted for St. Tropez." Cresta sported oversized sunglasses and a pink-and-lavender two-piece outfit consisting of a brief halter top and long pants which were cut low and very tight.

Eyeing him, Cresta retorted, "Well, you look like you're incognito." Josh was wearing a Yankee baseball cap, aviator sunglasses, and a designer shirt and jeans which she had bought for him.

A group of children appeared from behind the camper. There were four—three boys and a girl. They were barefoot and were wearing well-worn but clean clothes—a motley combination of home-made items, hand-me-downs and catalogue orders.

"Hi, kids," said Josh with false cordiality. Children made him nervous. He whispered to Cresta, "Should I give them some change?"

"Of course not, they're not beggars."

But they were odd. Their hairlines were low and uneven. Their eyes—all of them—were gray and flecked with yellow, and looked glazed over, as if they had been varnished. The lone girl, the oldest of the lot, stepped forward and presented Cresta with a purple wildflower. She was taller than her male companions and had a dark mane of hair which fell about her face like a heavy veil.

Cresta responded, "Why, thank you." The girl's extended arm was encased in a long sleeve, but Cresta could see that the hand which clutched the flower had only four fingers. The thumb was missing. Cresta managed a warm smile and took the proffered bloom. "I'm Cresta. What's your name?"

"Marinda," the girl replied in a husky voice and curtsied. Then she ran back to her male companions. They chattered in low, excited tones, then rushed away, playing tag as they ran. The thick yellow dust soon enveloped them and they were gone. "What's wrong with those children?" whispered Cresta. "They must be related."

"Closer than you think," Josh explained.

"They're probably products of incest." He guided
Cresta up the steps to the general store. The porch
was decorated with a discarded barbershop pole
and hand painted signs: "ice cole pop and beer,"
"pump gasolene," and "branch lettuse." They
pushed open a screen door, and a tinkling bell
announced their arrival. The interior was so full
of aromatic scents that it made them catch their
breath. Cloyingly sweet, tartly sour, pungently
spicey, all the sharp odors blended together into
one heady perfume.

They entered the apparently empty store and
began looking over the unusual items which were
for sale. Shelves and tables were laden with homemade cheeses, jars of sourwood honey, cider vine-
gar, and cough medicines. The rafters were fes-
tooned with dried leaves, herbs and pieces of bark.
Alongside were spiralling strips of sticky paper
randomly dotted with caught flies. Baskets and
hampers were filled to overflowing with late summer fruits and vegetables. A variety of preserves—
wild strawberry jam, blackberry jelly and apple
butter gleamed from their tightly sealed jars.
Open tin buckets containing sassafras bark and
ginseng root sat on the edge of the counter. On the
other end were glass containers chock-full of hard
candy, licorice, and brown and sugary chunks of
sea foam.

In addition to foodstuffs, there were other items
in the store: cornshuck mops, pinecone wreaths,
braided rugs and bolts of cloth. Part of one wall
was hung with a gigantic quilt in the striking
Double Wedding Ring pattern: scores of bright
circle overlaped one another to form an all-over
geometric motif. Cresta tugged at Josh's sleeve.
"Josh, I've never seen anything so beautiful."

"I bet the price is beautiful, too. I thought they didn't get many tourists up here, but this place is a souvenier shoppe."

"What a wonderful place to buy Christmas presents. You can't find things like this even at Bendel's."

Josh wasn't interested in the local handicrafts. "Christ, isn't there anyone around?"

"Why, I'm here."

Both Cresta and Josh were startled. They hadn't seen the woman sitting at a loom hidden in the cool shadows of the afternoon. She got up from her stool. "I should have lit a lamp, but I know the pattern so well that I can weave it by heart, uh huh, by heart."

She was an elfin woman, no bigger than an adolescent. Her age could have been anywhere from fifty to seventy. Her face was heart-shaped and her head covered with a cap of tight, gray curls. It was obvious that she had once been pretty, but now the vestiges of beauty had dried up and blown away. Her movements were flighty, her manner nervous, as if she were not only unused to strangers, but people in general.

"It's early for tourists," she said. "They generally come in the autumn to see the trees. Uh huh, to see the trees."

Josh stepped into the shaft of light streaming in through the window, so bright and golden that it almost seemed solid. The little woman peered at him through her tiny blue eyes. "Young man, who are you? What are you doing here?"

Josh replied, "My name is Joshua Holman, ma'am, and I'm looking for an aunt of mine who used to live up in these parts. Av—"

"Avarilla Chastain," the woman supplied. "Well

now, that explains it, uh huh. That surely does."

"Explains what?" asked Josh.

The woman smiled. "I'm Sophie Balock, nee Perkins." Her voice, squeaky and breathy at the same time, was a little girl's imitation of a grownup.

"And I'm Cresta Farraday," offered Cresta, feeling ignored.

"Aren't you pretty," Sophie said without looking at her. "Uh huh. Real pretty. I'm not from these parts originally," she confided. "My husband, Kalem Balock, brought me up here from Jericho Falls forty years ago. Then he up and died, leaving me stuck on this," she pursed her thin lips, "mountain."

"Aunt Avvie," Josh reminded her.

"Aunt Avvie, uh huh. She's the nicest person in this here place. The only . . . ." Sophie's voice trailed off.

"Then she still lives here?" asked Josh excitedly.

"Oh, yes, she practically runs this here community, uh huh. Avarilla's a real pillar."

"But where does she live?"

Sophie regarded Josh for a full minute. "In the Thicket."

"Yes, yes," Josh was getting impatient. "But where is the Thicket?"

"You just head the way your camper's pointed," Sophie explained. "Just head in the same direction, uh huh, for about a half a mile." She turned and saw that Cresta was examining the quilt hanging on the wall. "Most of the tourists we get are backpackers," Sophie said sharply. "They never have any money." It was more of an accusation than a statement.

Cresta was unperturbed. "How much are you

selling the quilt for, Mrs. Balock? There doesn't seem to be a price on it."

Sophie looked flustered. "Don't know. No one's ever offered to buy it. I'll have to ask Avarilla, I suppose. After all, she and the other granny women made the quilt, uh huh, she and the other ... granny women."

"Well, I'd like to buy it," Cresta said defiantly.

"Make me an offer. Cash, of course. No traveler's checks."

Cresta glanced at Josh. He held up ten fingers. "A hundred dollars, Mrs. Balock?"

The slightest trace of a smile played at the corners of Sophie's mouth. "Why yes, I think that would be quite adequate. Uh huh, quite adequate."

Even as Cresta paid the old woman, she knew that she could have gotten the quilt for less, but in New York it would have cost three or four hundred dollars.

Outside, the sky, a deep red-orange embroidered with lavender and gold, was as brilliant as a sorcerer's cloak. Since there were no street lights the village was fading into darkness, the houses becoming so much a part of the background, they might have never existed. The townspeople who had gathered around the camper quickly moved away when they saw Cresta and John emerge from the store. Then they too disappeared into the long shadows cast by the setting sun.

Sophie Perkins Balock stood at the screen door until the camper slipped from sight. Then she sighed and returned to her weaving. She checked the shuttles to make sure there was enough thread and sat down to her work ... throwing the shuttles, treading and pulling back the batten. Three easy steps which over the years had become the rhythm of her life.

As she worked, she rambled as she usually did . . . talking to herself and to her dead husband. "I never wanted to move here, did I, Kalem? I didn't want to leave Jericho Falls. But you had to leave. Uh huh, for some reason or other. Probably that Gatling girl, uh huh. I knew about it, and you knew I knew about it. But we acted as if we didn't neither of us knew anything about anything. Staying out late. Sometimes all night, uh huh, all night. Seems like I wouldn't be fool enough to think it would be different up here, but I was, uh huh, I was." Sophie paused to make sure the warp was taut then continued weaving and rambling.

When Sophie and her husband had moved to the Ridge, there had been more people in the community, as well as a small lumber company. The addition of a general store was—for a time—a profitable enterprise. But there was a gulf between the Balocks and the people of the Ridge. The women resented Sophie for her airy ways, and the men distrusted Kalem. He was not outgoing; a loner whose habits were considered strange even by the mountain folk. And he was too handsome by far. Tall and muscular as an oak, he had dark hair, light grey eyes and a face which caused women's hearts to beat a little faster.

Sophie sniffed with self-pity. "We were never liked, Kalem . . . I'm still not. Maybe kids would have helped, uh huh. Well, it wasn't my fault I couldn't have any. You didn't have to go off and never come back."

The screen door opened an inch. A long stick with a rag wrapped around the end deftly slid between the side of the bell and the clapper. The door opened wider and admitted the owner of the stick without announcement.

The whine of the unwinding thread, the soft whish of the warp and the dull thump of Sophie's feet on the treadle were joined by yet another sound—the creaking of the floorboards. Alarmed, Sophie looked up from the dark corner. She was a coward by nature. Every branch scraping against a window, every sighing wind, every flash of lightning struck terror in her heart. She cursed herself for not having lit the kerosene lantern. "Who is it?" she called out in a gravelly voice.

A muffled giggle translated by Sophie's imagination became an ominous growl. With trembling hands she reached for the kerosene lamp and struck a match. The wick sputtered for a few terrifying moments. Sophie was afraid that it wasn't going to catch. When it did, she turned it up to full, picked it up, and forced herself to walk toward the sound.

The girl named Marinda and her three male companions stepped into view. They smiled with sweet menace. Sophie reacted harshly. "What do you mean sneaking in here like that?"

The boys sniggered behind dirty palms. Marinda blithely answered. "We wanted to surprise you, Mrs. Balock. We know how *lonely* you get."

Sophie frowned and stared at the girl. Her eyes were so hypnotic that Sophie felt in danger of falling under a spell. While Marinda held Sophie's gaze, one of the boys wandered to a glass container of sourballs and opened it. The sound spun Sophie around. Defiantly, he stuffed one in his mouth. "Those cost a penny, Alex." He threw a lemon sourball to Marinda. She caught it without looking and slipped it between her glistening lips.

"What do you want?" Sophie asked.

A trace of a smile flickered on Marinda's mouth. She moved toward the loom. Sophie ran in front of her, instinctively stretching out her arms as if protecting her child. "Please go!"

The girl stepped around Sophie, leaned against the meticulously threaded and rolled warp. She began running the tips of her fingers through the threads and asked, "Why do you do the same pattern over an' over?"

Sophie opened her mouth to reply, but nothing came out. It was the first time anyone had asked her that question. Marinda stroked her hair as she watched the old woman. Sophie was puzzled. What did she want? She stole a cautious glance at Marinda's odd hand as she combed it through her tresses. "Do you want to buy a nice hair ribbon?" Sophie ventured.

The boys stood to one side, nudging one another and leering.

"What are you starin' at, Mrs. Balock?" Marinda said. "Do I look odd to you? Is there somethin' the matter with me?"

Try as she might, Sophie could not take her eyes from Marinda's hair. The right side seemed to be undulating with movement, although she knew the ceiling fan no longer worked. It hadn't worked in years. Then she saw what she thought was a small green ribbon emerge from between the strands. It had to be an illusion. The ribbon got longer and longer. Marinda turned over her hand and a writhing green snake crawled into her palm. Marinda, smiling crookedly, thrust it at Sophie's face. Sophie shrieked and staggered backwards. She flung out her arm and knocked over the jar of sourballs. It crashed to the floor. The glass splintered and the brightly colored candies went rolling in all directions.

Sophie, trembling with fright, leaned against the counter and held onto it for support. The boys knelt and began filling their pockets with the spinning candies. Marinda began laughing. It was a mocking, derisive sound. The three boys joined her, and soon the entire room rang with peals of wicked merriment. Then Marinda tucked the wiggling snake back in her hair. Still laughing, she and her companions ran out of the store.

After the door closed, Sophie fell across the counter and collapsed in sobs. At last she lifted her head, wiped her nose on a piece of fabric and asked plaintively, "What am I going to do now, Kalem, huh? What am I going to do now?" her mouth twitched and tears stung her cheeks. "I'm so afraid," she whispered to herself.

9

The labyrinth of trees that made up the Thicket grew close together and meshed their topmost boughs. They formed a cathedral made not of stone and mortar but of leaves and branches.

"You'll never get the camper through there," said Cresta.

"I don't intend to. We'll park here and walk to the house. I think I see a light. That must be it." Josh pulled off the road, and the two of them alighted from the vehicle.

"It looks like the entrance to Twelve Oaks," said Cresta.

"What?"

"You know, *Gone With the Wind.*"

"It looks to me more like an entrance to a primeval rain forest. As if we were going backwards in time."

As they entered the Thicket they were greeted by the sound of overlapping whispers—an overture played by myriad insects. The path, a greenish-brown smear, sodden with leaves, seemed to unwind before them. The last rays of the sun barely pierced the thick canopy of leaves; the light was diffused into a soft viridescent glow. The Thicket smelled of the wind and the rain, the sun and the shadows. It was the scent of death and rebirth. It was the scent of genesis.

Cresta walked ahead of Josh and kept glancing over her shoulder, encouraging him to catch up with her. Josh had the feeling that he was walking on the floor of the ocean, as if in a dream. His footsteps became labored, his legs nearly immobile. The light from the house seemed to pulse and Josh had the strange sensation that the house was moving toward him.

They had gone about a quarter of the way when Josh stopped. Cresta turned to look at him. His eyes were glazed and shining and he was breathing heavily, gasping for air. "Josh, what is it?"

"No air. Can't . . . catch my breath." He staggered to a tree and leaned against it, sucking precious oxygen into his mouth. His face was covered with perspiration, and his chest was heaving. Cresta became alarmed.

"Josh, what can I do? Is—is there any brandy in the camper?"

"Some amaretto," he gulped. "Please."

"I'll get it right away." She kissed him quickly on the lips. "I love you." Then ran as fast as possible back toward the camper.

Josh closed his eyes. Something rushed by. His fingertips went cold and then a strange insidious odor filled his nostrils. It was the suffocating smell of damp humus mixed with something else —was it fur? Yes, that was it. The scent of an animal which had been caught in the rain. A breeze, damp and brisk, caressed his flesh. The caress became a chilling embrace and Josh doubled over.

When Cresta reached Josh his eyes were closed, but he was breathing easily. She lifted his head and poured a bit of the almond liqueur between his lips. He swallowed a generous amount and sputtered; she took the bottle away. His eyes opened. "Wow!" he said. "I must have had an anxiety attack. The excitement of seeing Aunt Avvie and all."

"Do you think that's all it was, Josh? Your heart's all right, isn't it?"

He nodded.

"I've never seen a heart attack, but that's exactly what I would have expected."

"Naw, there's nothing wrong with my heart, love. My chest feels just fine. I was just doing a little hyperventilation number, that's all. I'm fine now." He took another drink of the amaretto and handed the bottle back to Cresta. She slipped it in her purse, then helped Josh to his feet.

"I'm all right, love. Really I am."

As they walked forward, Cresta kept her arm around Josh's waist. "I didn't know you were that close to your aunt."

"Well, I didn't see her that often. Like I said, mainly on holidays. I loved the way she loved me. I was better looking and smarter than my parents had any right to expect of their child, and they spoiled me—you know, catered to me. Aunt Avvie talked to me straight. No bullshit. 'Stop preening around, Joshua, and come over and sit in my lap,' she used to say, and of course I'd go. She'd hug me so tight I could hardly breathe. My parents, when they touched me, were always so careful, like they were afraid I was going to break."

"But they loved you."

"Sure, but from a distance. That can play tricks on your head. But Aunt Avvie, she was different. I remember one time in particular. Mom was sick and Aunt Avvie came down from the mountains to care for her. I was just a little shaver then, but ornery as all get out. Well, I'd had my own way ever since I could remember. Anyhow, Aunt Avvie did the wash and hung it outside to dry in the sun. Nearby was an apple tree and beneath that a small pond. I don't know what I was thinking of, but I climbed that apple tree, picked a bunch of apples and dropped them in the pond, which in turn splashed dirty water all over the fresh washing. Well, my Aunt Avvie cut herself a willow branch and switched me good and proper. My parents would never have done that. They would have let me get away with it. It was the only whipping I ever had, and it did me more good than all those pats on the head."

At the end of the tunnel of trees was the house. Although Josh and Cresta did not know this, it remained much the same as when Sissy's husband had built it for her, except that two small rooms had been added on either side. A kerosene lamp sitting in the kitchen window lit Josh and Cresta's way. Someone was sitting on the porch swing, humming a plaintive melody to herself. The light from the kitchen door spilled across a pair of slender legs—the legs of a young girl—pumping herself back and forth in the swing. But as Josh and Cresta neared the porch, they realized that the light had played tricks on them. The woman was older, much older than they had thought.

She was a middle-aged woman, cradling a corn-husk doll in her arm. Her once-blond hair was streaked with strands of pure white, and a limp ribbon decorated either side of her head. Her skin, youthful and pink, had lost none of its elasticity. But her face was bewildered, as if she had endured a perpetual hurt. The corners of her

mouth drooped delicately and there were fine
lines around her enormous eyes. Josh's eyes traveled to the slender hands holding the doll. They
were liver-spotted and laced with fine blue veins.
It seemed as if the woman had not aged uniformly.
A simple flowered shift added to the illusion of
youth, that and the fact that she was barefoot.

Josh cleared his throat. She looked up, startled,
as if she had heard a loud explosion.

"I'm looking for Avarilla Chastain," Josh said
with unaccustomed gentleness. The woman, still
clutching the doll, stood up and walked tentatively
toward them. She opened and closed her eyes,
which appeared ultimately shocked and blank. It
seemed to take time for her eyes to transmit what
she was seeing to her simple mind.

Her body suddenly went stiff. She drew back
her head and emitted a high-pitched cry, an un-
settling mixture of joy and agony. She dropped the
doll, ran to the edge of the porch and fell to her
knees. Her mouth moved soundlessly as she gaped
at Josh. Huge tears, as perfect as jewels, formed in
the corners of her eyes. She reached for Josh's
hands, pressed her soft cheek against them and began sobbing. Josh was touched. "There, there, we
didn't mean to frighten you. No one's going to hurt
you."

Cresta was surprised by Josh's kindness. Usually, he was intolerant of weak people. She
glanced at the fallen cornhusk doll. The hair was
made of dried cornsilk; a face was represented by
three dots for the eyes and nose and a narrow line
for the mouth. Either the doll had been given to
the woman unclothed, or the pitiful woman had
removed its clothing. Cresta wondered whether
she was seeing things. A small piece of cornshuck

had been attached between its legs and a bit of thread tied around the loose end. It was unmistakably a penis.

Another woman threw open the screen door. She glanced fleetingly at Josh and Cresta, then wrapped her arms around the kneeling woman. "Now, now, Sissy," she said. It was Avarilla. She pulled Sissy to her feet and headed her toward the kitchen. Over her shoulder she said, "Excuse us. I have to take her inside. I'll be back shortly."

Josh looked at Cresta. "She didn't recognize me."

"She barely looked at you. Besides, it's dark out here."

"I wonder what's the matter with that poor Sissy?"

"She looks retarded," replied Cresta. "You seemed to upset her. She took no notice of me."

Josh tried to make light of it. "I sometimes have that affect on women."

"Not funny. Shhhh, here she comes."

Avarilla Chastain came back, brushing a strand of hair from her face and smoothing her dress. At sixty-six she was still a formidable woman. Her stark white hair was piled loosely on her head and fastened with pins. Her eyes were as clear blue as a mountain stream, but they were also shrewd. Her mouth was broad and friendly, but her lips were narrow and uncompromising. Neither weight gain nor ill health had plagued her. Only her skin, as wrinkled as a dried apple, gave testimony to her old age.

"I'm sorry. Sissy is sometimes upset by strangers."

"But I'm not a stranger, Aunt Avvie." Josh stepped into the rectangular shaft of light streaming from the kitchen door.

Avarilla clutched her hands to her chest and her mouth formed a perfect O. "Josh? Joshua Allen Holman?"

Josh grinned. "The same, Aunt Avvie." They embraced.

Tears streamed from Avarilla's eyes, but they were twinkling with pleasure. "I never, never thought I'd see you again before I went to meet my Maker." They pummeled one another with questions, interrupted each other's answers and, alternately laughing and crying, quickly caught up with the highlights of their respective years. Cresta stood to one side, fighting off the feeling of being shut out. Finally, Avarilla looked at Josh and asked, "Josh, is this your wife?"

"No," Josh replied quickly. "A very close friend. Aunt Avvie, I want you to meet Cresta Farraday." Avarilla offered her hand to Cresta. She looked her up and down and pronounced, "You're just about the loveliest thing I ever seen." A smile creased her face. "An' I can just tell you're just as lovely inside."

Cresta was disarmed by the old lady and immediately liked her, not because of the compliment, but because of the warmth and kindness she exuded. She could actually feel it in the touch of her rough, careworn hand.

"Goodness, come inside an' sit. We'll have coffee. Oh, my goodness, my goodness." Avarilla retrieved the doll, then opened the screen door for her company.

The kitchen was large and cheerful. Dominating the room was a cast-iron stove, and in one corner sat a sturdy oak table and four chairs which had been made there in the mountains. The windows were hung with brightly colored curtains made from flowered feedsacks; bunches of field flowers in Mason jars decorated tabletops and window-sills. Avarilla set the coffee on the fire. "It's fresh. I just made it. I'll be back in just a minute. Sissy's sure to miss Only. That's what she calls her doll." She smiled sadly. "It gives her comfort."

Avarilla went into a connecting room and closed the door behind her. Cresta was about to mention the anatomically correct doll to Josh but thought better of it. Josh leaned back in an oak chair and sighed with contentment. Cresta thought that he looked very comfortable in the plain, homey sur-roundings and thought how wrong she had been to drag him to clubs and discos. Here was where he belonged.

Avarilla returned. "She's sleepin'. She always does after one of her spells."

"Who is Sissy?" asked Josh.

"Don't you remember me talkin' about her? Why, Sissy's my daughter." She poured three cups of coffee and set cream and sugar on the table. The coffee was strong and redolent of chicory. As they sipped from the delicate china cups, Avarilla said, "She wasn't born that way, you know. Why, when Sissy was little she was the prettiest, brightest thing you ever saw. Why, she crawled an' walked an' talked before any of the other children here-abouts. When she was five she used to call tunes at the square dances. She was the perfect child of God." Avarilla's face and her voice turned bitter. "But she wasn't meant to stay that way. When she was twelve a wasp flew into her ear. Just about drove the sweet thing crazy. I used hot oils an' I know I must have killed it, but it never did come out. An' Sissy, well, she was never the same. She always remained twelve. My little girl never grew up. Would you like some more coffee?"

They both acquiesced. Casting off her sadness, Avarilla got up from the table to refill their cups. Over coffee, Josh explained the purpose of his trip. It was an edited version, mentioning only the Indian mound and nothing of the discovery of the incredible bones and skull.

Avarilla was impressed with her nephew. "So you're goin' down to the old Indian mound. Goodness, you can't travel tonight. It's late an' the woods are dark an' sometimes dangerous. You'll stay for dinner, of course." She quickly added, "I'll feed Sissy in her room. I often do. You will stay, won't you?"

"Yes, of course," replied Josh.

"We'd love to," added Cresta.

Avarilla began gathering the ingredients for a stew. She went to the root cellar to retrieve a large basket of vegetables and a slab of meat. "Reuben will be in later. He's Sissy's brother-in-law. You see, he lived with Sissy an' her husband, Ben. And after Ben was killed in the war, Reuben stayed on. I moved in some time later to help take care of things. But it was such a small house that the men had to build a bedroom each for Reuben an' me. Of course, you're not plannin' to take your camper down the mountainside."

"No, we planned to backpack it," Josh said.

Avarilla laid the meat on a chopping block and began cutting it into cubes. Cresta started to explain that Josh was a vegetarian, but he stopped her. "Can't I be of some help, Avarilla?"

"Please, call me Aunt Avvie. Yes, you can scrape these carrots for me an' chop 'em into nice man-size bites."

Her knife poised in mid-air, Avarilla casually re-marked. "You know, Josh, it's remarkable how much you look like Sissy's boy, my grandson, Orin."

"Sissy had a child?"

"That makes Orin your second cousin."

"You say he looks like me?"

"Or you look like him. A trick of nature. Of course, it sometimes happens, an' what with your mother an' I bein' sisters . . . ." Josh frowned. He didn't like resembling anyone else. Avarilla sensed his feelings. "You're better looking, of course, Josh."

Cresta was intrigued. "I'd like to meet this cousin of Josh's."

Avarilla seared the meat in a frying pan, then dropped it into a huge iron kettle. Meanwhile, Cresta peeled the potatoes and cut them into large, white chunks. Then the old woman added a jar of home-canned tomatoes to the pot, plus a variety of seasonings. The scent of the simmering stew soon filled the kitchen like a holiday spirit. Avarilla tasted the mixture, added more pepper. "There's the Saturday social tonight at the Com-munity House. Maybe you'd like to come."

Josh shook his head. "Come on, Josh," pleaded Cresta. "It would be fun."

"There'll be square dancin' an' refreshments," tempted Avarilla.

Josh laughed. "How can I argue with both of you? Of course we'll go. But we can't stay late. We have to get an early start down the trail. This second cousin of mine, Orin, will he be there?"

Avarilla nodded.

The kitchen door opened and a man entered. Both his hair and his clothes were unkempt, and his face held the half-sly, half-desperate look of someone with more problems than he could handle. For a moment he looked as if he would back right out the door, but Avarilla stopped him. "Reuben, we got company. We're bein' paid a visit by my nephew, Joshua Holman, an' his friend, Cresta Farraday."

Reuben stared at Josh with something akin to shock; then he guardedly shook hands with them and mumbled his hellos.

A heavy odor of liquor exuded from Reuben like perspiration. Josh realized that he was probably not yet forty, although he appeared a decade older. His hair was thin and colorless and a network of broken veins covered his nose and cheeks with an encroaching illness.

"Dinner will be ready soon, Reuben," said Avarilla.

"No, no, I don't want anything to eat, Aunt Avvie. I have . . . things to do in the barn." His voice rose and fell like an out-of-sync recording.

Avarilla nodded with resignation. "I'll save you some stew, Reuben," she said but he had already gone. She began setting the table, looking slightly disconcerted. A silence stood among the three people like a folding screen. Finally Avarilla broke the quiet. "Reuben is a drinker," she stated flatly. "Has been for years. That's his work." Her voice caught in her throat. "He runs a still an' . . .," she forced a smile, "he samples his wares."

An hour later Avarilla sampled her stew and pronounced it done. She served the hearty meal—biscuits, cold buttermilk, a salad of dandelion greens and late tomatoes with a sharp cider dressing, and the stew—saying, "You all start. I'll just take a tray in to Sissy." After she had gone,

Josh began to eat the stew voraciously. Cresta watched with surprise.

"You're putting on quite an act."

"I can't offend Aunt Avvie." He speared a chunk of meat into his mouth. "Besides, it's good."

The old woman returned and sat down to her dinner. "She's fine. She's fillin' in her colorin' book."

"You love her very much," Josh said kindly.

"Yes, I do," replied Avarilla. "I think sometimes we love them more when they're . . . different."

"It can't be easy," said Cresta, meaning not only Sissy, but Reuben as well.

"We all have our crosses to bear," Avarilla replied stoically.

"This—ah—Orin. He live nearby?" asked Josh.

"Not far away."

"Married?"

"No, not Orin. He's still sowin' his wild oats."

Cresta said, "Another point in common."

"Yes," muttered Josh, clowning.

Avarilla stood up. "Your plate is empty, Josh. Let me get you some more stew."

The screen door slammed open, and a boy came into the kitchen. Josh and Cresta smiled in recognition. He was one of the youngsters who had been playing with Marinda in front of Sophie Balock's store. Avarilla put her hand on her hips and laughed. "Alex! As usual, you're right on time."

The boy sat down in Reuben's chair and said nothing until Avarilla had set food before him. Then, flashing a gap-toothed smile he presented a lumpy handkerchief to the old woman. "Brought Sissy some sourballs."

Avarilla said to her guests, "Sissy is a particular favorite of Alex's. He's always bringin' her presents. A blue-jay feather, a shiny stone, some-times something he's whittled himself. Alex, meet my nephew, Joshua Holman, an' his . . . friend, Cresta Farraday." The boy bestowed a quick half-smile and dug into his food, noisily smacking his lips and using his fingers to eat.

Cresta, sitting next to the boy, could not help looking at him. Alex's shirt was open and a shadow of hair covered his chest. Cresta was astounded. Surely he was no more than twelve years old. She looked at him more closely. His shoulders were broad and his arms well developed. Her eyes traveled downward. Alex's muscular thighs were encased in a pair of tight, bleached pants which emphasized the unmistakable outline of his genitals. Embarrassed, Cresta looked away. The boy appeared to be very fully a man.

Avarilla was talking. "You see, the childen of the community belong to everyone. Often they don't go home to either eat or sleep, but stop by any place that's convenient. Tonight Alex favored us with his presence."

"What a charming tradition," said Cresta.

"Yes," Avarilla continued speaking of the boy affectionately, as if he weren't there. "Alex also calls at the socials. He has a nice, clear voice." In an affectionate gesture more like a mother's than a neighbor's, Avarilla ruffled Alex's hair.

At first Cresta thought that Alex's dark brown hair had fallen over his ears. But no, it only appeared that way. The outer edges of his ears were completely covered with a silky down of dark brown hair.

The barn remained in darkness but then, there was no reason for Reuben to light the lantern. He

was contented in the dark . . . in the barn. He felt
safe there. The hay was warm, and its pungent
aroma was as comforting as a worn blanket. He
stretched out, still wearing his clothes. He always
slept in them. Clutched in his hand, like an ap-
pendage of himself, was a brown bottle containing
the top of his latest run. His illicit remedy for
life . . . his corn whiskey. He lifted the bottle to his
lips and drank.

Josh. Orin. It didn't seem right, them two looking so much alike. Reuben giggled. If he didn't
know better, he'd think Orin got himself up in city
clothes for a lark. His meditations confused him.
He pressed his cheek against the rough wood
planking beneath the window and scrunched up
his face.

He peered over the windowsill. The willow tree
was silhouetted by the moon, its silver tresses
trailing to the ground like the hair of a woman.
The two dark figures appeared again. One leaned
against a shovel, the other knelt on the ground.
Reuben grimaced. They often came when he was
watching the willow tree. Generally they came on
stormy nights. He narrowed his eyes and wondered why they never moved. They were as still as
carved figures in a graveyard.

Reuben grunted and lay back down on the hay.
Thinking gave him a headache. He closed his
fingers around the neck of the bottle and drew it
close to him.

10

Holding a kerosene lantern high, Avarilla preceded the young couple through the Thicket, toward the camper.

"It won't take a minute for me to change, Aunt Avvie," said Cresta.

"Take all the time you want, honey. I'll have me some fun lookin' over your camper. Just wear somethin' swirley—there's square dancin'."

"Won't they mind strangers coming to the social?" asked Josh, remembering the strange reception they had received earlier that afternoon.

"Goodness, no. It means two more young people to dance with. You're both goin' to be real popular, particularly you, Josh. There are a lot of widows up here on the Ridge."

"Why so many?" asked Cresta. "The war?"

"Oh no. We had a mine accident sixteen years ago. Killed every young man in the community."

"How awful," said Cresta.

"They closed down the mine after that. Orin an' Reuben were the only male survivors. Reuben, well as I said, he's self-employed. An' Orin wasn't to work that day, thank the Lord. He'd stepped on a trap only the night before an' he was having trouble with his foot. I guess that's why he's always had a rovin' eye. There's been so many women to choose from."

"How does Orin make his living now?" asked Josh.

"Oh, a little of this, a little of that. He does some carpentry—toys, furniture, coffins. You don't need much to live up here, no sir. If you live with nature, nature will take care of you."

"Did many of the men have families?" wondered Cresta. "It must have been terrible for the survivors."

"It was tragic, but we take care of our own up here."

"I can see that," said Cresta. "Like Alex this evening."

"Yes. Those of us that are left care for all of the children an' look after the young people, too." She smiled. "Even though some of them think they so grown up and they're beyond an old woman's advice."

"We saw some of the young people when we arrived today," said Cresta carefully. "Tell me, Aunt Avvie, are many of them . . . deformed?"

Avarilla stopped and turned around to face Cresta. "Nearly all of them," she replied quietly. "Most of the women were pregnant at the time of the mine accident. The shock of losin' their husbands left a mark on them children. But, as I said, when your dear ones are different you love them even more."

She stopped in front of the camper and moved the lantern about. "Is this it? It's so pretty! All white an' decorated so nice. The design'd do for a quilt . . . ."

"Oh, I bought a quilt this afternoon at Sophie Balock's store," said Cresta. "She should really charge more for such a fine piece of work."

"More than what?" asked Avarilla.

"I really didn't think one hundred dollars was enough. In New York that quilt would have brought three hundred at least."

Avarilla paused for a moment then said, "It's easy for us. We all get together an' sew them up in just a shake."

Josh unlocked the camper, stepped inside and switched on the lights.

Cresta hurried into the bedroom to find something to wear to the social. Josh offered his hand to Avarilla. The old woman seemed to need encouragement to enter the camper. "Ohhhh!" Avarilla exclaimed and clamped her hand over her mouth. "It's silly, but electricity always shocks me." She laughed at her unintentional joke. "It's roomy, really roomy." She ran her hands across the stove and examined the refrigerator. Her attitude was one of fascination, but not quite approval. Then she looked in the shower stall, turned on the water and shook her head. "Oh no, no. That would never do. Now my old copper tub—that's relaxin'." Josh offered her a drink of something, but she declined. Then he excused himself and joined Cresta to change.

After the door was closed, Cresta whispered, "I don't think Aunt Avvie approves of us sleeping together."

"You're reading her wrong, love. I don't think she's the kind of person who 'approves' or 'disapproves' of anything."

Cresta gracefully accepted Josh's putdown and went on searching through the small closet for something appropriate to wear. Josh kept on the same jeans but changed to a red-and-black lumberjack shirt and a pair of western boots.

Josh kept Avarilla company while they waited
for Cresta. She finally emerged from the bedroom,
wearing an extravagant gypsy costume purchased
from Bendel's, banded and ruffled in hot shades of
pink, orange and yellow. A kerchief was wrapped
around her head, gypsy fashion, and the inevitable
gold hoops dangled from her ears. Cresta smiled
apologetically. "I suppose it's a bit fancy, but it's
the only full skirt I brought with me."

Avarilla came to her rescue. "Goodness, Cresta!
Every male in the place is goin' to carry on like a
dog in heat. 'Course, they're real young, seventeen
being the oldest."

"Except for Reuben and Orin," smiled Cresta.

"You're ready, then," said Josh a little sharply.

When they had stepped outside, Josh started to
lock the camper. "Goodness," exclaimed Avarilla,
"you don't have to do that up here, Josh. I don't
think there's a single lock in the entire Ridge. No
one would think of stealin' from anyone else."

Josh shrugged his shoulders and left the camper
unlocked.

Avarilla marched ahead with long, striding
steps. Josh and Cresta tagged behind her. The
open, worn path led to a dirt road. To the left lay
the General Store. Avarilla turned right.

"How far is it?" asked Cresta.

"Just a good, healthy walk," the old woman replied. " 'Bout half a mile. Good for the circu-
lation." As they walked toward the Community
House, the Thicket gave way to forest on their
right. Avarilla pointed to a path among the trees,
lined with good-sized rocks and rhododendron
bushes. "That way takes you to the Lookout. It's a
great big boulder stuck to the side of the moun-

tain. Got the best view around here. You can see the whole valley an' Cheat River windin' down below."

"Could we take a look, Aunt Avvie?" asked Josh. "Maybe we could see Harry's campfire from there."

"Best not to go to the Lookout at night, Josh. You got to cross a swingin' bridge which spans a gorge an' a stream. Wait till daytime. Not much to see at night, anyway."

They walked on, a few scattered houses on their left, forest on the right, until the road came to a covered bridge. The worn floorboards echoed their footsteps. The bridge opened once again onto the road; it was now flanked by cornfields. The wind rustled the sword-shaped leaves, and the air smelled of the ripening corn. The road began to climb. Avarilla pointed out the Community House in the distance; the twang of country music rushed down to them like a welcoming hand. The joyful sound of banjo, fiddle and dulcimer easily seduced John and Cresta.

The Chestnut Ridge Community House was a large, six-sided building constructed entirely of split logs. "The young people built it themselves," Avarilla explained. "It took a lot of hard work. The men did the notchin', the layin' up, the cuttin', an' the peelin'. An' the women kept tables filled with good things to eat an' cold barrels of beer. Finished just about a year ago. We gather here every Saturday night for a social. It helps to keep the young people content, an' not lured by the ways of . . . *others*."

"You mean tourists?" asked Cresta. Avarilla nodded. "But what about your mountain crafts? Don't you want to sell them?"

"We hold one big sale a year. Summer's End, that's our local fair. It's comin' up in a couple of weeks. I hope you'll still be here."

"How long does it last?"

"Just one day. That's all we allow. We like to keep our community private. Tourists bring problems." Avarilla offered a quick smile. "Of course, I'm not referrin' to you two. I know that you respect our ways."

A group of young people stood outside the building. They greeted Avarilla warmly with hugs, kisses, and tender squeezes. She announced, "I want all of you to meet some visitors to the Ridge. This is my nephew, Joshua Holman, an' his good friend, Cresta Farraday. Now let's see, left to right, here's Harvey, Wilella, Annie, David an' Maude." Josh nodded automatically. Cresta tried not to stare: Wilella had extraordinarily thick eyebrows which grew together, and looked as though a fuzzy caterpillar were crawling across her forehead. Maude had a prognathous jaw, the lower half of her face thrust forward so sharply that her normally formed nose appeared foreshortened, squashed against her face. Cresta turned away only to encounter Annie, her cheeks shadowed by smooth patches of facial hair. Suddenly embarrassed by her own perfection, Cresta rushed to catch up to Josh. How, she wondered, was such a terrible thing possible? How could all the children be marked in such a manner? The two boys—Harvey and David—hurried to open the double doors for the trio. Cresta stared straight ahead, determined not to look too closely at either one of them.

The interior of the Community House was brightly lit; wagonwheels hung from the rafters

and supported numerous kerosene lanterns.
There were rows of plain wooden benches on
either side of the dance floor. At one end was a
raised platform where six musicians—three
elderly and three younger men—played. Directly
to the right was a long table laden with good food
and a giant galvanized tub brimming with a concoction designed to loosen up the crowd. Ten or
twelve young couples danced to the rhythm of the
infectious music. A group of people, perhaps sixteen in all, and mostly women, stepped aside for
Avarilla and her guests. The music slowed down
as the musicians shifted their attention from their
instruments to the most recent arrivals. Circles of
dancers lost their steps; conversations stopped in
midsentence and punch cups missed their marks.

Avarilla introduced the couple to everyone
within earshot: "I want you to meet my long lost
nephew an' his lady friend."

Josh and Cresta nodded genially and followed
Avarilla toward the refreshments. Josh was uncomfortable under the scrutiny they were receiving. Cresta, long used to audiences, paid little
mind to the stares.

At the table, two elderly women were dispensing
edibles and punch. Cresta eased away from the
group which was closing in around Joshua and
Avarilla. The women offered Cresta welcoming
smiles, and the young model realized that news of
their arrival in the Ridge had preceded them to the
social. Deciding to introduce herself, she crossed
to the table. "Hello, I'm Cresta Farraday."

The women looked startled by her audacity;
then they smiled. A narrow hand, rough and dry as
a dead leaf, shot out to take Cresta's proffered

one. Its owner said, "I'm Jewell Runion. Aunt Avvie told us you were here."

"An' I'm Faye Brooks," nodded the other. Wattles of flesh shook with every movement. "Nice to have you for a spell."

Josh and Avarilla joined Cresta. Suddenly the old women became quite disconcerted. They sucked in their breaths and exchanged frightened looks.

Avarilla introduced Josh to the astonished women as they stared at him: " . . . Oldest an' dearest friends . . . long lost nephew . . . New York City . . . all these years . . . Harley an' Leoma's boy . . . why of course, I've mentioned Josh . . . all of us gettin' forgetful . . . comes with age." Avarilla cleared her throat to command their attention. "An' isn't it a caution how much Josh resembles Orin?"

The women spoke in unison, "Yes, a caution."

Faye was the first to recover her bearings. "Would you enjoy a cup of punch, ah, Joshua?"

Josh smiled engagingly. "Yes. Cresta and I will both have one. It looks delicious."

Faye nudged Jewell; they filled two cups for the newcomers.

As Josh lifted his cup to his lips, he saw Reuben hovering in a corner and offered him a toast. Avarilla, who had witnessed the gesture, said, "Reuben donates a certain amount of his goods to each social. Goodness, a social isn't a social without a little bit of corn." With that she drained her cup.

The caller's voice cut through the hum of conversation: *"Choose your partners for the Georgia rang tang!"*

A mob of young men clustered around Cresta, including the two whom she had met outside the Community House—Harvey and David. Nearly all of them were muscular young men who moved with a certain sensual grace. They touched themselves affectionately as they spoke to her, lovingly caressing their own muscular bodies. They looked directly at Cresta with no self-consciousness; they appraised her body without embarrassment or apology.

Harvey, appointing himself host, quickly introduced his companions.

"This here's Junius an' Jake an' Grover; Will, Cal, an' Jim-Bob over there; an' that's Clifford. Behind him is Sam an' Rolly an' Lester." Cresta favored each of them with her famous model's smile.

At first glance many of them appeared normal. Then she noticed their deep-set eyes. They were startling in coloration—amber, yellow, grey—so that they seemed to change continually with the lights. They sported thick manes of glossy hair, ranging from deepest black to auburn to ginger. Apparently there were no blonds in the Ridge. Except for herself and Avarilla's unfortunate daughter, Sissy, Cresta had yet to see one. The older youths sported beards and/or mustaches in every possible style. Perhaps they were trying to disguise their unusual hairiness. Without exception, they wore long-sleeved shirts.

Still, they were strapping youths—strong, sinewy, vital. Robust health streamed from their pores with an almost visible aura.

"Well," she exclaimed. "Which one of you wants to teach me the dance steps?" They closed in on Cresta, wedging her in the exact center of their combined bodies. Cresta felt young, resilient flesh press against her and knew she had to make the decision. "I elect—Harvey," she gasped and a chorus of disappointed groans erupted from the rest. Cresta told herself that she had picked Harvey because he was the most outgoing. But unconsciously she had chosen him because he was the most normal looking of the lot. He was very nearly handsome. Only his teeth were strange. The upper incisors were abnormally long and rather pointed. Perhaps that was why he held his top lip tightly drawn over his teeth when he smiled.

Harvey was smiling now as he escorted Cresta to the dance floor. "How old are you, Harvey?" she asked.

"Fifteen," he answered proudly. He looked at least twenty.

"You look much older."

As Harvey was demonstrating the dance steps, Cresta noticed Faye and Jewell staring at them. "Harvey, who are those women?"

"Oh, them," Harvey shrugged. "Just a couple of granny women. They help out Aunt Avvie."

"Are they married?"

"They were. Both their husbands died real funny."

"Funny? How do you mean?"

"Sam Runion was rabbit huntin' when he got caught in a snowstorm an' wandered off a cliff."

"How terrible."

"Then ol' Simon Brooks, drivin' home from a beer joint in Jericho Falls, got himself buried by a landslide."

"God, no wonder they seem so strange."

Harvey stepped in beside Cresta to demonstrate variations on the two-step. He lowered his voice and said, "The funny thing about it is that when they got the bodies back, they weren't whole."

"What do you mean?"

"Big chunks of their flesh was tore away an' their hearts was missin'."

Cresta stopped dancing, turned toward Harvey and stared at him. He gazed at her evenly and she knew that he was not lying.

"Everybody says it was a bunch of wild dogs, but . . . ."

"But what?" exclaimed Cresta.

Harvey turned her to him and smiled enigmatically. "But I don't know."

Josh and Avarilla found space on one of the benches and sat down. The girls and young women waiting to be asked to dance began whispering among themselves. The object of their interest was, of course, Josh. Aware of the stir he was causing, Josh turned around and favored the buzzing group with one of his best smiles. As he did, he noticed that they were marked in much the same manner—deep hairlines, vitreous eyes, and misshapen extremities—as the young people he had already met. He also noted that a number of them were pregnant. He returned his attention to Avarilla.

"You feel comfortable here, Josh?"

"Yes, I do. It's much different from New York City."

Avarilla affectionately touched the young man's shoulder. "Then you should come back."

Josh laughed. "Leave my job? How would I live?

What about security?"

"The only security you can have on this earth is what nature gives you. It doesn't come from anywhere else, Josh. We must all return to nature or forfeit our very souls."

"You're probably right, Aunt Avvie. The city's an exasperating place to live . . . pollution . . .violence . . . rising costs."

"Then you must leave all that behind. There *are* more important things than a penthouse in the sky an' . . ." she glanced toward Cresta, who was dancing, "an' owning beautiful things."

Josh did not notice her insinuation. "I think the mountains are far more beautiful than anything New York has to offer. I hope I can stay long enough to see the leaves turn. Autumn's my favorite time of the year."

Avarilla stood up. "Let me fetch you another cup of punch." Josh started to protest. "It will do you good to have a little more of our mountain dew."

Cresta saw that the caller was the previously taciturn Alex. Now his face was animated, his voice clear and the words smartly delivered:

"Chicken in the bread bowl peckin' out dough.
Granny , won't your dog bite? No, chile, no.
No, chile, no.

Chicken in the bread bowl peckin' out dough.
Granny, won't your dog bite? No, chile, no.
No, chile, no. No, chile, no."

She and Harvey danced closer to the platform, and Cresta got a closer look at the musicians. There were six in all. Three old men played banjo, fiddle and dulcimer; the younger trio played on duplicate instruments, intent on learning the fine art of "pickin'" from their elders. The old men, somewhere in their seventies, were completely expressionless despite the lively music they were producing. The faces of their teenaged disciples were split with ebullient grins. Cresta suddenly missed a step. The young fiddle player's thumbs were useless, shrunken like pieces of dried fruit.

She broke away from Harvey. Clutching her chest and feigning exhaustion, she led him to a bench where they sat down. They were quickly joined by some of the other young men. Harvey asked Cresta, "Would you like some punch?" As soon as she said yes, several hurried away to fetch her some.

She looked at her companions. "I understand that you have one of these socials every Saturday night?"

Clifford, who was sitting on the floor staring at her legs, replied without raising his head. "Every Saturday night."

"And what do you do the other six nights of the week?" asked Cresta.

The question hung in the air like a piece of laundry. Then two of the young men—Junius and Jake—covered their mouths and snickered. Cresta wondered what she had said that was so amusing. Harvey quickly answered, "There's lots of things to do, but mostly we like to hunt."

Five glasses of punch arrived. Cresta accepted the nearest one and began looking around the room. Across from her was a seated group of women, aged from late twenties to early forties, who did not seem to be part of the festivities. They were dressed in black. Several carried on conversations without actually looking at one another.

Others seemed to stare blankly at the dance floor. One woman, thin to the point of emaciation, twitched her shoulders as she clenched and unclenched her fists. Their eyes looked stunned; there was a weariness in their faces, as if they had suffered. The line of slender figures could have served as a chorus in a Greek tragedy. She asked Harvey, "Who are they?"

"Why, they're our mothers," came the reply. His voice held no hint of warmth.

"Of course," Cresta muttered more to herself than to her informant. "The mine disaster." She absently sipped the punch and suddenly realized that the punch was alcoholic. "Why, this stuff is spiked!" The young men nudged one another and giggled.

Josh had been ignoring Avarilla for some time. He was staring at a young woman of the Ridge.

She was just sixteen, but her exotic face and lush body made her seem older. Her hair was black and glistening as if it had been kissed by moonlight. Her complexion was olive, and her jet-black eyes were streaked with green and gold and heavily fringed with thick black lashes. They were the eyes of a Byzantine mosaic.

Her nose was perfectly straight, and rather demure, except that her nostrils flared sharply. Lips full, moist and exquisitely sculpted had been painted carmine. As an accent, a small round mole was positioned just below the left corner of her mouth. Her hair was parted in the center and fell past her shoulders in thick, corrugated waves. It resembled an exotic headdress of a perverse religious order. She wore a plain dress, but the color was a deep, rich reddish-purple and was designed to show off her coloring and figure. It had a high neckline, long sleeves and a cinched waist above yards and yards of material which formed the skirt. The words "forbidden" "dangerous" flashed through Josh's mind. She was coming towards him.

Before Avarilla could introduce them, she extended her hand to Josh. He quickly stood up. "I'm sorry. I didn't mean to stare."

"But I did," she replied.

"I suppose I more than resemble Orin."

"I think you look exactly alike, but I'll have to see you together."

"When will that be?"

"Soon. Very soon. I'm Roma Underwood. You're Aunt Avvie's nephew from New York City." She lowered her lashes. Her voice was dark, husky. "An' Orin's second cousin."

Josh suddenly became conscious that he was still holding Roma's hand. The back was covered with a fine down of hair, almost imperceptible unless felt.

Roma pulled her hand from his grasp. "Why are you here?" she asked with surprising bluntness.

"I'm investigating some Indian digs down on the Cheat River."

"An' your woman?"

Josh looked across the floor. Cresta was watching them. "She is also investigating. You'll meet her. Here she comes now."

Roma took Josh's empty cup. "I'll get us some punch," she replied smoothly and swept away.

Cresta's eyes were flashing. "Who's the hillbilly sorceress?"

"Don't be bitchy. You're not doing so bad, if only by sheer numbers."

Roma returned, carrying two cups. She handed one to Josh and kept one for herself. Josh made introductions. "Roma Underwood, this is Cresta Farraday."

"Roma?" queried Cresta.

"Like the city," replied Roma. "Cresta?"

"Top of the line," Cresta shot back.

Roma turned to Josh. "Josh, come, dance with me." She handed Cresta her empty cup and pulled Josh toward the dance floor. Cresta was smoldering as she watched them take center position. The other couples began to circle around them and the dance began.

He certainly can pick up fast, Cresta thought, not without admiration.

Josh swung Roma in an unending circle as the other dancers spun around them. Everything was a blur except for Roma's face, which remained fully in focus. Josh began laughing with high spirits and stopped spinning. Roma pressed her body against his. Josh savored the pressure of her warm flesh. He was intoxicated by the closeness of Roma's body and the hypnotic tune the musicians were playing . . . or was it merely the punch?

Sophie Balock wended her way through the crowd with all the aplomb of an aging countess. In her bright, mail-order dress, a bit too young for her, she looked as out of place as a formal servant.

She cornered Avarilla and said, "Avarilla, I sold the Double Wedding Ring quilt. Uh huh, the young woman from New York bought it. And she paid eighty dollars for it! Here," she pressed the folded bills in Avarilla's hand. "That's minus my ten per cent commision, uh huh, ten percent. Oh, I think it's a good sign, Avarilla. It's going to be a good fall. The tourists will come again, uh huh, the ones with money. Not those hippie types. I'm sure the tragedies have been forgotten by now." She paused and licked her lips.

"The river is treacherous," responded Avarilla solemnly. "Why, in my lifetime alone, countless people, young an' old, have been drowned in its swift currents, an' they never came back to the surface."

Sophie shivered. "You know I don't like that depressing dead talk, Avarilla." Then she hurried toward the refreshment table to boost her spirits with whatever was in the punch.

Cresta, having refused all offers from her admirers to dance, stood leaning against the post, watching the festivities. The dancers formed a promenade; leading the couples were Josh and Roma. Cresta contemplated returning to the camper but didn't want to make a scene, not on the first night there. She feared that Josh was drinking too much of the potent punch and Roma looked like a very willing temptress; Cresta feared how the evening might end.

A sudden gust of wind caused her to turn toward the back entrance. Standing in the open doorway with the strong rays of the moon at his back was Josh. But Josh was dancing with Roma. Of course . . . it was Orin. He had made his appearance at last.

His black hair was wild and tangled as if it had been blown by the wind, or perhaps stirred by an amorous hand. It was longer than Josh's, and thicker. Although his eyes were partly shaded by his errant hair, Cresta saw that his gaze was fixed upon Josh. He seemed incapable of blinking.

Orin's skin was bronzed, making his large, white
teeth appear even larger. He moved forward on
the balls of his feet, his pelvis thrust forward.
Sexual arrogance radiated from him like electricity.

He wore no shirt. His massive chest was covered
by a snakeskin vest, and his pants were made of a
soft, clinging leather. Circling his waist was a
wide belt with a huge buckle of polished brass
which caught the light and drew the eye to his
crotch. Cresta suspected that it was meant to do
so.

He reminded her of a woodland diety, a god of
the forest, a veritable grown-up faun. Had he
appeared nude, wrapped in nothing but damp
leaves, Cresta would not have been surprised.

She knew that he embodied the darker side of
her sexual fantasies. He was Josh the intellectual
become Josh the brute. Cresta watched Orin as he
scanned the congregation and knew the exact
moment when he saw Josh. What was the emotion
which altered his face? Anger? Shock? Curiosity?
All those and something more. It was an expression of defiance. With visible effort, Orin rearranged his face into a pleasant smile of welcome
and strode forward to meet his lookalike.

Josh and Orin stood before each other without
speaking for several minutes. Had they been separated by an empty frame, and had their clothes
been the same, it might have appeared that one
man was gazing at himself in a mirror.

The musicians put down their instruments and
the dancers stopped dancing. Slowly tension
spread to fill the Community House. Cresta half-
expected the men to circle and sniff one another
like warring animals. Instead, they extended their

hands to each other. Then, laughing, they
embraced, parted and looked at one another once
again. Then everybody laughed and the tension
disappeared.

Roma sidled up to Cresta. "My, my, seein' them
together like that, I just don't know which one I
like the best, do you?" Without waiting for an
answer, she sashayed over to the musicians and
made a request for a moderately slow two-step.
The band began to play.

Orin stepped in front of Cresta. "Would the lady
from New York like to dance?" He grabbed her
waist and swept her onto the floor.

Orin's flesh was so warm that he felt like he'd
been lying in the hot sun, and his scent was powerful—the smell of burning leaves in autumn. He
pressed his body against hers. "Where is Josh?"
she asked weakly. "I promised this dance to Josh."

"Roma is entertainin' my cousin," Orin replied
blandly. Then he swung her around, and she saw
them. Roma had her arms around Josh's neck and
he had his hands placed firmly upon her hips.
Cresta pressed closer to Orin. She came to the re-
alization that Orin danced exactly like Josh. He
held her hand low and intertwined their fingers.
His other hand stroked her waist to the rhythm of
the music. Even the foot movements were the
same. Orin, just like Josh, veered to the left.

"How do you feel about having a lookalike?" she
asked.

"It's a surprise. A blow to the ego, perhaps. Two
of myself, it's hard to imagine." Orin's voice, although colored by his accent, was similar in pattern and intonation to Josh's. Cresta looked at
Orin's face. Except for the hair length and complexion they looked exactly the same . . . and yet

there was a difference. Orin's right eyebrow was slightly higher than the left. Josh had just the opposite. A small mole decorated Orin's left cheek. That same mole rested on Josh's right cheek. Their hair fell in the same manner. If Orin employed a part, he would have been forced by his hair's natural fall to part it on the left. Josh parted his on the right. They were exactly the same except that everything was the opposite. They were mirror images.

"Is my cousin a good lover?" asked Orin.

"Don't you think that's an impertinent question?"

"No. Aren't you curious about me?"

"Who should I ask?"

"Any of the girls here, the fetching ones."

"Roma included?"

"Ask her first." He pulled her closer and moved the flat of his hand in a circular motion against the small of her back. Cresta started. It felt as if he had pressed hot coals against her flesh. Cresta's eyelids fluttered shut, the lashes casting tiny shadows across her cheeks. She had to part her lips in order to get enough air. She held onto Orin, inhaling his scent, tasting it. Orin began running his fingertips up and down the indentation made by her spine, and as he did, he ground his pelvis against her.

"Don't," she murmured weakly. "Please *don't*."

The body heat he generated poured into her until it seemed that her veins flowed with liquid fire. Beads of perspiration broke out on her temples, merged and trickled down her neck. Cresta was afraid that she was falling under his spell and would be lost forever. She was becoming dizzy. She had to open her eyes, had to make sure that she was on a country dance floor and not drowning in a lake of liquid sensuality.

Her eyes snapped open. Orin was staring directly into them. For a moment she felt as if she were going to faint. His lips parted and she felt his breath burn against her face. She inhaled, sucking his breath into her mouth.

"I want you," he said. The words frightened her. They were neither a question nor a compliment. They were a command.

"No!"

Cresta broke away from Orin's grasp and hurried to Josh, who was standing with Roma near the refreshment table. Defiantly, Roma handed Cresta a brimming cup of punch. Cresta emptied it into the galvanized tub and said, "Josh, I want to go."

To her surprise, Josh agreed. They said goodbye to those who were nearest, and Josh made Avarilla promise to join them in the camper for breakfast. On the way out, Josh waved to Orin, who did the same with a grin.

Orin took Roma's hand and pulled her to the center of the dance floor. They looked at one another and smiled. Then Orin raised his arm and signaled the musicians. The older men left the platform; their young pupils took over. Gathering close together, faces creased with concentration, they began to play.

Avarilla nudged Reuben. He quickly poured another bottle of his brew into the nearly empty punchbowl. Avarilla added spices and apple cider. She tested it and pronounced "Right perky." Then she returned to her seat to watch the young people dance.

The ensuing music was intense, pulsating, almost savage in its liberation. It filled the night with primitive vibrancy.

11

Sissy's glazed eyes were fixed on the intricate patterns overhead. Random moonlight spilling into her room covered the ceiling with patches of yellow mold. Sissy grunted and pushed her body upwards. She tossed her head from side to side until her hair was sodden with perspiration. Her cries of pain reverbated around the room; now the patches seemed to be moving.

She was lying in the center of her bed, her feet drawn up to her buttocks; her hands gripped the headboard. The nightshift she wore was so twisted it looked as if it had been wrung out with Sissy still in it.

She let go of the headboard, ran her hands over her stomach and stroked the taut flesh. She could feel them inside her, each struggling to be the first one out. Throwing her head back, she cried out in agony and relief. The pains were coming quicker now and she remembered: that was the way it had been before, so many years ago.

"Ahhhhh, God in Heaven!" Sissy wailed. "Soon. Make it soon!" The room seemed to be panting along with her, urging her on, giving her support. A cool breeze had entered through the window and chilled the sweat-soaked sheets. Sissy began shivering. "Sweet Jesus, please make it happen now, *please!*" She kicked her swollen legs out flat and drew them up again, banging the calloused heels of her feet against her writhing buttocks. Sissy ground her teeth together and pushed hard, so hard that she could feel her sphincter contract and begin to throb.

"Help me! Help me!"

Sissy began squeezing her belly. The pain returned, so intensely that her entire body was lifted several inches from the bed. "Please—stop—the—pain!" she gasped.

Sissy was having difficulty breathing. How soon would it happen? Why weren't they coming out? Her stomach muscles tightened into a spastic knot. She dug her fingers into her abdomen and squeezed until her self-inflicted pain was greater than the labor. Suddenly she knew they were starting to be born.

The camper, white and glowing in the moonlight, appeared to float among the waves of foliage which surrounded it like a dark green ocean. A mist of fog swirled over the tops of the trees; on higher ground fireflies flashing signals resembled the lights of a distant harbor.

Cresta lay on the bed, watching Josh as he undressed. She was feeling passionate, but dared not admit to herself the reason. Josh's movements were slow. Cresta knew him well enough to realize that he had consumed just the right amount of alcohol to make him sleepy.

"Would you like a cup of coffee, Josh?"

"No thanks, love, it will keep me up."

He sat down on the bed and struggled out of his jeans. Cresta pressed her cheek against his back and stroked his smooth shoulder.

"Cresta, please. We have to be up in a few hours."

Cresta drew back. "All right, but would you refuse the mountain girl, I wonder?"

"No more than you'd refuse my cousin," replied Josh tersely. Then he got under the light blanket and turned so that he was facing the wall.

Resigned, Cresta went into the bathroom. Her nerves were taut, and she knew that she would have trouble sleeping unless she had a little help. She opened the medicine cabinet and found the Valium. She took two, feeling guilty. She had vowed at the beginning of the trip that she would stop putting anything artificial in her body.

After checking that the doors were locked, she turned out the lights and returned to the bedroom. She was tempted to lie close to Josh but knew that that would only frustrate her more. She ached to press her lips against his marble-smooth back and wrap her arms around him.

Cresta tried to think of soothing things, but images of Orin kept invading her mind. She closed her eyes tightly and with all her willpower tried to force the thoughts away. She was not successful. Orin's scent, Orin's flesh, Orin's overpowering sexual presence possessed her. She imagined his weight on hers. Would it be the same as it was with Josh, or would it be different? Did Orin embody that forbidden fantasy that many women harbor? That of being ravished by a brutal, coarse and bestial man?

Cresta shuddered and turned to Josh. She touched him, but he didn't stir. She pressed her cheek against his back, trying to regulate her breathing to his. Within ten minutes she was matching

Josh's slow, easy pattern. The Valium began to take effect. Cresta's eyes fluttered shut and she, too, slept.

At the Community House, Reuben leaned against the post where Cresta had stood. He gazed dully at the dancers, unmoved by the twangy rhythms of the music. He did not tap his feet; he did not clap his hands. To a casual observer, Reuben might have been deaf and blind.

But he was reacting to what he saw. Each time Orin and Roma rounded the dance floor, Reuben blinked his eyes, and when he did, Orin changed to Josh and then back again. Damn it, which one was it? Why were they playing tricks on him? He narrowed his eyes to slits and tried to get a clear image, but they continued switching back and forth. Orin, *Josh*, Orin, *Josh*, Orin, *Josh*. He willed his eyes closed. The sweet scent of Cresta's hair still clung to the post. He sniffed the rough wood and pressed his open lips against its surface. A thin ribbon of drool ran down his chin. He didn't dare look back at the dance floor, or else he would be lost forever to a memory that he could not allow to return.

Reuben heard a moan and thought how odd that it had come from his own lips. He shaded his eyes with his hand, stumbled to the back door and never looked back. The astringent night air made him feel better. He had started back to the Thicket and his soft bed of hay when he remembered that he had brought all his bottles to the social. He would have to make his way through the darkness to his still. He started to go back and collect his lantern, but he didn't want to return to the Community House. The clouds suddenly parted and

the moon, high and bright, cast strange yellow
shadows across the landscape. The moon would
show him the way.

Avarilla scanned the Community House, searching for Reuben. She asked Faye and Jewell if they
had seen him. They looked at one another uneasily
and shook their heads. Sophie interrupted. "I saw
him, Avarilla, uh huh, I saw him. He left just a
little bit ago. Looked like he needed to get some
fresh air."

Avarilla frowned. It was the unspoken code of
the hills not to acknowledge the frailties of one's
relatives. Sophie bubbled on. "Looks like you'll
need company going home, Avarilla. I'll be glad to
walk with you."

"Nonsense," Avarilla replied, knowing that it
was Sophie who wanted the company, not her.
"I'm not a schoolgirl." Then, without preamble,
Avarilla picked up her cup of punch and hurried to
the other side of the building.

Sophie, realizing that she had angered Avarilla,
became flustered. She turned to the two granny
women and said, "Goodness, here I am a'lolly-
gaggin', and I came to lend a hand."

"Got plenty of hands," Faye replied tersely, and
Jewell nodded in agreement.

Sophie forced a smile and looked away from the
two women to see Marinda clutching her sides and
laughing. *Laughing at her.* Sophie backed away
from the table. "Well . . . ," she murmured and
ducked behind a partition made from stored sacks
of feed. She opened her drawstring bag and retrieved a cardboard fan. It came from a funeral
parlor in Jericho Falls and featured a hand-tinted
portrait of Jesus Christ. She bit down on her lower

lip. She wasn't going to cry. *She wasn't.*

Sophie sat down on a sack of corn. It was time to go. Who would walk home with her? She hated the nighttime in the mountains—the noisy blackness, the dark cries, the sounds with no names. Perhaps she'd ask Orin. Of all the people on the Ridge, he was the most polite and thoughtful. Yes, that was it. Orin would walk her home, even if that Roma Underwood didn't like it.

From the other side of the feed sacks came Jewell's voice, made harsher by alcohol. "Orin's second cousin, my foot! They're alike as two peas in a pod."

"Shhhh, Jewell. Not so loud," admonished Faye.

"It made my blood run cold, seein' the two of them together, made me remember what we both should have forgotten a long time ago."

Sophie leaned around the wall of sacks as far as she dared. Their voices rose and fell in crackling tones, like an old-time radio program. At first Sophie eavesdropped out of sheer curiosity; then, as their words began to take on darker meanings, she listened in earnest.

After a time Sophie fled from the Community House, more afraid of what she was hearing than the night.

Arm in arm, Jewell and Faye approached the covered bridge. Faye's house lay off to their right, down a narrow path by the cornfields. Jewell lived further down the road, opposite the Thicket.

"After all, Jewell," Faye was saying, "Rev'rend Hooper tol' us hisself that the deformed baby died. Praise be to God! He swore that him an' Aunt Avvie buried it somewheres on the grounds."

Jewell was still worried. "Maybe so, Faye. But

ever since that night, so much has changed. Every-thin' is different."

"The times have changed, Jewell. The young people think different than us, just as we grew up to think different from our folks."

"Not that different," muttered Jewell.

"It sometimes happens. You remember the Jutes from over Cheat Holler? All of 'em looked exactly alike—snub noses, pig eyes, big fat butts. Why I could tell a Jute if I ran into one in Hawaii."

"You've never been to Hawaii," giggled Jewell.

"Well, if I was an' ran into someone with a snub nose, pig eyes an' a big, fat butt I sure as shootin' would know they was a Jute."

"Remember that oldest Jute girl? I don't remember her name, but everyone called her Petunia—Petunia Pig." Jewell laughed. "Don't know what ever happened to the Jutes. We used to see 'em every year at the Spring Picnic. 'Member, it was at one of them Spring Picnics that Sissy got that wasp in her ear."

"I remember," replied Faye, "and she never was right after that. Aunt Avvie's sure got her cross to bear—an idiot for a daughter, and that Reuben. His brain is plum pickled from alcohol—just never know how she manages to stay the same sweet angel from God."

"She certainly is. Remember how she attended us in our grief when our husbands was killed?"

"I do," replied Faye. She looked at her friend. "Who do you suppose fathered those twins of Sissy's?"

"I always thought it was Sophie Balock's husband."

"I did, too. He always had a hot eye on Sissy."

"Well, here's your path," said Jewell. "Now, you

sure you don't want me to walk you, Faye?"

"'Course not. Why I know this old path so well that if I was struck blind I could find my way home." The two women kissed one another on the cheek.

Faye hiccupped. "I started to say, I'll see you at church in the morning. I wish things hadn't changed so. I miss it."

"I do, too," Jewell replied. Then she began to sing, "I'm gonna see my Jesus, when I get home."

Faye, getting into the spirit of the moment, joined her, and the two women began harmonizing. "I'm gonna see my Jesus, when I get home. I'm gonna see my Jesus, I'm gonna see my Jesus, I'm gonna see my Jesus, when I get home."

Still singing, the two women parted and eventually Faye could hear only her own high, thin voice in the night. " . . . Gonna see my Jesus . . . . "

The kerosene lantern divided the dark as Faye made her way. She sang to the heavens. The sky had become frosted with stars, and a sudden falling star caused her to gasp with delight. She made a quick secret wish and hurried on, anxious to put her weary body to bed.

" . . . See my Jesus, when I get home. I'm gonna . . . ."

Suddenly Faye's pudgy feet flew out from under her and she went sprawling. The lantern fell on its side and went out. She lay on the ground for a full minute before recovering her breath. Then she felt for her lantern, found it, but couldn't relight it because she hadn't brought matches with her. Exploring with her hands, Faye examined the pathway to find out what had caused her fall. She grasped a small, hard, round object and then found several more. What were they? Marbles?

She held them close to her face and sniffed. The round objects smelled of citrus. "Sourballs," she muttered with surprise. "One of the youngsters must have dropped them." Groaning, Faye got back on her feet. Her heavy body ached from the fall, and she feared she'd have to stay in bed the following morning nursing the bruises. Still, nothing was broken.

With only starlight to guide her, Faye hobbled carefully down the path. A sudden wind rushed past her like a questing animal. Faye wished that she had let Jewell walk her home. "Now, now, Faye," she told herself, "you're becomin' another Sophie Balock." She forced herself to pick up the song again.

"I'm gonna see my Jesus, when I get home. I'm . . . ."

As she passed a clumb of blackberry bushes, Faye saw that the leaves were shivering. But the wind had passed. She drew in her breath and increased her pace. She had to walk through a brief patch of forest before reaching home. The woods, like a tiny peninsula, jutted into the Hogans' cornfield. For years Ol' Man Hogan, who was as lazy as a hound, had talked about cutting it down so that he would have more space for corn. But like so many other things, Hogan didn't get around to doing it before he died. And the Hogan boys were just as shiftless. They had no interest in felling the trees. Of course Faye could take the long way around, through the cornfield, but that would mean climbing through a barbed wire fence in the near-dark. Also, the corn stalks when they brushed against her skin made her itch. She was too tired to bother bathing again that night and, if she would admit it, too drunk.

As Faye entered the forest, the treetops blotted out the stars and she was plunged into blackness. She stopped and considered backtracking, detouring through the cornfield after all, but it would take much longer, and she was so anxious to get home. As she pushed onward, a low-hanging tree limb slapped her in the face. She must have taken a wrong turn. She backed up and expelled her breath sharply. Something was pressing against her. Faye turned; it was nothing more than the stump of another limb. She was trying to get her bearings when a rhododendron bush to her left moved for no apparent reason. She rushed away from it, but became entangled in grapevines, which encircled her like serpents. Gasping, she pulled herself free. Where in the devil had the pathway gone? Another step, and her feet found smooth ground once again. Nearly smiling, Faye knew where she was. She'd be through the trees in no time.

As she stumbled on, she heard movement on either side of her. She strained her eyes to see, but the darkness of the forest was so ominous, so heavy, that it made her feel like she had been struck blind. Then she heard it again—the distinct sound of shuffling and breathing.

"Who's there?" she asked in a strangled voice. Her nerves quivering, Faye stopped. For a moment there was utter silence. She was oddly aware of the scent of summer—the ripened corn, the wild-flowers, the loamy earth . . . then something else, a smell that had a sickish sweet undertone. It was the smell of her own fear.

She moved forward again, cursing the burned-out lantern with each painful step. She increased her stumbling pace, but did not dare to run in the cover of darkness. Sobbing with relief, Faye reached the edge of the trees at last.

The clouds which had earlier obliterated the moon now blotted out the stars. Faye made her way to the cornfield on the right of the path. Its fence would lead her home. She stretched out her arm, cried out in pain and quickly drew back. Her palm had caught on one of the many barbs. She pressed her hand to her mouth and sucked the salty blood.

Something was moving between the corn-rows, rustling the sword-shaped leaves. They've followed me from the forest, Faye thought wildly. Pitching the useless lantern aside, she ran along the fence. Suddenly she crashed into the post and was seized by metal talons. She cried out in surprise and pain, and then realized what held her. The Hogan boys had not finished wiring the posts, and three great curls of barbed wire, each about the size of a tumbleweed, had been left carelessly lying on the ground.

The loosely wrapped wire caught Faye's dress and its barbs dug into her legs. Shrieking with pain, she tried to disengage herself, but she fell to the ground. The more she struggled, the more the deadly wire coiled around her body. The horror of the moment was worse than any nightmare she could imagine.

Those who had been pursuing Faye emerged from the cornfield and surrounded her. Faye felt her stomach turn and her bowels rumble uncomfortably. Abruptly, the wind rose; the clouds were blown away and the moon came out. Faye's screams were transformed into thin, birdlike shrieks by the night winds.

A low, deep growl came from the leader.

Faye began to cry in terror, tears mercifully blurring her vision.

The leader, loping cautiously around the wire, seized Faye's ankle between strong teeth. They cut through her flesh and scraped against the bone. Another one crept forward and reached toward her face, ripping her cheeks away. The others grunted and drew closer. At last Faye knew what had profaned her husband's body and what had happened to his heart. As they drew nearer she could feel their hot, fetid breath burn her flesh. Faye closed her eyes and forced herself to sing. "I'm gonna see my Jesus, when I get . . . . " Her words ended as her throat filled with blood.

Avarilla hurried through the Thicket towards home. She shouldn't have stayed so long at the Community House. As community leader she was expected to attend the socials, and she did so willingly; still, she didn't like to leave Sissy alone for too long a time. Alex had offered to sit with Sissy, but he was, after all, the caller at the dances and an energetic young man, to boot. It was right for him to be out enjoying his youth while it lasted. It was natural.

She entered the kitchen, set the lantern on the table and glanced at the Big Ben alarm clock. It was past eleven; Sissy would be asleep by now. After taking off her shoes, Avarilla crept quietly into Sissy's room to kiss her goodnight.

The bed was empty. Sissy was sitting in a chair by the window, bathed in moonlight. Her hair was wet; it hung about her face and shoulders like the tendrils of an underwater vine. Her face was pale, her eyes glazed and shining, and a proud smile curled the corners of her mouth.

"Why, Sissy, what are you doin' up so late?"

"They came, Mama," said Sissy. "They finally came."

Apprehensive, Avarilla went to her daughter. As she neared, she saw that Sissy cradled something in each arm. "What have you got there, Sissy?"

"My boys," Sissy giggled. "My baby boys."

Avarilla stared at the offerings. In one arm Sissy held the corn husk doll, in the other a shapeless mass of fur. The old woman touched it and drew back. It was a dead squirrel, crawling with maggots.

"And I already named them, Mama." She held up one. "Josh." And then the other. "Orin."

Avarilla heard a piercing scream and realized that it had come from her own lips.

Part Two

"Surely the serpent will bite
without enchantment;
And a babbler is no better."

ECCLESIASTES, 10:11

12

The sun exploded in a shower of golden needles through the treetops. The dusty path resembled a strip of beaten bronze until it was disturbed by Avarilla's footsteps. Carrying a huge basket, she hurried toward the camper, through the spangled sunlight.

The old woman tapped lightly on the door.

Josh answered it. "Aunt Avvie! You're up early." He was wearing cutoffs, a tank top and sandals.

"You'll forgive me, Josh," she said kissing him warmly on the cheek. "I brought you breakfast." She held up the basket. "Fresh eggs, country bacon, homemade bread, red raspberry jam, an' a tub of butter. I hope that's to your likin'."

"Sounds wonderful. But you shouldn't—"

"Of course I should have," interrupted Avarilla. "This is quite an event for me. Your comin' back to the Ridge." She set down her basket and rolled up the sleeves of her plain, homespun dress. "Now, if you'll just show me where everythin' is, I'll get breakfast on. Looks like your coffee's finished perkin'."

"But Cresta and I—"

Avarilla smiled. "I always say there's nothin' so nice as wakin' up to the smell of bacon. She's still asleep, is she?"

"She was tired out—the trip and all."

"And the dancin'. Goodness, she had a lively time last night."

Josh poured coffee for himself and Avarilla. "Did the social last much longer?"

"It was still goin' when I left."

"How did Orin react to meeting me?"

"He took it in stride, just like you. I guess I never stopped to think that nobody really likes to look like anybody else."

Josh started to answer her, thought better of it, and began taking down dishes, frying pans and forks and spoons.

Even though Cresta was groggy from the Valium, the seductive aroma of bacon brought her to her feet. She quickly pinned up her hair and put on a robe of Chinese silk. Then she opened the sliding door and stuck her head out. "Did I oversleep? I was supposed to cook."

"No, love," said Josh. "Aunt Avvie brought all sorts of good things for breakfast. We thought we'd just go ahead with it."

"It smells wonderful. I'll be with you as soon as I take a quick shower."

After Cresta had disappeared into the bathroom, Avarilla remarked, "I must say, she's one of the few women I've ever seen who looks just as beautiful in the morning."

"That was her main selling point," grinned Josh.

Avarilla insisted on serving the young couple first, before sitting down herself. Josh ate with gusto, and Cresta was surprised to see that he ate half a dozen strips of bacon. Well, it *was* delicious. The old woman ate lightly herself, explaining, "Better to eat less as you grow older. It sustains one's health." Then she turned serious. "Josh, I

want you an' Cresta to be real careful climbin'
down that mountainside to the river. You'll be
takin' the old mining trail, but don't go explorin'
any of those boarded-up mine shafts. They're dangerous. I guess the mountain took offense at
gettin' all cut up like that. An' dress in somethin'
sturdy. You'll need high boots. You got to watch
out for the brambles an' the snakes." Cresta shivered, and Avarilla added, "They won't bother you
if you don't bother them. They're just creatures of
nature. How long are you plannin' to stay down on
the river?"

"Well, we'll want to visit with Harry and his
assistants . . . ."

"You shouldn't try to start back this afternoon.
You wouldn't make it back to the Ridge before
dark. Better wait an' come back in the morning. If
you'll fetch me a piece of paper, I'll draw you as
good a map as I can recollect."

Cresta cleared the table and washed the dishes
while Avarilla, brow knitted in concentration,
drew a crude map. "You start off goin' toward the
store—away from the Community Center—but
you'll see a little road goin' off to the left. You turn
there. It'll take you to the trail." She added,
"You'd better be takin' some food an' blankets."

"I've already packed the necessaries in the backpacks."

Avarilla gathered her empty basket. "Well, I'd
better get going. It's at least eight o'clock. I've got
wood to chop, chickens to feed, an' a cow to milk."
She lowered her voice. "An' I don't like to leave
Sissy alone for too long a spell. She'll be wantin'
her breakfast." She embraced them both and left.

Cresta remarked, "I hope when I grow old, I
grow old with as much grace and kindness as Aunt

Avvie. She makes me feel guilty for all the petty things I fuss about."

Doing as Avarilla had told them, the couple dressed in long-sleeved shirts, jeans and high boots. They strapped on the backpacks and, after locking the camper, were on their way.

The sun-scorched little road came to a fork. Josh and Cresta stopped, wiped their dusty faces with handkerchiefs and looked at one another. The fork hadn't appeared on Avvie's map.

"Which way to Oz?" wondered Cresta. She glanced around and suddenly began laughing. "Look, Josh, look! There's even a scarecrow. Is that prophetic or what?"

A dissolute scarecrow stood sentinel above the rows of tassel stalks. Arms stretched out, body dangling down, it was dressed in a threadbare jacket, baggy pants and a misshapen hat—all black. The head was made from a flower sack stuffed with husks. Somebody had added yarn to represent hair. The face had been painted on in bold, rough strokes, and the "artist" had given the scarecrow a disturbing expression. The eyes were wide and staring, the nostrils flared and mouth open and twisted into a silent scream.

Cresta muttered, "Someone has a wild imagination."

"Or a macabre one," added Josh. "By the way, they don't call them scarecrows around here. They're called scarebuggers."

"Scarebugger! That one certainly is. It's scarier than anything I've ever seen outside an amusement park." She looked at the paths. One went uphill and the other down. "Let's take the high road." Josh nodded, and they walked on. About ten yards further on, the trees cleared and they saw that they were approaching an old country church. "This can't be the way," exclaimed Cresta. "The path ends at the church."

"We needed to go the other way. I wonder why Aunt Avvie didn't mention the fork?"

The path looked as if it hadn't been used for a very long time. The church was set on the crest of a hillock. Its front was windowless, but there was a covered entrance and several steps leading up to it. Paint hung in scabs from the warped boards. The grass and bushes near the structure were brown and paper-dry.

"That's odd," said Cresta. "It looks abandoned. I thought mountain people were fervently religious."

"They are. I expect the preacher's a traveling man and doesn't get up here too often. Either that, or they've built a new church somewhere else. Come on, love, let's go." He wanted to leave. The church reminded him uncomfortably of his parents' home in Jericho Falls.

"Oh, Josh," pleaded Cresta, "let's look around." She walked around the side of the church and called, "Josh, here's a graveyard. Please, I'd like to see."

Josh sighed and followed her.

"Oh, Josh, it's in absolute ruins. It looks as if its been bombed or something. Why on earth don't the townspeople take care of it?"

The burial ground contained roughly fifty graves, which were overgrown with leaves and thistle. Crosses, stones and wooden markers were staggered at odd angles. Here and there graves were covered with an iridescent moss which glistened like a dragonfly's wings. Cresta shuddered, and Josh slipped his arm around her. "I was hoping to make some rubbings of the gravestones," she said sadly. "When they're framed they make wonderful decorative pieces." Hand in hand they walked in through the rusted iron gate. Some of the graves had sunken several feet into the ground. One section of the hillside had eroded, and rotting caskets were clearly visible.

"Josh, how ghastly. Don't they care anything for their relatives?"

"Maybe they're planning on moving the graves to the new church," Josh suggested.

"Lord, I hope so! It looks so desolate. This does it. I've made up my mind to be cremated once and for all."

They took off their heavy backpacks, set them on the ground and turned to face the back of the church. This side had a stained glass window. It was not large; it looked as though it had been fashioned by local craftsmen. Still, the work was remarkable. It was a life-size depiction of a simple, childlike Christ wearing a milky-white robe, standing alone on a road, his arms outstretched in a gesture of welcome. A small, cuddly lamb lay curled at his feet. The colors were bold, startling in their intensity. They added to the pleasing, if primitive, effect.

"Josh, it's beautiful. It makes me want to cry or get religion."

Josh did not answer. He stooped and gathered up his backpack. "We'd better get going, Cresta. Harry's undoubtedly made a call to the institute by now, and he'll be expecting us. Cresta?"

Cresta started to turn, and then out of the corner of her eye she saw movement. "Josh! *Josh!*" Josh looked up. Cresta stood clenching and unclenching her fists. Despite her natural high color, her face was ashen.

"Cresta, what is it?"

"His face," she gasped. "It's alive! Jesus was looking at me."

"What in the hell are you talking about?"

"Look. Look at his face."

Josh stared at the glass face of Christ. "You're seeing things. It's nothing but a window."

"Josh, I know what I'm talking about. The face was looking at me. The eyes moved, the lips moved, the whole face shifted."

"Cresta," said Josh patiently, "the sunlight is playing tricks on you. Come on, we've got to go."

Cresta allowed herself to be led away.

"Come on, love, I'm going to sit you down in the shade, and I'll give you a nice cold drink of water." Josh led Cresta to the front of the church, made her sit down on the bottom step. He opened his canteen and handed it to her.

Cresta took a long drink, wiped her mouth with the back of her hand, and said evenly, "I don't care what you say. I saw what I saw."

"Maybe I'd better take you inside. It's probably cooler in there. You might have a touch of sunstroke." Josh tried the church door, but it was locked. He looked up and read the sign over the door. "The Holiness Church of Sweet Jesus Savior." His expression changed: filthy words and vile epithets had been scratched into the sign with sharp instruments. As he started back down the steps, his foot hit against a pie tin. The tin, burned black with age, was empty save for a few small, polished bones. "They must have a dog here, keeping guard against vandals."

Cresta eyed the bones and replied dully, "It

must be an awfully neat dog."

"You're feeling better, then?"

"Yes, let's get on with it."

Further down the path, Cresta glanced over her shoulder. The church, silhouetted against the blazing sun, resembled a giant tombstone.

The inside of the church was as bleak and chill as winter. The Sin-Eater climbed down from the ladder which stood next to the stained-glass window and headed for the pulpit. The weight of his boots made crunching sounds upon the sheddings which were strewn about the floor like long cellophane wrappers. He moved carefully. His companions uncoiled and slithered out of his way.

A swarm of copperheads, rattlesnakes, blacksnakes and garter snakes constituted all that was left of the congregation of the Holiness Church of Sweet Jesus Savior.

Several were draped from the rafters like morbid party decorations. Others wound around moldering songbooks like satanic rosaries. Still others clustered together in unholy wreaths.

Reverend Hooper ascended the steps to the pulpit. A copperhead unwound with intricate grace and slid away, allowing him access to his Bible. He opened the brittle book to St. Matthew. A waterstain, like a dark yellow birthmark, blemished the pages. The preacher cast his watery eyes downward. He recognized the section only by the number of letters in its name in the upper righthand corner. The reverend recited from memory, often paraphrasing the passages to suit his feelings of the moment. The shocking events of the past years had so scrambled his mind that he could no longer read.

He parted his cracked lips and spoke in a hoarse, fanatic voice. "An' I say! For where three or four of you are gathered together here in My name, then I am here in the midst of you." He scanned his congregation, and his distorted memory filled the pews with people. "Yea, Lord. There are spirits that are created for vengeance an' in their fury they lay on grievous torments. I say that they are the enemy of God an' must be scattered!"

As he preached, the reverend punctuated his words with vigorous gestures. He slapped his hands together, balled them into fists and struck his cheeks. He pulled at his shoulder-length hair and stamped down the steps of the pulpit. The serpents, long used to the preacher's histrionics, did not stir. His words became a choked babble, as he began to hop about the church on one foot. The snakes, pointing their seed-like eyes at him, darted out of his way. Some hissed and struck at the preacher's heavy boots, angry at being disturbed.

"I will rise again in glory and they will reap the punishment of their iniquity!"

Reverend Hooper had once been a tall man, broad-shouldered and roughly handsome. Now he was stooped, thin as a starved bird; all vestiges of his good looks had long since disappeared. His pallid skin looked repulsive and artificial. His hair, knotted and unwashed, grew about his head in rank profusion and intermingled with the matted hair of his beard. It was hard to tell where one left off and the other began. He had the wild eyes of a fallen saint . . . vacant, opaque, the pupils cast up as if waiting to be imprinted with the image of paradise.

He wore a pair of bib overalls, foul with sweat

and mottled with food stains, a white shirt now as yellow as old ivory, a string tie, and a jacket whose seams sprouted black threads.

In one sense, Reverend Hooper had descended into hell on the night of September twelve, nineteen seventy and four. In another, his ruination had begun many years earlier.

There had been a burial on that September day in 1974. Wilma Gillespie's favorite child, Fern, twelve years old and an epileptic, had died, when she suffered a convulsion. There had been no one to help her and she had choked on her own tongue. Following the funeral, the preacher had attended the grieving mother for the remainder of the afternoon and well into the evening. Then, exhausted, he had gone to the church to pray for the young girl, as he had promised Fern's mother and father.

The interior of the church had reeked of flowers and something else—the scent of death. Fern's distraught mother had refused to give up her child to the earth, and it wasn't until the granny women had talked to her that she agreed to let her daughter be buried. Bodies were not embalmed in the mountains. Because of the delay, the casket had to be closed and sealed. Still, the air had become permeated with the unmistakable smell of the dead.

He took a long swallow from the bottle of Reuben's strong blend which he carried with him for "medicinal purposes." Then he knelt and began to pray for Fern's immortal soul. The alcohol helped work up his fervor.

"Sa-weet Je-sus! Take this little gal unto your bosom. Amen. Praise the Lord an' Hallelujah! Take little Fern an' set her right next to You on

Your golden throne." He took another sip from the bottle, which he set on the floor. Perspiration coursed down his face. The bandanna came loose and fell to the floor, which was littered with flower petals like so many split communion wafers. He reached for his bandanna, swabbed his brow and raised his mighty voice again.

"You remember, Fern, Lord? The youngest gal on the Ridge to find salvation an' give testimony. Only twelve years old, Lord, an' she knew enough to test her faith in You. An' they shall take up serpents, an' they shall speak with new tongues an' in Thy name they shall cast out devils!"

Fern had given her testimony only a few weeks before her death. Too tall for her age, elbows jutting, wrists thin and angular, frizzy red hair framing a valentine face—Fern had eased her way down the aisle toward the preacher, toward the rattlesnakes coiled around his arms. Her eyes were rolled back in her head, as if she was having one of her fits, but her expression was serene.

The choir started up the upbeat mountain version of "Gimme That Old Time Religion"; the worshippers, gathered in a crescent around the preacher, clapped and praised and pressed close together.

Fern approached Reverend Hooper and calmly placed her bare arm next to his. The rattler uncoiled and swiftly wrapped itself around her wrist. Fern was transfixed. Hallelujahs and amens burst from the congregation. The preacher's voice boomed out: "An' a little child, I say, a little child shall lead them!"

It had been a memorable testimony, and the preacher had recalled it on the night of her funeral with swelling pride. "Her soul was purified, Lord.

Amen. I know You will stretch forth Your hand and take Your anointed one. Fern Gillespie was a true believer."

An unearthly howl interrupted the preacher's prayers for Fern. He gave a violent start. The stench of corruption, hideously evocative, was overpowering.

He rose to his feet. The sound had come from outside the stained-glass window overlooking the graveyard.

A series of howls more like mocking laughs erupted outside. The preacher pressed his face against the glass. He could see nothing but the bright moonlight outside, now turned a ghastly shade of green by the glass. He looked up at the face of Christ. He would be able to see through that lightly tinted oval. He dragged the stepladder from behind the organ, set it by the window, and started to climb. Terror shook his body. Why did fear consume him? The preacher was not a coward. Indeed, little on the earth caused him trepidation. When he reached the top rung he pressed his face against the face of Christ.

Had God been toppled from his throne? Had Satan's messengers been released from the burning pits to plague the living?

Creatures—their bodies covered with hair, their limbs grotesquely misshapen, their faces masks of degeneracy—had dug up the grave of Fern Gillespie, dragged her body from its resting place and were dancing around it. Shredded and bloodied and only partially covered by her communion dress, Fern had been placed on a fallen tombstone. They were devouring parts of her.

The preacher opened his mouth to cry for help, but no words came out. Who would have answered? In that moment he lost his faith. God had deserted His earth. Reverend Hooper pulled his face away from the window and retched, but his body found no relief in sickness. He knew that he should tear the cross from the wall, march into the graveyard and defy them. But he was gripped by fear unlike anything he had ever experienced. The mocking howls reverberated throughout the church and chilled the preacher to the very marrow of his bones. Try as he might; he could not quit the scene. His eyes were drawn back to the graveyard. He watched, his mind crumbling with horror, through the rest of the night.

Toward dawn the creatures dispersed and their hold over the preacher was broken. He climbed down the ladder and crouched at the foot. He stayed there, shivering, until the sun was in the center of the sky.

In the years after Fern's death, his torments had continued—strange birthings, violent deaths and hideous night sounds of digging in the graveyard. Graves were ripped asunder, bodies withered and atrophied were desecrated and sometimes devoured. And there were the orgies—unholy couplings of the things upon the gravesites.

Ashamed of his cowardice and his loss of faith, the preacher had closed the doors of the Holiness Church of Sweet Jesus Savior and became an outcast in the community, an object of ridicule. He was pressed into the bitter role of "Sin-Eater." When someone in the community died, the Sin-Eater had to be the first to enter the house after the dead was laid out. He had to eat a bit of each dish provided for the wake. Symbolically, he was eating the sins of the dead.

One night his house burned down, whether by

accident or plan Reverend Hooper never knew. It mattered little. He had already adopted the church as a shelter. He existed on food which the older members of his dispersed congregation left on the church steps. He never bathed. He rarely left the sanctity of his own madness.

Now the only human inhabitant of the Holiness Church returned to the ladder. He was watching for some sign that would tell him that God had returned to the Ridge and had driven away the infidels of the night. Balancing himself on the top of the ladder, his eyes fixed on the unmoving eyes of Christ, he began to sing in a wavering voice, "Amazing Grace! How sweet the sound, come save a wretch like me!"

At the melody the serpents stirred. They began moving rhythmically, in time to the preacher's voice.

Cresta and Josh reached the site of the coal mine just before noon. The tunnels and shafts had been boarded up. A ruined trestle, a damaged and rusting bulldozer, and a section of track were all that testified that the mine had existed. Deep fissures in the mountainside, washed deeper by rain, resembled great, angry scars.

Josh and Cresta sat in the shadow of the trestle and ate a lunch of hard-boiled eggs, cheese and iced tea, plus butter-and-jam sandwiches.

"You'd think they'd put up some sort of a memorial or something," said Cresta. "I mean, all those men who died here . . . ."

"They probably wanted to forget it," said Josh., He glanced up at the tipple. "Thank God Dad got that job in Morgantown, where there were better schools and a university, or I might have very well ended up working right here."

Cresta shuddered. "What a life, digging in the ground. It makes a man old before his time."

Josh laughed. "What do you know about mining, love?"

"I read, you know. And I see movies. Remember watching *How Green Was My Valley* on television?" Josh shook his head. "That's right. You were out that night." It had been one of those nights when Josh hadn't come home until dawn. She pushed the unpleasant memory out of her mind. "In a way, I'm glad the mine didn't continue. It would have ruined the beauty of the setting."

"We'd better get going," said Josh, swinging his backpack into place.

Cresta groaned. "How far is it to the river?"

"Not far. Look down there, through the trees. You can see it winking in the sun."

"I don't see anything."

"You will, love, you will."

An hour later they had reached the Cheat River. It sparkled as if in reward for their efforts. Despite their exhaustion, they were exhilarated by the beauty of the river. They broke into a run and at the river's edge knelt to splash cool water on their faces. "How long did it take us, Josh?"

He looked at his watch. "It's nearly two. God, we've been hiking for more than five hours." Cresta touched Josh's arm. They looked at each other and smiled; she realized that she had experienced more pleasure in being with him today than she had since the early weeks of their courtship.

"I think I see the mound," cried Cresta, pointing down the river. "See there, to the right? It sort of looks like a giant Reese's Cup."

"That has to be it," agreed Josh, shading his

eyes against the sun. "But I don't see the camp."

"It's probably further on, behind those Christmas trees." Josh grinned at Cresta's catchword for every evergreen, but he was uneasy. Harry was a man of convenience. He would not have made camp far from the subject of investigation.

On their way downstream they came upon some blackberry bushes and stopped to sample a few berries.

"I wish I had something to put them in," said Cresta. "We could take some to Harry and his assistants. What *are* their names, anyway?"

"Ted Dwyer and Amy Parrish," replied Josh. "A very nice young couple."

"A boy and girl?" queried Cresta.

"Isn't that the usual setup?"

She began laughing. "For God's sake, and I always accuse you of being chauvinistic. I assumed that they were both men."

The sun had sunk to the treetops when the couple reached the area which had been the campsite. Josh was puzzled as he looked around the clearing. "They would have set up here, Cresta, near the burial mound. That inlet in the river would have been a perfect place to moor the canoes."

"Perhaps they moved," suggested Cresta. "Maybe they shifted to those trees beyond the mound."

Aggravated, Josh kicked at the sandy earth. His foot uncovered the remains of a campfire. He knelt down and examined the rocks and the partially burnt wood. "They were here, all right. It had to be them." At that moment, almost as a confirmation of his suspicions, a sudden breeze from the river lifted a scrap of paper and sent it spinning through the air. Like a bird it first dipped and then glided over the campsite. Josh caught it. "What's this?" he muttered and turned the paper over. "Hmmmm, Mail Pouch Tobacco." He looked at Cresta. "That's Harry's brand."

"You mean he *chews tobacco?*"

"Only when he's in the field. He worries too much about forest fires to smoke." Josh smiled. "That's the way good old Harry is."

They looked over the ground and found other evidence that the group had been there—a bright hair ribbon, a razorblade caked with soap and stubble, and a page torn from a paperback novel.

"Well, that proves it," Josh said at last. "They were here. But where the hell did they get to?" An insinuating kind of fear crept into his thoughts. What would have caused the group to move on? Had it been something related to the mutant skull and bones? He wanted to take Cresta into his confidence, but decided that there was no need to upset her unnecessarily.

They approached the mound. The ladder was lying there; Josh picked it up and secured it in position. Then he climbed to the top of the mound, made his way across the boards and looked around. "No sign of them. They must have been recalled by the institute. We must have just missed them, damn it."

Cresta sat on a pile of stones at the base of the mound, flexing her tired feet. Behind her, the wall of the mound shifted beneath Josh's weight as he started down the ladder. She didn't look around. Thus she missed seeing a crack appear at the top edge of the mound; powdery, dry earth began to trickle downwards. As the rent in the mound deepened, Harry Evers' grasping hand, stiff with rigor mortis, seemed to push through the earth.

Below, Cresta went to hold the ladder steady. "What are we going to do now, Josh?"

"Well, it's sure as hell we can't start back tonight, love. Avarilla was right. I'm tired, and I know you are. And I wouldn't want to try finding my way in the dark."

"But where will we sleep, Josh?"

"We brought blankets. We'll sleep beneath the stars. Isn't that what you wanted?"

"The prospect seemed more romantic in New York."

"Let's just hope it doesn't rain. When we get back to the Ridge I'll have to drive down to Jericho Falls, call New York and find out what's going on. But right now I'd better see to dinner." He grinned. "I said we'd get in a little fishing."

"But we don't have any fishing poles."

"I brought some line and tack. I'll cut a straight branch and put one together Huck Finn style."

"What can I do?"

"We'll need a campfire. You can gather some medium-sized stones and some dry twigs."

Getting into the spirit of the adventure, Cresta headed off towards the woods. She passed the burial mound. The dirt had continued to trickle down, and Harry's hand was fully exposed, but Cresta didn't notice.

By twilight, freshwater bass, which had been slathered in clay, were baking on the coals. A bottle of wine was chilling in the rapids.

"You amaze me, Josh," complimented Cresta. "I didn't know you were such an outdoors boy."

"Dad used to take me on fishing trips. It's good to know you can still live off the land."

"You sound like Aunt Avvie."

"I guess I do."

They dined with gusto on the fish and the wine. Afterwards Cresta asked, "How's the water? Is it warm enough to bathe in?"

"If you take a deep breath first," replied Josh.

Josh and Cresta stripped out of their clothing, just as Ted and Amy had done, and went to the river to bathe.

Beneath the trees near the burial mound, shadows shifted and moved. They crept forward for a better view of the couple in the water.

Josh and Cresta emerged from the river. As they walked toward their fire the night air, still warm with the day, caressed their bodies and dried them. They hid their blanket down on a bed of leaves, and pulled the other one over them. "Josh," breathed Cresta, her pink tongue passing quickly across her lips, "make love to me."

"I intend to." Josh leaned on his elbow and looked at Cresta's alluring body. In the soft light of the moon her skin was alabaster white. His eyes moved from the rose-tipped mounds of her jutting breasts down to her flat stomach to the small blond triangle between her rounded thighs. His breath came in sharp, quick gasps.

A tremor passed through Cresta's body as the tip of his tongue flicked over her nipples. She turned to Josh and pressed her pelvis against his. The leaves, shifting with the weight of their bodies, made delightful crunching sounds as they thrust their hips against one another.

The act of making love outdoors (something they had never done) stimulated their senses and released their inhibitions. Cresta demanded more fervor, more passion, than Josh had ever given her before. Josh, in response, gripped Cresta's waist and roughly entered her. Cresta's legs tightened around him and she emitted a long wailing cry of ecstacy.

Gleaming ghosts in the silver moonlight, they stood at the edge of the forest. At the sensual sounds they gathered closer together, nuzzled and bit at one another. Saliva dripped from their jaws. Their legs trembled with excitement, their muscles coiled and they seemed to grow bulkier. The females knelt to allow the males to mount them. An acrid odor of musk emanated from the group.

One of the pack, not yet old enough to mount a female, slipped away from the others. Padding softly across the dry ground, he occasionally glanced over his shoulder to see if he was missed. He wasn't. He reached the section of the mound where Harry Evers had been buried and, quivering with anticipation, ran his tongue over his lips. He had smelled the exposed hand. Saliva dripped from his mouth as he sniffed the air for the origin of the scent. He looked up and saw it protruding from the earth. Whining with anxiety, he pushed against the base of the ladder and moved it several yards. Then he clambered up the ladder halfway, steadied himself, and began to chew on the rigid flesh of the rotting hand.

13

Alex strolled up the path to the church. As he walked, he kicked loose some stones, gathered a handful and put them in his overall pocket. The youngster had never been inside the church, or any church, for that matter. He reached the bottom of the steps and contemplated the ruined building without emotion. Then he cried out in a harsh voice, "Rev'rend! Rev'rend! Come on out here!"

There was no immediate response. Alex walked to the back of the building. A blackbird perched on a tombstone tugged at a dried piece of vine. A hard, humorless smile formed on the boy's face. He selected a stone from his pocket, took aim and threw it. The bird fell to the ground. It righted itself and tried to fly, but the stone had broken its wing. The bird hopped away to the safety of the underbrush.

Satisfied, Alex turned his face to the stained-glass window. The symbolism was completely lost upon him. He called out once again, "Rev'rend!" There was still no response. Alex threw another stone; it broke a small hole in the sky-blue glass surrounding the face of Jesus.

An eye and part of a crusty cheek appeared in

the opening. "Who is it?" the preacher called in a tremulous voice.

"You got a job, Rev'rend!" grinned Alex. "Faye Brooks is dead. The wake's at seven o'clock at her house. You clean yourself up an' get in an' out by then."

There was a pause. Finally the preacher asked, "How did she die?"

Alex hesitated. The Sin-Eater wasn't supposed to talk to anyone. Still, he was all too willing to share the morbid news. He scratched his genitals affectionately and replied, "She got drunk, fell down an' broke her head."

The preacher cleared his throat and opened his mouth.

Alex pretended to throw another rock. The preacher flinched. Alex ran away, his laughter trailing behind him like a sour odor.

The remains of Faye Brooks lay on a plain plank, covered by a muslin sheet. Nearby, Orin Chastain, wearing only blue jeans and boots, worked on the plain pine coffin. He finished padding the inside with cotton and lined it with a smooth white material held down with carpet tacks. Then he painted the outside black with jet oil.

Orin stepped back to admire his work. His beer was sitting on the edge of the plank supporting Faye Brooks; he picked it up and finished it. Using the edge of the cloth which covered her, he wiped the perspiration from his face, and returned to the casket to touch up a spot he had missed.

When the coffin was dry, he picked up Faye's body and unceremoniously dropped it inside. Then he put the lid into place and, with swift, even strokes, nailed it shut. The shed echoed with the hollow sounds of the hammer.

The interior of Sophie's General Merchandise Store reverberated with the sound of the loom. The sharp tinkle of the bell cut through the drone as the front door was opened. Sophie rose, hoping that the caller was the postman. She was expecting her latest order from Sears—a pink sundress and a pair of white patent-leather shoes.

She stopped short, her smile of anticipation melting.

"Good mornin', Mrs. Balock," Marinda said cheerfully. "An' how are you this beautiful Monday mornin'?"

"What do you want?" asked Sophie.

"Why, to make a purchase, of course."

"What kind of purchase?" Sophie asked guardedly.

Marinda walked over to a case of notions. "I want a length of black ribbon. Something shiny, 'bout two inches wide, or wider." She pursed her lips. "I suppose a foot an' a half of the stuff should do. After all, there's only myself an' Alex."

Sophie quickly went behind the counter and opened the case. "I have this," she said, and held up a spool of two-inch satin ribbon. "It's thirty cents a yard, so that would make it . . . ."

"Fifteen cents for a foot and a half," supplied Marinda. She unclenched her four-fingered hand, revealing a tarnished nickel and dime. Sophie measured and cut the ribbon. "Please cut it again, Mrs. Balock. Exactly in the center."

"You want me to cut it into two pieces?"

"That's right. Two pieces the same length."

Sophie did as she was asked and placed the pieces of ribbon on the counter. She hoped that Marinda would not hand her the money. The thought of touching the youngster's hand repulsed her.

Marinda smiled engagingly as she let the coins slip from her palm to the counter. Sophie scooped up the money and started back to her loom, hoping that the girl would leave.

"Can you spare two straight pins, Mrs. Balock?"

"Straight pins?" Sophie repeated.

"Yes. Straight pins. Two, please."

Sophie nervously opened the pin jar and managed to jab her fingers several times before withdrawing two. She placed them on the counter and stepped back, hoping again for Marinda's departure.

Marinda took one of the lengths of ribbon. Then, deftly, she pinned the ribbon around the sleeve of her upper left arm. Sophie frowned. Marinda stretched out her arm to admire the ribbon.

"It looks pretty, don't it, Mrs. Balock?"

"Yes," Sophie replied hesitantly. "But what's it for?"

Marinda's smile curled upwards. "Why, it's for Faye Brooks. Didn't you hear? She's dead. Yes, some children found her early this morning along the path. Seems like she got herself drunk at the social an' fell down an' hurt her head."

The words swarmed around Sophie, stinging and paralyzing her. "Faye . . . dead?"

"I thought you knew. As a matter of fact, I was surprised that you weren't in the kitchen makin' somethin' for the wake." Marinda glanced at Sophie's grandfather clock. "Why, it's after ten, Mrs. Balock. You better get started if you're goin' to bring a covered dish. It's expected, you know."

Sophie covered her eyes and turned away. Her elbow hit one of the keys on the old-fashioned cash register, and with a noisy clang the drawer flew open, striking her in the side. She was suddenly possessed by images of flowing blood and broken skin.

Marinda paused at the door. "Mrs. Balock, why don't you make something sweet?" It was more a threat than a suggestion. "You know how us children enjoy sweet things." A smile clung to her lips like powdered sugar. With that she let the door slam. Casually, she tipped over a display of baskets Sophie had painstakingly arranged earlier that morning. Then she hurried across the porch to Alex, who was waiting there for her.

Jewell Runion had already ruined three spice cakes, which she had planned to be her contribution to the wake. Now, using the last of her flour, she tried to concentrate on what she was doing. She was eaten up with sorrow and guilt. She should have walked Faye all the way home. She should have known that she'd had too much to drink. Such a sad and futile end.

Earlier that morning a group of children playing in the woods had found Faye's body. They had called for Orin, and he had carried her to his shed. Ordinarily the granny women—Jewell and Avarilla—would have prepared Faye for burial, would have washed her and dressed her in her Sunday best, but Orin sent word that Faye's face had been badly bruised by her fall, and he didn't want to upset them. And so, he had nailed the coffin shut. Still, it didn't seem right. The granny women had always attended the dead. But then, times had changed. A nameless fear insinuated itself around

Jewell, but steadfastly she refused its company. Carefully, she counted her strokes. "Easy now, not too many," she said to herself. "That's what ruined the last one."

Jewell's garnet ring was lying on the kitchen table. She always removed it when doing chores. The sight of it caused her to cry. Jewell had intended to will it to Faye, who had so often admired the beauty of its sanguine stones. But now Faye was gone. Tears coursed down Jewell's withered cheeks and fell into the batter.

Through her kitchen window, Avarilla glanced uneasily at the sky. It had suddenly become overcast and held the promise of a hard rain. The Big Ben ticked away the afternoon. It was now past two o'clock. Avarilla hoped that Josh and Cresta would make it back from the river before the storm broke. She checked the ham she was baking in the oven, poured on more glaze, and sat down to sip her fourth cup of coffee. She knew that she shouldn't drink so much coffee, but it was the only thing that had kept her going through the day.

Sissy was on the porch, playing with her "babies." Avarilla had substituted an old beaver hat for the foul, maggot-infested squirrel Sissy had somehow acquired. Her daughter had been strangely calm since the previous evening. She might even have been called serene as she devoted her complete attention to her "toys"—Josh and Orin.

Avarilla finished her coffee, then opened three jars of home-canned beans—green, white, and red —for a cold bean salad. As she was cutting onions into paper-thin slices, Reuben came into the kitchen. Avarilla looked at him with exasperation.

He looked more haggard than ever and his clothes were filthy. "Let me fix you sometin' to eat, Reuben."

He shook his head. "I was wonderin' how much corn I ought to bring over."

"Two or three gallons should be God's plenty."

Reuben shifted his feet. "Who's going to pay me?"

Avarilla didn't bother concealing her irritation. "Pay you? Why, that's your contribution to the wake."

"Seems like I been doin' a lot of contributin'."

"Since that's your only good deed," Avarilla replied tersely, "I suggest you cling to it. Now hurry, an' get the stuff over there before it starts to rain." Reuben slouched out of the kitchen.

Avarilla had finished the onions when the first heavy drops of rain spattered against the window-pane. She went to the door. "Sissy. You come inside now. The wind's risin' an' you'll get drenched out there."

Roma Underwood had never learned to cook properly. Her kitchen was a suburban housewife's nightmare. The kitchen table was littered with dirty dishes, sewing and containers of kerosene. Unwashed pots and pans, old magazines, gardening tools, and a black-and-white cat, who watched Roma through passive eyes, sat on the unscoured sink.

A shelf holding canned goods was cluttered with bags of dried herbs, burnt and unburnt candles, and pieces of homemade jewelry. Clothing, some dirty, some clean and waiting to be pressed, hung around the room on nails. Above, stuck to the walls by a flour-and-paper paste, were pictures of dark and sultry sirens cut from magazines. They paid homage to Roma's own egotism. A washboard balanced across two chairs held a mirror, a kerosene lamp and Roma's few cosmetics.

The windows were so streaked and dirty that it was a while before Roma realized it was raining outside. She shrugged and finished washing the few dishes needed to make her specialty—caramel apples.

Water had splashed against her thin shift; the material clung to her full breasts and rounded belly like wet tissue paper.

While the mixture of sugar and Karo syrup was cooking on the stove, Roma washed twenty or so apples. Then she laid them aside, along with the sticks Orin had cut for her, and went to the stove to check the caramel mixture. She lifted the wooden spoon to her lips, blew on the sticky brown substance and licked it.

Roma stabbed the sticks into the apples and dipped them, putting them on butter-greased plates to cool in front of the window. Even though it was mid-afternoon, the sky was as black as endless night. The wind whipped the rain against the small house; the sound of it had made Roma drowsy. She sat down on a kitchen chair and contemplated the neat rows of apples as bright and golden as Christmas tree ornaments. She picked up the nearest one. Her pink tongue slid out and stroked the gleaming surface. With a sigh she let it drop in her lap and savored the weight pressing against her there. As she flexed and unflexed her shapely legs, Roma's eyes were drawn to a photograph which had captured the New York skyline. She continued flexing and unflexing her legs and thought of Josh.

The sun had been swallowed up by the turbulent clouds, and the wind tore across the mountains. As the storm came closer, the trees writhed and struggled as if in agony.

Josh and Cresta hurried up the trail, hoping to reach the mine before the storm broke. They were nearly there when the clouds broke, and the heavy rain pelted them like gunshot. Within seconds they were soaked clear through to their skin. They couldn't see where they were going; the earth became as slick as grease.

Clutching one another, half-stumbling, half-crawling, they reached the mine. The mud surrounding it was like quicksand. Cresta slipped and fell. Josh grabbed her arms and dragged her to the entrance of the main shaft. He struggled with the boards haphazardly nailed across the opening. The wood was rotten and came free with little effort. Josh pulled Cresta inside.

"Josh, do you think it's safe?" she gasped.

"It's dry." Josh opened his backpack. The canvas had kept everything dry. He withdrew a flashlight and flashed the beam around the interior of the mine. The main area was about twenty feet high and twenty feet wide. Further on, the mine branched into three tunnels. The ceiling looked solid and the timbers which supported it were still intact. Dry leaves had been blown inside by several seasons of wind. Josh began gathering them up and collecting loose boards. He soon had a fire going. Cresta was huddled against the wall, shivering. He gave her a dry blanket from the pack and said, "Here, love, strip out of your clothes and wrap up in this. The fire should be giving off some heat soon. I'm afraid it's going to be a bit smoky in here, but at least we'll be warm and dry."

Cresta stripped and wrapped herself in the warm blanket. She made an attempt at a joke, but her teeth were chattering. "Your face is all sooty, Josh. You look just like a minstrel man." Josh laughed in response and wrapped his arms around her. He was alarmed at how cold her flesh felt.

"I'm going to brew you something hot. I'll fill the canteen with rain water and boil it over the fire. At least you can have a cup of hot tea."

"Good. I'm chilled to the bone. That rain feels like it came straight from the North Pole."

After tea and a meager meal of cheese and dry bread—the last of the supplies—Cresta professed to feeling better. Josh felt her forehead. She was running a temperature. He looked over his shoulder to the mine opening. The rain was still coming down in silver sheets. "It looks like we're on the other side of a waterfall," remarked Cresta.

"I hope to hell it lets up soon. I want to get you back to the camper and to bed. I'm afraid you're liable to end up with a cold, or worse."

"I never get colds," said Cresta. "I'm as healthy as all get out."

Josh regarded her. Her face was paler than he'd ever seen it. Two great spots of red glowed hotly on her cheeks, and her eyes were glazed. He stood up. "I'm going to look in the tunnels for some more loose boards in case the rain doesn't let up."

"Oh, Josh, be careful. You know what Aunt Avvie said."

"I won't venture far, love."

Cresta watched him until he disappeared into the shadows, and only the distant flickering of the flashlight identified his whereabouts. She drew the blanket around her and moved closer to the fire. Cresta knew she was getting sick, and she was unreasonably irritated with herself. She never fell ill. She disliked being a bother to anyone, even those closest to her. The yellow flames danced in slow motion before her eyes, and Cresta nodded off. She drifted into unconsciousness, her head resting on a knapsack and her body drawn up in a fetal position.

Josh followed the center tunnel for thirty yards without finding any loose wood. Even in the belly of the mountain he could hear the wind hurling itself against its side like a demented animal. Trickles of water seeped through the tunnel ceiling and down the walls.

Blackness yawned before him. It was so dark that the light would not penetrate it. Josh eased one foot in front of the other. Suddenly he felt nothing but space. He pitched himself backwards and fell on his buttocks. Then he examined the path with his hands. A sheer drop lay just ahead of him. It was impossible to ascertain its depth.

Shaking with relief, he backed up until he came to the main cavern. This time he chose the left tunnel, which veered sharply away from the center of the mountain and went steadily downward. He laid aside several planks which he would pick up on his way back. He wanted to make sure there was enough wood for the fire. Cresta must be kept warm.

The tunnel suddenly widened and opened into a cave which was about the size of a modest living room. Here Josh's nostrils were assailed by a scent which was excruciatingly vile. Josh held his breath and felt his confidence evaporate.

At first the floor appeared to be covered with

snow. Then, as a faint wind stirred the billowy
white drifts, he saw that it was not snow, but
feathers—thousands of feathers, with occasional
sharp flashes of polished bone. Some were broken,
some were whole, and some remained strung
together: a raccoon's skeleton here, a snake's
there . . . it was a hideous underground graveyard.
He surmised that the cave was a den used by a
pack of wild animals who returned here to eat
their prey.

He forced himself to move forward. Feathers
stirred around his feet, bones snapped beneath his
weight. He felt as if he were wading through the
surf of the River Styx, towards the land of Death.
The stench was overpowering.

Suddenly Josh found its source. A stretch of
bare earth was covered with excrement.

The feces did not look like any animal's. It
appeared to be human waste.

One thought and one thought alone possessed
him.

He must get himself and Cresta away from this
virulent place as quickly as possible.

14

Reverend Hooper tugged on the thick rope. The bell in the steeple tolled loudly, but the somber sound was muted by the roar of the departing storm. Thirteen times the bell tolled, mourning for Faye Brooks.

It was just past six thirty when the preacher left the church. The rain had abated; the sky was white and glowing in its wake. The trees dripped as though it were still raining, and the preacher's boots made squishing sounds as he hurried through the evening, Sin-Eater to the dead.

There were about twenty people gathered on the porch of Faye Brooks' cabin. They moved aside to make room. No one spoke to him, and few looked at him. Reverend Hooper did not look at them, either. Their deformities appalled him. God had surely cursed the Ridge. He removed his flat, black hat and pressed it under his arm as he entered the kitchen.

The kitchen was permeated with the odor of home cooking. But a more formidable scent was evident, one with which the preacher was painfully familiar. It was the smell of death. He looked through the door leading to the parlor. The closed coffin was propped up on sawhorses and a cluster of figures in black knelt beside it. They were the four oldest women on the Ridge—Avarilla, Jewell, Sophie and Sissy. Avarilla looked up and smiled directly at him. The preacher nodded, grateful at being acknowledged.

In the kitchen two tables had been pushed together to hold the food brought by the mourners. From the ceiling above, strips of paper unfurled, speckled with limbs and wings and bodies of summer flies—flags of the vanquished. The preacher filled a plate with a sample of each food. He did not choose from personal taste. The amount of each sample was exactly the same. He mixed sweets and starches together, often eating them in the same bite. He took a bite out of one of Roma's caramel apples and followed it with a mouthful of cole slaw. The preacher did not sit, but rather stood in the middle of the floor while slowly, methodically, he ate everything on his plate. When he had finished, he placed the plate and fork in the sink, although he knew that they would not be washed and used again, but taken away and buried with the corpse.

Reverend Hooper bowed his head and offered a prayer. It was as much for himself as Faye Brooks. His lips moved in a silent litany: "Oh Lord, why won't You return to the Ridge an' drive out the beasts which have taken over the night? When will You return? What can we do to bring You back? What sacrifice must we make? Sweet Lord, what sacrifice do You want from us?"

He put his hat on, and once more eased his way through the silent crowd on the porch.

As soon as the figure in black had departed, the younger people began to file into the kitchen. They grabbed plates and began heaping food onto them.

Reuben's jars of liquor were opened; substantial tots were poured into jelly glasses and quickly consumed. The middle-aged women, the mothers of the youngsters, followed their children inside. Solemn and drab in their mourning clothes, they ate little and spoke even less.

The four women at the casket finished their prayers. Sissy retreated to a rocking chair in the corner and watched the young people with placid interest. Alex brought her a plate of food and cajoled her into eating. Sophie, Avarilla and Jewell began clearing away the used dishes.

Jewell went to the sink, took off her garnet ring, placed it on the windowsill, and began stacking plates. She wished that she had given the ring to Faye while she still lived. As she washed the dishes, she eyed the young people reflected in the kitchen window. Not for the first time, Jewell resented them. True, they hadn't been brought up with the traditions and the beliefs which she and her peers had been given by their parents. But that wasn't what bothered her. They seemed completely bereft of normal feelings. They weren't there to mourn Faye, but rather to eat and to drink. She bit down on her lower lip, flung the dishrag aside and hurried through the house to Faye's bedroom, where she closed the door behind her.

Avarilla, collecting plates, saw Jewell's actions. She gave the stack of dirty dishes to Marinda, saying, "Would you put these in the sink, dear? Jewell needs some attending."

The young girl carried the dishes to the sink and began to scrub the plates. She hummed a sprightly tune to accompany her work.

Sophie, her face strained and anxious, brought a

stack of dishes to the sink. She sucked in her breath as she saw Marinda.

"I sure enjoyed your apple pie, Mrs. Balock. Perhaps next time you'll add some raisins."

"The . . . next time?" Sophie whispered.

"Yes, I'm just wild for raisins."

Avarilla shut Faye's bedroom door behind her and looked around the small, neat room. Jewell was sitting on the floor next to the window. Thin rays of late sunshine surrounded her like a cage. "Jewell," Avarilla began.

Jewell looked up, grief and misery in her face. "Nobody cares," she sobbed. "Faye's dead an' nobody cares."

Avarilla knelt beside Jewell and cradled her in her arms. "That's not so, Jewell," she said soothingly. "Everybody liked Faye. You an' I loved her."

"She was like a sister to me," Jewell sobbed.

"I know, I know," croned Avarilla. "She was a sister to everyone."

"I should have give her my garnet ring, Avvie. She always admired it. But I can't now. The coffin lid's nailed shut. It's too late."

"I'm sure Faye understands, Jewell. She doesn't need it now."

"Where's Orin—Roma?" wailed Jewell. "They haven't come by. Where are they?"

"Shhh. They'll be here soon," said Avarilla. "I'm sure they just wanted to wait till the crowd had thinned out. They were very fond of Faye, you know."

"Yes, I know. I guess," Jewell sniffed, "everybody was."

"The young ones show their grief in a different way. Goodness, Jewell, you have to remember that they're so different from us. Havin' no fathers an' bein' marked has made them—well, a little strange. We got to be tolerant of them."

"I suppose," Jewell conceded.

"It's not like Faye was really gone from us, you know. She's in heaven now. She's with the Lord."

"Amen, sister. Amen."

"An' you'll be seein' her soon. You know that, don't you, Jewell?"

Jewell nodded. "You know, Avvie, I don't mind dyin'. Now that Faye's gone, the sooner I go, the sooner we'll be together."

"Not to be rushin' things," Avarilla said gently. "You'll go in your time. Here, take my handkerchief an' dry your eyes. We ought to be gettin' back to the wake."

"You think Orin an' Roma has come yet?"

"I'm sure they have," Avarilla tenderly stroked her friend's hair back into place. She stood up and helped Jewell to her feet.

Jewell kissed Avarilla on the cheek. "Avvie, you're a tonic for everythin'."

When they returned to the parlor, the last of the mourners were filing past Faye's coffin, paying their final respects, going home. Avarilla took her friend into the kitchen, sat her down and poured her a cup of coffee. While Jewell was drinking it, Roma and Orin entered.

Roma came to Jewell and hugged her. "Jewell, I'm so sorry." She glanced at Orin. "We both are."

Orin touched the old woman's narrow shoulder. "Faye was a good soul. We'll all miss her."

Once again Jewell broke into tears. Roma comforted her while Avarilla drew Orin aside. "You're both late comin'." It was a gentle chastisement.

"I'm sorry, Grandma. The storm washed out the road. Me an' some of the boys went to see if we

could right it, but seems like the whole mountainside slid down. We'll have to wait till it dries up
before we try to clear things away."

"Why was Roma so late?"

"A chunk blew off her roof, an' she spent most of
the afternoon up in the attic movin' things about so
they wouldn't get spoiled."

"Well, you're here now, an' I'm sure that makes
Jewell feel a whole lot better." She lowered her
voice. "She's really torn to pieces. They were so
close, as close as sisters. Goodness, I've got to get
you two young people somethin' to eat." She
touched Orin on the arm. His clothes were damp.

"I didn't have time to change."

"You'll catch your death."

"A shot of old Reuben's juice'll fix me up." Orin
looked over the table and grinned. "I see Roma
made her caramel apples again."

Avarilla smiled indulgently. "Roma tries, but
she's just out of place in the kitchen." Orin said
nothing. "Your ma's inside. Why don't you go say
hello to her? She gets upset when you don't come
around."

Dutifully Orin went into the parlor. Sophie was
sitting on one of the side chairs, staring at the
casket; Sissy, still occupying the rocker, was
toying with her hair. As Orin approached she
looked up, and her usually dull face became bright
and animated. Orin, who had always been
somewhat repelled by his mother, gritted his
teeth, then bent to kiss her forehead. "How you
feelin', Ma?" Sissy smiled in reply. "Can I get you
somethin' to eat?"

Sissy rubbed her stomach and smacked her lips.
"I'm full, Orin. Good an' full." She ran her fingers
through Orin's thick black hair. He stifled the

impulse to draw back.

"I'll let you alone now, Ma," he said and returned to the kitchen.

Sophie got up and followed him.

"Is there anythin' I can do?" she asked Jewell. "I
can stay all night with you, if you'd like. I don't
mind at all. Uh uh, not at all."

Jewell looked up wearily. "No thanks, Sophie.
I'm not goin' home for a while. I want to stay here
with Faye."

No one else spoke. Reluctantly Sophie said,
"Well then, I guess I'll go, uh huh, go." The
assembly mumbled their goodbyes. Sophie started
for the screen door, stopped, and uttered a nerve-
shattering scream.

Framed in the doorway, looking like a specter of
the night, was Josh. His hair was matted, his
haggard face streaked with dried mud; mud and
leaves clung to his clothes. He opened his mouth
to speak, but no sound came out.

Avarilla jumped up from the table. "Josh, what
is it? What's happened?" She guided him to a
chair. The others clustered around him. Josh was
finally able to speak.

"Cresta and I, we got caught in the storm.
Soaked to the skin. She caught a fever. I'm afraid
she's very sick."

"Where is she?" asked Avarilla.

"I got her back to the camper. She's in bed. I
came looking for you. I'm sorry about Faye. One of
the children told me."

Avarilla took charge. "Roma, get Josh a glass of
whiskey an' stay with him. Orin, you see Sophie
home. I'll take Sissy by the house an' get what I
need to tend to Cresta." Josh started to stand.
"No, Josh, you stay here an' rest. I'll see to

things."

"But I should drive down to Jericho Falls and find a doctor."

"You can't," said Orin. "There's been a landslide. The road's completely covered. Besides, there ain't no doctor as good as Grandma. She can take care of anythin'."

Avarilla turned to Jewell. "Jewell, you sure you want to stay here?"

Jewell nodded, "Yes, I'm goin' to spend the night. I don't want to leave Faye alone. I'll be fine. You all go do what you have to do an' Avvie, please don't worry about me. I'll be just fine."

Sophie interrupted, "Can't I do anythin' to help?"

"No," said Avarilla sharply. "Orin will take you home."

Sophie started to protest, but Avarilla's face stopped her. She turned to Orin with a small smile.

On his way back to the church, Reverend Hooper detoured to cut several branches from the huge willow tree which stood as the only marker to the secret grave he had dug many years before. Upon returning to the church the preacher stripped to his boots. He carried the branches to the center of the altar rail, sat down and, using a pen knife, began cutting away the leaves, leaving the resilient branches bare. As he worked he prayed. "I beseech you, brothers, by the mercy of God, present your bodies as a living sacrifice, which will be holy an' acceptable unto God." Then slowly, methodically, he began to flagellate himself.

15

Avarilla opened the door of the camper. "Cresta?" There was no answer. She stepped inside. She could hear the young woman's labored breathing coming from the bedroom. She set a worn carpetbag and a bundle of quilts on the kitchen table, then hurried towards the sound. "Cresta?"

"Who is it?" Cresta's voice was weak and rasping.

"It's Aunt Avvie." She went to sit on the bed. Cresta was wrapped in a blanket. Her face was mud-smeared, her eyes red and glistening. "I'm goin' to nip that fever in the bud."

"Where's Josh?"

"I told him to stay away. It's a bother havin' men underfoot when there's illness. Now, if I help, do you think you have enough strength to get in that shower contraption?"

Cresta nodded. "If you help me."

Avarilla put her arms under Cresta's and lifted her out of the bed. The young woman could hardly walk. "You're burnin' up with mountain fever. It's a caution, but trust me. I'll break it up. Just trust me."

"I do, Aunt Avvie."

Avarilla set a wooden stool in the shower stall and said, "You sit on that an' wash yourself. Make the water as hot as you can stand it. Meanwhile, I'll brew a special tea an' have your bed ready."

While Cresta was showering, Avarilla put a kettle on to boil. She had brought her own teapot to brew the tea from the leaves of boneset, ground ginger root and pine needles. To that she would add honey and whiskey. It should break Cresta's fever. If not, she would have to resort to more drastic measures. She spread the quilts on the bed. The teakettle whistled; Avarilla poured the hot water into the teapot and left it to steep. Cresta came out of the shower.

"Here, honey, I'll help you dry."

"I'm so c-c-c-cold," Cresta shuddered.

"I brought you an old flannel nightgown. It'll keep you warm."

"Did Josh tell you that they left camp?"

"They're not there?"

Cresta shook her head. "No they must have gone back to New York. We just missed them. I wish we'd missed the storm."

Avarilla helped Cresta on with the nightgown, then practically carried her to bed. "You'll be warmer in a minute, honey. The tea must be steeped now."

Avarilla brought a large mug of the steaming brew to Cresta. "Sip it if you have to, but drink it all."

"Hmmm, what's in it, Aunt Avvie? It has some bite."

"A lot of good things, darlin'."

"I can barely hold the cup. It's so heavy."

"I'll hold it for you." Avarilla sat next to Cresta. Steam rose from the mug and caused beads of moisture to form on Cresta's forehead. With her free hand Avarilla dabbed them away with a clean handkerchief. When Cresta had nearly finished the tea, the old woman set the mug aside and made her scoot down into the bed. She tucked the quilts and blankets around her and switched off the overhead light.

"Don't go, Aunt Avvie. Stay with me."

"I'll stay as long as you want, Cresta." She sat down on the edge of the bed.

"Oh, I hope I don't get real sick. It's been such a wonderful trip coming here. It's meant so much to Josh."

"You love him very much, don't you, my dear?"

Cresta smiled softly. "Yes, I do."

"How did you meet?"

In slow, dreamy phrases Cresta started to tell Avarilla of that morning in Central Park, but her words began to run together. Her eyes closed and she was asleep, her breathing sonorous and strained. Avarilla turned out the lamp and slipped out of the room.

In the kitchen Avarilla made herself a cup of regular tea. She was hungry. Even though she had cooked all day, she was not one to sample her own cooking, and she'd eaten nothing at the wake. She looked in the refrigerator and found a container of raspberry yogurt. She looked at it curiously, held it up to the light and read the label. "There's nothin' in there that could hurt me." She sat down on the couch and sampled it. It was tasty for store-bought food, she thought. Her hunger satiated, Avarilla curled up on the couch and, finally allowing her exhaustion to take over, she fell asleep.

Josh, Roma and Jewell sat around the table in

Faye Brooks' kitchen drinking from the remaining jug of Reuben's whiskey. Round wet marks made by their glasses decorated the tabletop like interlocking prizes from a carousel.

Josh was worried about Cresta and felt that he should be at the camper, but his exhaustion, combined with the lure of the whiskey, kept him where he was. And he was beguiled anew by Roma's sensuality. He wanted her with more intensity than he had ever wanted any woman, and he knew that she wanted him. All the signals were there—half-lowered eyes, parted lips.

Roma regarded Josh through a fringe of heavy lashes. She had ceased to be impressed by his remarkable similarity to Orin. There were differences, and it was those differences which interested her. There was an evasive quality about Josh that made him irresistible. He seemed like an innocent ready to be corrupted. This thought alone excited Roma more than anything. He was also important. She liked that. And he lived in the fairytale city of New York. Could she make him fall in love with her?

She touched his hand, which was clutching an empty glass. "Josh, can I pour you some more whiskey?"

"I think I've had more than enough," he replied, but he was unconvincing.

Roma hoisted the gallon jug and filled the glass to the brim. Her tongue outlined her lips; she smiled at him. He returned the smile.

Jewell was completely oblivious to the interplay between Josh and Roma. She was immersed in the whiskey and in her memories of Faye Brooks. They covered the past fifty years of her life. Their relationship seemed to be a series of shared firsts

. . . the first dance, the first date, the first "crush." And then marriage—they had had the first and only double wedding ceremony to take place in Chestnut Ridge. The births and eventual loss of their firstborn, the deaths of their husbands, and finally the closeness between them which allowed them both to face an old age together with a kind of hope. They were bittersweet memories.

Jewell spoke more to herself than to the others. "I remember the first time Faye an' I went berry-pickin' together. We came across the biggest copperhead you'd ever seen . . . ."

"You look tired," Roma murmured to Josh. "You need a bath."

"Well, sir, Faye picked up a rusty sickle which somebody had left stickin' in a fence post an' . . . ."

"I'd better be getting back to the camper," Josh responded without conviction.

" . . . She whacked that sucker right in two!"

"Not yet. Come back to my house. I'll boil water an' give you a good bath."

"It was the biggest copperhead ever seen in these parts."

"You'll bathe me yourself?"

"Set some kind of record."

"Yes," whispered Roma. "I'll bathe you with my own hands."

"Pa was going to have it stuffed, but being that it was chopped in half . . . ."

"How can I resist such a tempting offer?"

"It began to stink before nightfall an' he had to take it out in the yard an' bury it."

"An' I'll give you fresh clothes to wear."

"Just whacked it right in half, she did."

"Where did you get a closet full of men's

clothes?"

"Faye was always braver than me. At least I think she was."

"Not a closet full, just a few things."

Josh smiled thinly. "What are we waiting for?" He drained his glass and turned it upside down on the table.

Jewell rambled on. " . . . Cut it right in half."

Roma stood up. "Jewell, we're going to go now. Will you be all right?"

"Surely, surely. I'm goin' to stay an' watch over Faye. I must do that. You understand, don't you, Roma?"

Roma kissed the old woman. "Yes, of course, you must."

Josh got to his feet unsteadily. The rigors of the afternoon combined badly with the alcohol, but his desire for Roma far surpassed his exhaustion. He nodded to Jewell, knowing that his words of goodbye might very well tumble out as words of lust.

Josh walked very close to Roma as they headed toward her house, but he did not dare to touch her. He would not have been able to restrain himself from completing the sexual act, once it was started. They crossed the covered bridge; Josh realized they were nearing the Community Center. Josh asked, "Where will Faye be buried?"

"Why, in the graveyard," replied Roma.

"You mean the one behind the church?" She nodded. "But it's in terrible condition."

"I know. There's underground erosion. We think it was brought about by the diggin' of the mine an' the explosion, but there's some plots which are still good."

"I don't understand about the church, Roma."

"What do you mean?"

"I mean, doesn't anyone attend anymore? I thought mountain people were very religious."

"We have our own kind of religion," Roma replied sharply. "We don't need churches. Besides, the preacher went crazy an' closed it up. We couldn't go even if we wanted to."

"Is he still alive?"

"Oh yes. He lives in the church."

"Lives there!" exclaimed Josh. "But how does he exist?"

Roma did not answer. "Here's the pathway to my house." She turned and lightly brushed her breast against his arm. He forgot the church and the preacher.

Orin and Sophie stood on the porch of Sophie's General Merchandise Store. He spoke with a forced smile: "All safe, Sophie. No goblins, no haints."

"You must come in, Orin." She saw the hesitation in his eyes. "Please, just for a moment. Let me make you a bite to eat."

"I'm not hungry, Sophie."

"Some dandelion wine, then. I make it myself, and if I say so, it's the best I've ever tasted. Uh huh, the very best."

Orin sighed. "I'd enjoy a glass of your dandelion wine, Sophie. But just one. I got a lot to do before mornin'."

"Mornin'," Sophie repeated. "Oh, yes, the buryin'. I just don't think I'm up to goin'." She led him through the shop and into the back where she kept house. "Sit down, Orin, an' make yourself comfortable. Take off your boots if you like. I know how men like to take off their boots, uh huh.

A little comfort never hurt nobody."

Orin scowled and looked away. "I'm fine as I am, Sophie. How about that wine?"

Sophie offered a coquettish smile to her guest and hurried to the pantry. A bottle of wine was handy, and so were jelly glasses, but Sophie took the time to open a dusty box labeled "Seneca Glassware." The box contained half-a-dozen goblets which a now-forgotten relative had sent her as a wedding present. They had been used once on her wedding night, and then had been packed away along with her expectations for a happy life with Kalem Balock. She returned to Orin. "I'll just be a moment. This glass wants rinsin'."

"Any glass will do, Sophie."

Taking his remark as politeness, Sophie elaborately washed and wiped the crystal goblet. She set it down on the table, then uncorked the wine and poured a taste into the glass. Orin looked at it questioningly. "You're supposed to taste it," she bubbled, "an' let me know if it's all right. Then I'll pour you a proper glass. That's how they do it in movies."

Orin tossed down the wine, smacked his lips and pronounced, "Ahhhh, right fine." Then he held out the empty glass to Sophie.

Sophie sat down opposite Orin and gazed at him appreciatively while he drank. "It's nice havin' a man in the house." She rattled on. "The sound of heavy boots, the smell of leather and tobacco."

Orin stood up. "I don't smoke, Sophie."

Looking for any excuse to delay him, Sophie held up a length of cloth she had just woven for Orin's approval.

"Now, that's a nice piece of work," he said politely.

"I was thinkin' maybe you'd like for me to make you somethin', Orin. Perhaps a poncho, uh huh, like they're wearin' now."

This time Orin did not conceal his irritation. "That was a long time ago, Sophie," he said. "Nobody wears ponchos anymore. I have to go now."

"Yes, you must go. You have things to do. Uh huh, things to do." There was a note of envy in her voice.

After Orin had gone, Sophie was suddenly consumed by an overwhelming loneliness. She told herself she had acted silly with Orin, but it wasn't that she had been trying to seduce him. Really she wasn't. It was only that Orin stirred something within her, something which had been dormant for so many years that Sophie could no longer identify it.

Orin walked through the village toward the Jericho Falls road, intending to check for more landslides. But then he turned around and walked in another direction, the length of his stride increasing with every footstep. Orin knew where he was headed, where he had been headed all along.

16

"You may now kiss the bride."

She lifted her wedding veil and pursed her lips. No one kissed her. The congregation stirred. Sibilant whispers rustled the pages of prayer books, a child giggled, a parent hissed a reprimand.

Cresta was standing alone at the altar, a bride without a groom. Puzzled, she looked around. She was beneath the wisteria arbor in Central Park. Slowly she turned. Middle-aged widows served as her bridesmaids, faces blank, eyes hollow. They were dressed in black and carried bouquets of dead flowers held by black, serpentine ribbons trailing to the ground. There was a rustle of material. The child Marinda, clutching Cresta's train with her hideous four-fingered hands, grinned at her. Cresta scanned the wedding guests. They were the deformed young people of the Ridge.

These aren't my friends.

A mountain tune began playing, slightly off-key. The musicians were the six who had performed at the Community House social—the three old men and their younger counterparts. That's the wrong music, she wanted to scream. *It isn't appropriate.*

"You may *now* kiss the bride."

It was Alex's voice, speaking in a singsong manner like the caller at a square dance.

Where was Josh? Cresta began to cry. She ran from the grape arbor and into the park. A sudden wind whipped around her, pressing the organdy and lace wedding gown against her body like the petals of an unopened flower. Completely alone now, she stood in the center of the running path and listened to the sound of approaching footfalls, running shoes slapping against hard earth. Josh!

But the sound of the running feet passed her by. Cresta wrapped her arms around her shoulders, shivered and exhaled. Her breath floated on the air like a puff of dandelion down. Underneath, the damp carpet of grass chilled her feet. Why hadn't she worn shoes?

She felt so alone. She began to tremble, bit down on the inside of her lower lip and was surprised by the taste of her own blood. Her heart was pounding, and she felt a sharp pain underneath her breast.

"Josh!"

Cresta woke up gasping for breath. For a time she was unable to shake off the dream, and then she saw the band of light, and beyond, the living area of the camper and Avarilla asleep on the sofa. She remembered. She was sick and the old woman was caring for her. But where was Josh? Where—was—he?

The small bedroom blurred. She pressed her damp cheek against the pillow. Time stopped for Cresta and then carried her away on its endless journey.

Roma moved about the kitchen, making preparations for Josh's bath. He watched her. Buckets and pots filled with water sat on top of the stove. The wood fire was burning with a furious intensity, providing an orange light. She had given him a glass of whiskey.

"Where's the tub, Roma?" he asked. She crossed the room to a flowered curtain which hung from a length of clothesline and concealed the far corner. With a flourish Roma pulled it aside, revealing a unique bathtub. It was a large scoop of copper balanced on four claw feet and higher by at least a yard at the back. The tub was one of the few things that Roma bothered to clean; it gleamed like a treasure from a Pharaoh's tomb.

"It looks like an antique," said Josh.

"It belonged to my Ma an' her Ma before her. Come all the way from Boston."

"It's a very interesting piece."

The words were conventional, but their tone and cadence were filled with hidden meanings and taut emotions. Their voices were husky and the words were broken by the effort of breathing. The inevitable conclusion was at hand.

Roma moved back to the stove. The glow surrounded her and cast her body in silhouette. She had changed from her black mourning dress to a pale shift worn shadow-thin by too many washings. She tested the water. "It's hot enough. Not yet boiling, but hot enough." Then she began carrying the buckets and pots to the tub. As she emptied them, a white mist rose to dampen her hair and her dress.

Josh began unbuttoning his shirt. Still watching Roma, he removed his muddy boots. Roma turned to him, holding a cake of homemade soap in the palms of her hands like an offering. Josh stood up, undid his belt and peeled off his jeans.

Roma's eyes flickered as she dropped her gaze. Her lips separated and her cheeks flushed red. Josh walked toward her, took the soap and stood in front of her. Still they did not touch. It was as if a strain of masochism caused them to put off something pleasurable for as long as they could stand it.

Josh stepped into the tub and as Roma watched, he slowly immersed himself in the water. Roma took off her shift and was completely nude. She walked to the copper tub. Roma had much more body hair than most women. A light spray of hair shadowed the valley between her breasts and still more, fine as down, covered her rounded stomach. Josh did not find it disagreeable; rather, it heightened his desire. Roma knelt by the tub and, using a natural sponge, she began to wash Josh, starting beneath the surface of the water.

Orin stood outside the camper and listened. No sound came from within. He looked in the window and saw Avarilla asleep on the couch. Then he moved to the far end of the camper and looked inside. In a pale half-light he saw Cresta asleep on the double bed. Sliding his hand down over his abdomen, he began to stroke himself through his trousers.

He tried the door. It was unlocked. As he stepped inside he glanced at his grandmother. She didn't stir. Orin walked softly into the bedroom and closed the door behind him. Cresta turned over so that she was on her back and her beautiful face was lit by the pale moonlight streaming through the high window. Her flesh glistened as if powdered diamonds had been sprinkled over it. Orin removed his vest and let it drop to the floor.

Then he bent over to take off his boots. Because of his erection his pants were difficult to remove. He walked to the edge of the bed. Cresta's hair was spilled across the blankets. He rubbed his knee against her tresses. They felt softer than anything he had ever imagined. He touched her face, and she smiled in her sleep. Then he unbuttoned the top of her flannel nightgown and cupped her right breast in his hand. His thumb and forefinger secured the nipple and he began exerting the slightest pressure. Cresta groaned, her eyes partly opened. "Josh," she said. Her voice sounded detached as if it were coming from somewhere else.

"Yes, Cresta," Orin replied. "I'm here." Then he lifted the covers and climbed into bed.

Jewell's hand reached out in her sleep and knocked over the glass of whiskey. The amber liquid spilled across the tabletop and washed against her cheek. The sting of the liquor woke her up.

"Faye? Faye? I was dreamin' about that time you an' me an' Avvie decided to enter that quilt makin' contest at the County Fair." She chuckled in remembrance. "It was the Lone Star design. Pretty ambitious, considering that you an' me couldn't sew a decent stitch. We all agreed to do a third of the quilt an' Avvie got real angry because we couldn't keep up with her. Then the night before the contest, we pasted all them triangles into place. Avvie was just amazed that we got our part done. Hah! Then when they hung it up at the fair the weather was so hot an' dry that those triangles began fluttering off the quilt like leaves from a tree." Jewell began to cry. "Oh, Faye, Faye, you're dead. You can't hear me. I loved you better than my own family. You stayed, they all went away. An' now you're gone too." She stood up, sobbing, and looked around the kitchen until she found the jug of liquor. She poured herself another drink. It made her gag, but she drank it anyway. She went to the sink for a rag to sop up the spill on the tabletop and saw that her garnet ring was still on the windowsill.

"I wanted you to have that ring, Faye." She picked it up and held it to the light. "I *want* you to have it."

Jewell looked under the sink and found a hammer and the metal wedge Faye had used to split logs into kindling. Going into the parlor, she shoved the wedge between the top and side of the coffin and said, "Oh, dear Lord, forgive me for disturbin' sweet Faye, but I just got to give her the ring. Please, *please* understand."

She pried the coffin lid open an inch or so. Setting the tools aside, she gripped the lid and, working it to the left and right, managed to free it. She pulled it aside and laid it on the floor. Then Jewell looked into the casket.

A terrible cry flew from her throat. The garnet ring slipped from her grasp and spun away from her. She staggered backward, clawing at her eyes, trying to obliterate what she had seen.

Faye Brooks was hardly recognizable. Her hair was matted with blood. Her cheeks had been torn away, so that the bones were visible. Her lips had been ripped away, and her teeth hung loosely from discolored gums. One of Faye's eyes was missing. The other, hanging from its socket, was staring at Jewell. A jellied mass of gore was all that was left of her throat, and her chest was rent by wounds so deep that part of her spine was exposed.

Jewell stood motionless, staring at what had once been her friend. She denied her eyes, convinced that what she was seeing was a figment of imagination and liquor. But the ghastly vision refused to change. Jewell at last had to accept that the mangled thing in the casket was Faye Brooks. Her soul could not do so.

Jewell spun around and fell to her knees. Sobbing and screaming, she crawled into the kitchen where she sought shelter beneath the table. She held onto one of the wooden legs and bared her teeth. She worked her jaws against the wood with such force that finally the table leg began to splinter.

The sound of the camper door closing awakened Avarilla. She rubbed her eyes, unsure of where she was. Then, realizing she was in the camper, she hurried into the bedroom to check on Cresta.

The young woman was sprawled across the bed, lying on a tangled mass of quilts and blankets. The flannel nightgown was around her waist, and her flesh was covered with perspiration. Avarilla touched her skin. Cresta was more feverish than ever. After pulling the blankets and quilts over her charge, Avarilla hurried into the kitchen to make a poultice. In her experience it had never failed to rout a fever. She combined kerosene, turpentine and pure lard, the latter to prevent blistering. Then she soaked a wool cloth with the mixture.

Avarilla managed to get Cresta in a sitting position. She lowered the nightgown, placed cheesecloth on her chest for protection, and added half of the wool poultice. Cresta became conscious. She spoke in a hollow voice. "Josh was here, Aunt Avvie. He came to see me."

"That's nice, darlin'."

"He—he made love to me."

Avarilla shook her head with pity. The fever was causing the poor girl to hallucinate. "Now, just lean forward."

Avarilla drew in her breath. Cresta's back was covered with deep red scratches. "Goodness, darlin', how did you hurt yourself?" Cresta said nothing. Avarilla stared at the markings. They were evenly spaced and were in series of fives. She dabbed the wounds with alcohol before applying the other poultice. "The poultice will help heal those marks." Then she gave Cresta another cup of the tea. Once again Cresta fell into a deep sleep.

After tucking Cresta in, Avarilla returned to the living room. It was then she saw the damp footprints which stained the carpet. The prints were made by a man's boot. Avarilla became troubled. If Josh had been here, why didn't he stay? It seemed unlikely that he would take advantage of Cresta's illness. Or *was* it Josh?

The stars were fast losing their sparkle—diamonds becoming glass—as dawn bleached the sky. Josh, racing the daybreak, hastened through the forest with heavy steps and aching thighs.

Never before had Josh experienced such intense passion. And yet, the act of their lovemaking was indistinct, amorphous, like a half-remembered dream. What remained was exhaustion and guilt. He knew that Avarilla would have stayed with Cresta throughout the night. But what would Cresta think if she awoke and didn't find him there? As Josh increased his pace, he began manufacturing excuses. He spent the night with Jewell Runion, giving her comfort and support. No,

Cresta wouldn't buy that. He got lost in the forest and slept in a tree. No good; his sense of direction was phenomenal. Perhaps he could just say he got drunk and passed out. That she would believe. Josh wondered if she would suspect that he had spent time with Roma. He would deny it vehemently, of course, but he was so tired. Could he convince her? It required effort to lie.

Thrusting his thoughts of guilt aside, Josh hurried through the forest and reached the road leading to the covered bridge they had crossed earlier. It was the quickest route back to the camper. As he stepped inside the dark entrance, his footfalls echoed hollowly against the walls and ceiling of the structure. The sound unnerved him. Cursing his own paranoia, he hurried toward the arc of light at the other end. Halfway there he heard a noise. A growl? A groan? Josh's heart slowed down, and then began to beat faster. A sudden fear rushed through his body. His mind flashed back to the dreadful things he had seen in the cave, and to the abnormally shaped skull which had brought him here. Despite the coolness of the morning, he began to perspire.

Josh looked over his shoulder. The sound came again. It was louder, more intense and closer. A wave of dread lapped at Josh like a physical force. Instinctively he thrust out his arms. Something clutched his hand. He uttered a cry and drew back, but his hand was caught. He backed up frantically, dragging the heavy creature with him, until he reached the light from the entrance.

The creature was Jewell Runion. Her eyes burned with madness, and her lips were encrusted with dried blood. He shook her hand loose and she fell in front of him. Her chin hit the boards hard and the impact seemed to jar her into speech. She began babbling.

"The garnet's turned into blood . . . Faye knew . . . she knew the answer . . . not dead and buried . . . the preacher lied . . . *lied!* Accursed twins . . . Orin . . . Josh . . . ." She lifted her face, recognized Josh, and began tearing at her hair and screaming. Spittle mixed with the dried blood; a pink foam oozed from her lips. Josh, horrified, stepped around her and ran the full length of the covered bridge, pursued by her terrible gibberish. The death of her friend had obviously unhinged her mind. He knew that he should try to get her home. But, after all, she was not his worry, and he didn't want to become involved with her insane grief.

Josh sprinted past Avarilla's house and the Thicket until, gasping for breath, he entered the camper. Avarilla was at the sink, washing a cup. She looked at him sternly. "Where have you been till this hour of the mornin', Josh?"

"I stayed on at Faye Brooks' house," he lied. "How's Cresta? Is she better?"

"Her fever's broke, thank the Lord. An' she's restin' easy now. You don't look none too good yourself. Why don't you let me fix you a cup of my special tea? I'll make up a bed for you here on the couch." Josh glanced toward the bedroom. "Don't go wakin' her up now. She's goin' to be all right. But I don't want you sleepin' in there. There's no use in you catchin' what she has."

Josh didn't argue. He sat down at the table. When Avarilla had prepared the tea, he drank it.

"By the way, Josh," the old woman said smoothly, "Cresta thinks you were here earlier."

"Me? Here?"

"Of course she was hallucinatin'." Josh didn't

respond. "She was hallucinatin', wasn't she, Josh?"

"Of course she was. I told you I was at Faye Brooks' house." Josh finished the tea and lay down on the couch. Avarilla covered him with a blanket.

"I'll be by later with some homemade soup. Right now I've got to see to Sissy an' attend Faye's buryin'. You stay there an' sleep it out. If Cresta takes a turn for the worse, you come an' fetch me, hear?"

"I will, Aunt Avvie. Thanks for everything you've done." Avarilla knelt to kiss Josh on the forehead and was struck by the strong musky odor which clung to his flesh like a perfume. She wondered anew . . . who was telling the truth? Josh? Cresta?

Perhaps they both were.

Somehow Jewell Runion stumbled back home, still muttering with terror, but the familiar surroundings brought her no comfort. The empty house only served to emphasize how very much alone she was.

She stood in the front hall breathing raggedly, one hand pressed to her heart, the other holding on one of the brass coathooks jutting from the hall rack. Her heart slowed down until its beat was very nearly normal. Jewell licked her dry lips. Her mouth was stale with liquor and the coppery taste of blood. She turned to look into the mirror centered in the rack. But it wasn't herself that she saw reflected. It was the grinning corpse of Faye Brooks.

Jewell threw back her head and howled.

The hall was suddenly filled with the unmis-

takable aura of decay. Jewell had a tenuous grip
on her sanity and prayed that reason would re-
assert itself. It was a hallucination, nothing more.
She looked back into the mirror.

In the mirror Faye was visibly rotting. She
glowed with a certain phosphorescence, and a
putrid yellow slime began to ooze from the open
wounds. The spoiled flesh began to curl and drop
in chunks from the rapidly decomposing body.

Jewell flung out her arms, shielding her eyes
with the backs of her hands, and ran into the
parlor to escape the apparition. She stumbled
over a low table and went sprawling to the floor.
Jibbering with fright, Jewell dragged herself to
her feet and fled into the kitchen. *Faye Brooks lay
across the sink and draining board.* Her head
turned toward Jewell, the lone eye staring at her
intently. The rotting features were blending,
merging, running together like melted tallow. She
didn't look like a person at all; she looked like a
bundle of rags and butchered meat. Flies tracked
across the gaping wounds, buzzing sonorously as
they deposited their eggs.

The hair on Jewell's arms and neck rose. Her
mouth worked frantically, but nothing came out
except a bloody froth. Nausea overcame her, and a
bitter bile began to fill her throat. Jewell pressed
her body rigidly against the wall. The moldering
arm moved upwards and stretched toward her.
The hand was folded except for the extended ring
finger. Jewell tore at her hair and shrieked. She
lurched to the door and stumbled into the weedy
back yard, featureless save for the stone well. Her
heart pounded like a jackhammer, and an in-
credibly sharp pain tore through her chest. She
made weak, gurgling sounds as she stumbled

through the tangle of weeds. She twisted her ankle on what might have been a ground squirrel's hole and fell down. Something slithered through the dry grass and touched her shoulder. Even before she turned, Jewell knew what she would behold.

The moonlight had become brighter. The resurrected visage was flaked with putrefaction. Maggots fretted the remaining flesh, which glistened with slime. Jewell screamed and pulled away from its touch. Bits of rotting flesh clung to her shoulder. She got to her feet, clamped her hands to her head and rocked it back and forth. There was only one way to escape.

The well.

Jewell flung aside its wooden covering and fumbled for the rope which held the bucket. She was surprised how easily the rope freed itself from the handle. She wrapped it around her throat once, tied a bulky knot and clambered up onto the rock rim. Her hands hung loosely at her sides, her arms twitched aimlessly. She cocked her head sideways, as if listening to someone calling her from far away.

The cadaver was coming toward her, shedding flesh and maggots as it shambled through the weeds. A maniacal laugh erupted from Jewell's lips. She jumped.

As she plummeted downward, Jewell saw Faye Brooks' grinning skull reflected in the still waters. And she knew she hadn't escaped after all.

There was no escaping death.

The rope was jerked taut. Jewell's body was suspended half in the water and half out.

Crawfish swam toward the partially submerged body and began their work.

17

Josh was painfully aware that everyone in the diner was listening to him. The pasty waitresses, the burly truck drivers and the beehived cashier were all giving him their undivided attention. Why wasn't the phone enclosed by a booth? He turned his back on his audience and cupped his hand around the mouthpiece. The help and the customers leaned forward and strained to hear the stranger's words.

"What! . . . What, operator? . . . No, it's a collect call, person to person, to Dr. Raymond Phelps." Josh sighed and patiently repeated the number. "It's the direct line to Dr. Phelps . . . Jesus." Muttering, Josh looked over his shoulder. Everybody turned back to their plates, their order pads and their grills. Josh drummed his fingers against the coin box and waited.

It was the third day after the storm. The mountain road still hadn't been cleared; Josh had borrowed a horse from Orin. His only experience with riding had been canters on horses more used to non-riders than riders. Orin's lumbering black gelding was just the opposite. Josh rubbed his aching buttocks. The uncomfortable journey had made his vile mood worse.

The illness had left Cresta in a weak and nervous condition. She looked terrible. There was a pallid cast to her skin, her hair was dull and lusterless, and she had lost several pounds, making her face look drawn.

Because of her fever, Cresta and Josh had not been sleeping together. And that circumstance had become an integral part of their bitter argument this morning.

Josh had eyed Cresta as she picked at her food. "Try to eat more, Cresta. You need it to gain back the weight."

"Where were you last night?"

"Where?" Josh had replied uneasily. "Why, right here."

Cresta had pushed back her chair. "Why are you lying to me? I got up in the middle of the night to get a drink. You weren't here. The couch was empty, and you were gone."

Josh had run his tongue over his lips. "Oh, that. I couldn't sleep. I took a short walk."

"That short talk took almost three hours. I know. I sat up watching the clock."

"That's not going to make you better."

"I know what I need to make me better," she had retorted.

Josh had risen from the table and attempted to kiss her. She had pulled away, saying, "And did you meet anyone while taking your walk?"

"What do you mean?" Josh had snapped. "Who in the hell would I meet wandering around the mountains in the middle of the night?"

"Weren't you with that girl, that Roma?"

Josh had sighed. "Cresta, I think the fever's affecting your judgment."

She had slammed down her coffee cup.

"Goddamn you! You're not going to make me think I'm paranoid. I saw the looks you were giving each other."

"What looks?"

"I'm going to Jericho Falls with you," she had said defiantly.

"What in hell for?"

"I'm going to call Jason and accept those bookings in Europe."

"You're not going anywhere. You're not well enough to go horseback riding down the mountainside."

Cresta had lain her head down on the table and begun to cry. "It seems like I'm too sick for anything, and I look like a Goddamned hag!" She'd run into the bedroom, slamming the door behind her. He hadn't followed her.

What in the hell was taking so long? "Operator! Operator . . . The call's to New York City, not Nagasaki. What? . . . Phelps! Dr. Raymond Phelps!" He scratched the back of his head in exasperation. Finally the connection was made. The operator garbled his name to Elsa Krupp, who had answered. Josh yelled, "Elsa, this is Josh Holman. I'm trying to get through to Dr. Phelps . . . Well, find him!" Josh turned back to the fascinated diners. He crossed his eyes and let his tongue loll from the corner of his mouth. They quickly returned to their blue-plate specials.

"Dr. Phelps . . . I'm at a pay phone in Jericho Falls . . . What? . . . There *are* no phones up on the Ridge. Listen, did you call Harry and company back from the digs? . . . No? Well, I wonder where the hell they are . . . . No, they aren't there. I trekked down the mountainside several days ago.

The burial mound was there, but no camp . . . .
Yeah, yeah, I find it strange, too. Well, I guess
Harry has his reasons, and I'm sure you'll be hearing from him soon. If he's had half as much
trouble trying to reach you as I did, he may very
well have given up and sat down to write you a
letter. Christ, what a production!" Josh lowered
his voice. "No, nothing so far." He started to
mention the cave, but decided better of it. After
all, there was no proof that it was linked to the
strange bones. "I'd like to stay on for . . . . Stay
on!" There was a crackling on the line, followed by
a dull metallic buzz. "God damn it, I've been cut
off! Operator! *Operator!* Shit!" Josh hung up the
phone, swung around and caught the diners
watching him. He smiled sarcastically and offered
them a deep bow before leaving.

Josh paced aimlessly for several blocks, trying
to come to terms with his anger, his guilt, the fight
with Cresta. He found himself standing in front of
a tavern colorfully named Big Tilly's. A couple of
beers would put him in a better mood.

From behind the bar, a broad muscular man
sporting a crewcut said, "We ain't open till twelve,
pal."

Josh looked at the clock. It was five to. "It's
almost that now."

The bartender shrugged. "So sit down an' wait it
out."

Josh sat. He cast a friendly smile in the bartender's direction and asked, "What time does Big
Tilly get in?"

"I'm here," growled the bartender. "It's short
for Tilford, pal." Then, despite the two minutes
remaining until noon, he drew two beers and set
one down in front of Josh. "Here. You look like

you had a rough night." Josh drank it greedily and was finished before Big Tilly even lifted his glass. The bartender gave Josh his untouched beer and went to draw himself another one.

"What's your business?" he asked bluntly.

"I've just come down from the Ridge to pick up a few things," replied Josh easily. "I'm up there snooping around the Indian burial mound."

"Oh, yeah? The one on Cheat River? Not a very lucky place for tourists."

"What do you mean?"

"They have a way of disappearin' in that part of the country."

"What do you mean?"

"Disappearin', you know . . . poof! Gone! Just like they never existed. No bodies, no nothin'. Everybody thinks they somehow got drowned, but I think different."

"Oh?" Josh pushed a five-dollar bill across the bar, indicating that he was buying the next round. He hoped that Big Tilly would expand on his viewpoints.

The ploy worked. Big Tilly downed his beer and drew another. "I remember the first bunch. It was in '48-'49. I was fresh out of the army an' had just bought the place." Josh stared at him; he hadn't figured Big Tilly to be that old. "A group of kids from Wesley College. They stopped in here the night before they took off on a canoe trip up the river. Not an easy trip. The river looks calm, but there are a lot of surprisin' currents. Yeah, they all got pretty drunk that night on beer an' bourbon. Nice bunch of kids. Let's see, there were seven or eight of them. Three girls, the rest guys." He paused to take a swallow of beer.

"So what happened to them?" asked Josh.

Big Tilly wiped the foam from his upper lip. "Dunno. They were never heard from again. Their canoes were found all battered to shit, but no bodies. Not even pieces of bodies."

"Then they must have drowned."

"That's what I thought, everybody thought, until it happened again." Big Tilly bit into a beef jerky, swallowed his mouthful and continued. "It seemed like it became a regular thing. Tourists an' such goin' up to the Ridge an' never comin' back."

"Did anybody do any investigating?"

"The sheriff's office." The bartender snorted. "The sheriff an' his men couldn't find a flea on a hound dog."

"So how did they explain all those disappearances?"

"Drownin'."

"And never any bodies recovered?"

"Nary a one, pal."

What if Harry, Amy and Ted weren't on their way back to New York City? What if they were also among the missing? "You didn't happen to run into a guy named Harry Evers, did you? And his two assistants, a couple named Ted and Amy, hippie types?"

"From New York, were they?" Josh nodded. "Yeah, they was here. The state store was closed. They stopped off an' picked up some sixpacks of beer." Big Tilly's face clouded. "Say, they were goin' up the Cheat River."

"They went there all right, but they're not there now."

"I take it they're supposed to be."

"That's right."

They stared at each other.

Josh said, "Maybe I ought to stop in at the

sheriff's office and report them missing."

"For all the good that'll do."

"Ah, they're probably driving through the Lincoln Tunnel at this very minute."

"Probably." Big Tilly wasn't convincing.

Another beer, and Josh's inherent optimism surfaced. "Yes, probably hitting the Lincoln Tunnel right about now." He finished his beer, overtipped Big Tilly and left.

On his way back to the borrowed and tethered horse, Josh made a stop at Jericho Fall's only drugstore to buy a present for Cresta. A peace offering. They had Je Reviens, Cresta's favorite perfume. He hoped that would do the trick. Sure, he'd spent the last few nights at Roma's, returning to his bed on the couch just before dawn. But Cresta hadn't missed him until last night. He just had to be more careful.

Josh reached the local feedstore where for a few dollars, they had taken care of Orin's horse. The gelding eyed him with suspicion as he prepared to mount. The store owner laughed. "I don't think that horse much cares for you."

"Well, that makes it mutual," replied Josh.

The trip back up the mountain took most of the afternoon until it was nearly dark. Orin was out, so Josh left the horse in the stable and hurried back to the camper. Cresta was gone, but she had left a note.

"Josh, I went to Aunt Avvie's for dinner and will stay there until you get home—Cresta."

At least the note didn't seem unfriendly. He tucked the bottle of perfume in his back pocket and decided to have a drink before picking up Cresta. After all, it was seven o'clock, way past cocktail hour. Josh poured a double vodka and sat down at the kitchen table. From his vantage point he could see the bedroom and the unmade bed. Josh frowned. He didn't like being around people who were sick or incapacitated in any way. Perhaps when Cresta was well enough he'd let her go back to New York on her own. He'd stay in Chestnut Ridge for a few weeks and complete his investigations. He wished he hadn't missed old Harry. What a drinking companion he was. Josh poured another double.

As Josh made his way down the Thicket, he realized he was high. He hadn't eaten lunch; the liquor was acting faster than usual. The misshapen branches hovering above the pathway did not frighten him as they had when he'd first arrived, however; instead, the close-knit trees gave him a sense of security. The house in the distance with its brightly lit windows seemed like the face of an old friend.

Despite the closeness of the night, no one was sitting on the front porch. Josh had started up the steps when he heard someone whisper his name. "Josh! Over here!" He turned and saw Roma, half hidden in the silvery tresses of the willow tree. He ran to her.

They embraced, holding each other tightly. Josh covered Roma's face and neck with biting kisses. "What are you doing out here?"

"Waitin' for you."

"Why aren't you inside?"

"*She's* in there." Roma slid her hands down to his buttocks and squeezed. "What's that?" she asked, feeling the outline of the bottle in his back pocket.

"Perfume," Josh stammered.

"You brung me a present!" Josh didn't tell her

otherwise. He turned around and let her dig the bottle out of his pocket.

Roma held the bottle up to the moonlight. "Oh, it's so pretty. How do you say it?"

"Je Reviens. It's French. It means 'I will return.'"

"Je Reviens," Roma mispronounced. She opened the bottle and smelled. "Josh, it's wonderful. I never had such a sweet present . . . *never.*" She kissed him passionately and pressed her body against his. Immediately Josh became aroused. Roma slipped her hand down to his crotch. "We'll save *that* for later," she murmured.

"I hope I can get away tonight."

"You got to. I'll be waitin' for you."

"I'll go in first, Roma."

"Yes, that's smart. An' I'll come in shortly. Like I was just arrivin'."

Josh stood on the porch, composing himself. Under the willow, Roma doused herself liberally with the perfume.

In the parlor the quilting frame was suspended from the ceiling. The women were gathered around it, working on a quilt of the Flying Bird design. Avarilla, her work glasses balanced on the tip of her nose, was sewing a large triangle into place. Cresta, next to her, was sewing a smaller triangle onto a larger one. Using cardboard patterns, Sissy was carefully cutting scraps of fabric into triangle shapes with a huge pair of shears. Josh stood in the doorway, smiling to himself. Cresta looked so out of place. He had never known she could sew.

Sissy was the first to see him. "Here's Josh," she cried gaily.

Avarilla got to her feet. "Goodness, I was hopin'

you'd be back before dark. Let me fix you some dinner."

"No thanks, Aunt Avvie, I'm not hungry." He smiled at Cresta. "You're looking better, love." Cresta gave him a controlled smile in return.

"I made her sit in the sun today," explained Avarilla, "Sunshine's a great healer." She stroked Cresta's hair with affection.

"I'm helping make a quilt," Cresta said brightly.

"Quilt, quilt," Sissy crooned.

"It's a Flying Bird design," Cresta went on. "See the triangles? Don't they somehow resemble birds in flight?"

Josh kissed Cresta's forehead. "You seem to be feeling better too."

"Yes, a whole lot better."

Slamming the screen door, Roma called, "I'm here." She entered the parlor and smiled sweetly at everyone.

"I was just about to make coffee," said Avarilla. "Roma, you do it for me."

"Of course, Aunt Avvie," Roma replied. "Now, who wants coffee?"

Everybody did, including Sissy. Avarilla whispered to Roma, "Make Sissy's mostly milk." Then louder, "An' there's some fresh ginger cookies in that jar on top of the cabinet. Fill up a plate of those, too."

Roma went into the kitchen. As she worked, she called to Avarilla: "I stopped by for Jewell. I thought she might want to come, but she wasn't in."

"She might have hiked over to her sister's in Cheat Holler," said Avarilla. "Times like this, she probably wants the comfort of her family."

Josh looked at his feet.

Roma began serving the coffee. First Josh, since he was the only man in the room, then Sissy, then Avarilla, and finally Cresta. Cresta looked up to thank her and was suddenly aware of her scent.

"What a nice perfume," she said drily. Roma smiled thinly and went to fetch the cookies.

Cresta looked at Josh, who was standing in the doorway looking at Roma. Once again the sharp pangs of jealousy cut through her. She forced her attentions back to the quilt and made up her mind that she was going to test Josh's love later that night.

Josh rolled off of Cresta and murmured into the pillow. "I'm sorry, I'm just too worn out."

Cresta was filled with hurt and anger. She balled her hands into fists and began hitting Josh on the back. "Get out! Go sleep in the living room or wherever you want! You'd rather be with that mountain slut than me!"

"Cresta . . . don't."

"Get out!" she screamed and burst into tears.

Josh climbed out of bed and stood looking at Cresta. "Why are you carrying on like this?"

"I saw what I saw, and I smelled what I smelled. Did she go to Jericho Falls? Or did you bring the perfume back with you?"

"Of course she didn't go with me. And I didn't bring her anything."

Cresta sat up in bed. "What do you think I am, Loony Tunes? Roma was wearing Je Reviens. That's my scent."

"I didn't notice."

"Didn't notice?" growled Cresta. "*Didn't notice?* You always compliment me when I wear it. *Always*. I will return. Hah! That's sure as hell prophetic." She threw a pillow at him.

Josh ducked. "I'm too tired to fight, Cresta."

"Apparently you're too tired for anything." Her voice dripped sarcasm.

Josh bent over, picked up the pillow and dropped it back on the bed. "I can't deal with you when you're in your moods." He walked out of the bedroom, shutting the door behind him.

Cresta lay back on the bed clutching the pillow. If she was going to get any sleep she would have to take a Valium. She slid her hand between the mattress and the box spring and withdrew the nearly empty bottle. She swallowed the pill without water and lay back.

I could be wrong about Josh and Roma, she thought. The perfume could have been a coincidence. Sure, but the looks they give one another are real enough. Oh God, *please* let me be wrong. I don't want to lose Josh and I don't want to drive him away. I love him so much. Please, God, let me be wrong.

Then, like a little girl, she folded her hands beneath the covers in prayer.

Something was scratching on the door of the camper. Josh, disturbed by the noise, lifted his head sleepily. The scratching became louder and then it abruptly stopped. He opened his eyes and glanced at the kitchen clock. It was nearly two A.M. The scratching began again, with renewed vigor. Josh sat up and rubbed his temples. The noise stopped. Nude, he padded across the floor and opened the door. There was no one there. The moon was so bright that it hurt his eyes. He started to close the door; then he knelt and touched the deep scratches in its metal. The metal was warm where the paint had been scraped away. Puzzled, he stood up and looked toward the woods.

The sultry night air surrounded him like a lover's embrace. For a moment he imagined he was lolling in a tub of warm water. Roma's tub. He stepped onto the ground. The earth, soft and warm beneath his feet, seemed to infuse him with a sudden vitality. The sounds of the night beckoned him. Josh walked past the entrance to the Thicket. The night sounds were louder now, the air warmer and permeated with an intoxicating aroma. A mixture of evergreen, moss and honeysuckle. And something else.

Je Reviens—I will return.

Josh reached the edge of the forest and began running through the black numinous void. Leaves stirred around his legs, stones tore his feet and branches scratched his flesh. He stopped to catch his breath. His heart was pounding more blood than his veins could handle. Leaning against the base of an elm tree, he inhaled deeply. The scent of the perfume was stronger than ever. Josh continued on until he reached the edge of the path which led to the Lookout.

The effulgent moon, floating on a swell of clouds, was traveling westerly like a solitary ship on an endless voyage. Josh blinked and shielded his eyes against the harsh light as he groped his way toward the swinging bridge. He stopped at the end of the path and let the delirious scent of the perfume wash over him.

Standing beyond the bridge, near the edge of the giant boulder, was Roma. She was nude, bathed in moonlight and framed by the twisted branches of two dead trees. Josh made his way across the swinging bridge toward her outstretched arms.

And when they touched it was like two stars colliding.

18

It was a sleepless night for many in Chestnut Ridge. The gibbous moon, humpbacked and a loathsome yellow, cast a repellent glow which dispelled nearly every shadow.

A series of howls, carried through the mountains on the back of the wind, punctured the stillness.

Reverend Hooper, stretched out on a pew, was aroused from his tortured dreams. As he lifted his head, his eyes became wide circles of fear. He knew that what had happened so many times before was about to happen again. He righted himself and lowered his feet carefully to the floor. The serpents slithered out of his way.

He walked down the aisle, stepped over the altar railing and made his way toward the ladder in front of the stained-glass window. His hands gripped the rungs, but he could not bring himself to climb. And yet, he must. If he did not climb the ladder and serve as witness to the blasphemy, he would be rejecting his duties. The preacher took a deep breath. "The Lord said, ye shall be witnesses unto Me."

He began to ascend. With each step he prayed

for the courage and the stamina to see him through one more night of horror. He reached the top rung; his face was but a foot from Christ's stained-glass countenance.

The sulphurous moon lit up the cemetery as brightly as a stage setting. The creatures had gathered in a far section of the burying place, the section that was still used. The wooden marker on Faye Brooks' grave had been uprooted and cast aside. The grave had been dug up and the coffin exhumed. It now lay on its side, open and empty. The shredded lining had been scattered over the dead grass. The cadaver was serving as a toy, a plaything, for some sort of terrible ritual now in progress. Two of the beasts had caught Faye's blood-clotted hair between their snarling jaws and were dragging the body around the graveyard. The others ran behind the moving cadaver, yelping and snapping at the tattered flesh and trailing entrails.

Reverend Hooper closed his eyes and bowed his head. "Oh, God, what do you want of me?" he wailed. He straightened up on the ladder and, in supplication, thrust out his arms so that they were perpendicular to his body. The harsh moonlight streaming through the multicolored window cast the preacher's shadow across the floor. Then he looked down and saw his silhouette. It was the sign of the cross. A rattlesnake, as thick as a man's arm, crawled across the shadow and the holy pattern was destroyed.

The piercing howls infiltrated Sissy's dream and altered it, turning it into a nightmare.

The flowered pathway suddenly twisted, leading her into a grove of skeletal trees. Sissy knew with heart-rending certainty that she was lost. The contrast between the cheery brightness of the flower-drenched path and the cool darkness of the grove was absolute. It was like stepping into a pit. The trees seemed to enfold themselves behind her. The darkness pressed upon her; the air became thicker and harder to breathe.

A black rain began to fall. The twigs, limbs and trunks of the trees were eaten away.

Danger!

She had to find shelter from the rain. She began running, stumbled over a root, but continued on. The stinging rain was flung into her face and further impeded her sense of direction. Then she saw it . . . the outline of the coal tipple, even blacker than the black sky. She hadn't realized she'd come this far. That part of the mountain was forbidden to her.

Sissy was frightened. She called out to her mother and then to her husband, Ben. She began crying, her tears mixing with the rain. She had forgotten that Ben was dead, he'd gone off to the war and hadn't come back. There was no one to tell her what to do.

Sissy took a step toward the opening of the mine and then ran headlong with all the speed she could muster. She crawled inside, grateful to be safe and dry. She sat on a pillow of dead leaves, her knees drawn up to her chin, and wished the storm away. A soft sound, discernible above the wind and the rain, caused her to turn around. She strained her eyes in the darkness, watching the shadows.

One shadow extricated itself from the others and began taking on a distinct form—that of a man. No, not quite a man. The head was lower than the back, the arms were long and trailed to the ground. And even as it came nearer to the faint

source of light, it remained a shadow, its flesh
dark, its features indistinct. Only the eyes were
definite. Large, yellow and blazing, like brush
fires seen from far away. But they weren't far
away, they were close and coming closer.

Trembling with fright, Sissy clutched herself
tighter.

It reached out to touch her. Sissy stiffened. Its
hand made her flesh crawl because it wasn't like a
hand at all, it was more like a paw.

Sissy woke up. The dream always ended in exactly the same place. Her instincts told her that
perhaps it was not just a dream. Perhaps it was
something more. She desperately wanted to
understand. Why did it always stop when she was
sure there was more? She'd questioned her
mother; Avarilla had told her to put it out of her
head. But how could she forget it? She made up
her mind to ask someone else about the dream.
Didn't all stories have an ending? And she had to
know the ending of this one. Perhaps she would
ask Alex. Yes, she would ask Alex. He was her
friend, he would explain things to her.

Heavy woven drapes shielded Sophie's bedroom
from the moonlight. The small kerosene lamp
which she kept burning throughout the night had
gone out, and the room was in total darkness. It
was impossible for her to read her alarm clock,
but Sophie reckoned it must be about three
o'clock in the morning. Her ears caught the sound
she was waiting for.

There it was again—the sharp creak of a floor-
board. Sophie's worst fears were confirmed.
Someone was in the store.

She lay frozen in bed for another minute; then

she slipped out of bed and eased the drapes open. The metal hooks made a harsh sound. She sucked in her breath. The room was suddenly filled with the jaundiced moonlight. Shuddering, she tiptoed to her closet, eased the door open and felt inside for her husband's shotgun. It had not been used or cleaned since his disappearance, although it was still loaded. Sophie silently prayed that she would not have to use it.

Mustering her courage, Sophie crept into her kitchen, holding the shotgun. She breathed a sigh of relief when she saw the pale strip of light under the curtains leading to the store. At least the kerosene lantern in there still burned—her guardian against the night.

The nose of the shotgun went through the feedsack curtains, then Sophie's white-knuckled hands, and finally her face.

"I've got a gun," she announced in a shrill voice, her eyes darting wildly about. The place appeared to be empty and she relaxed somewhat. It was just her imagination working overtime. She stepped into the room and had started to smile when she saw what looked like a dustrag lying on the counter. Had she left one there? She hadn't dusted that day. Still, she had to admit that she didn't remember things as clearly as she used to when she was . . . well, younger. Sophie's tidiness overcame her fear. She leaned the shotgun against the wall and went to clear away the object.

Sophie smelled death before she saw it, the sour stench stinging her nostrils.

On the counter lay the deformed chicken she heard the children talk about, the one which had been born with two heads. Now both hung limply from necks which had been wrung. Tied to each broken neck was a wrinkled length of ribbon. Black satin. Nine inches in length. Two inches in width. Fifteen cents worth.

The gnarled trees were groaning and bending against the wind in chorus; a row of curtseying witches.

Roma looked down at Josh. His eyes burned hot from narrow slits, his mouth was wet and slack. She smiled, revealing a moist tongue and glistening white teeth. She began moving her pelvis. Josh groaned. Roma threw back her head in triumph. She reveled in being in the dominant position. She increased the pace of her movements, and Josh bared his teeth in ecstacy. He began to pant, sucking in the sultry night air as heedlessly as a drowning man sucks in water. Roma raised herself higher, arched her back and, moving her hips in a circular motion, thrust herself downwards. She rubbed her breasts with her left hand, roughly dragging the palm across her swollen nipples. Her right hand pressed against Josh's chest. His heart beat wildly beneath it like a caught bird.

Roma flexed her fingers, curved them downwards and let her sharp nails penetrate his skin. She raked her nails down his chest. Josh's flesh was rent and five thin welts of blood appeared. Roma lowered her head and licked the blood flow. Then she fell upon him, pressing her red, red mouth against his.

The saffron moonlight paled to cream as dawn chased away the night. Cresta licked her dry lips, then opened her eyes. Her mouth and throat were parched. It was her particular side effect from taking Valium. She lifted her head; it felt wrapped in cotton batting. She staggered into the kitchen to the refrigerator, withdrew a Tab and drank about a third of it before noticing that Josh was missing from the couch. Furthermore, the door was wide open. She went to the door. The light made her wince. The prints of Josh's bare feet marked the ground. Also the prints of something else—an animal, perhaps a large dog.

"Josh?" She followed his footprints through the woods. When she reached the last trees before the hanging bridge, she saw them.

The rising sun cast them in silhouette. They were standing locked in a passionate embrace. Cresta's hands flew to her mouth and muffled the cry which rose in her throat. Her eyes stung with hot tears. "Josh, oh Josh," she whispered.

She wanted to be sick, but her body would not allow her the physical release. Blinded by her tears, she ran back to the camper, slamming into the side of the vehicle. She felt for the open door, found it, and stumbled inside.

Her one thought was flight. She had to get away from Josh. From Roma. From the Ridge. Cresta felt ashamed, ashamed that she had put so much love and effort into a relationship which she should have known was doomed from the beginning. Finally she was left with this. She had loved Josh, and he had betrayed her. Now what was she going to do?

She tore off her nightgown and turned on a cold shower. She had to do something, anything, to shock herself into action. In the shower Cresta pounded her head against the wall and screamed in despair, the sounds muffled by the falling water. She eased on the hot water, and gradually she stopped shaking. When she stepped out of the shower, she knew what she had to do. She dried herself, hurried into the bedroom, and dressed. She would be out of the camper before Josh returned.

Even when she had accused him of being unfaithful with Roma, she had never, *never* really believed that it was true.

Cresta took a wicker suitcase down from the closet and began to pack, thinking of the apartment, the lease, the furniture, the magazine subscriptions . . . .

She searched for her credit cards and found them, along with the neatly folded fifty-dollar bills that she had brought with her. That was all that she really needed to get back to New York City. She glanced at herself in the mirror and decided that she needed a bit of rouge and lipstick. The camper door shut. She dropped the lipstick tube. Cresta sucked in her breath, closed her eyes and listened to the sound of her own heart beating. Her anger overcame her hurt.

Why am I acting so guilty? I wasn't screwing in the wide open spaces. *He was.*

She picked up the lipstick and used it, took a deep breath and braced herself. Josh was just scrambling under the covers as she entered. Employing a sleepy voice, he said, "You're up early."

"And you're up everything," she replied acidly.

His eyes traveled from the expression on her face to her clothing, and finally to her suitcase. He sat up. "Where are you going?"

"I'm leaving, Josh. You see, I got up in the middle of the night and decided to take a little walk myself. I . . . ." Her voice broke. "I saw you and Roma." Josh opened his mouth. "No, don't say anything. There's nothing you can say."

"Cresta," Josh began miserably, "don't do this."

"Oh, you want me to stay? I see, Roma and I could draw lots for your services. No thanks, I'm not into open relationships." She shook her head sadly. "I thought you knew that."

Josh whispered. "I'm sorry."

Cresta turned on him. "Are you? Or are you just sorry I found out?" Her lips formed a twisted smile. "Well at least you don't need to use alcohol as an excuse anymore for screwing around." He looked up. His eyes were filled with tears. "Don't cry, Josh. I don't believe it. Oh, I wish I *could* hurt you. I wish I could. But you can't hurt someone who doesn't love you. And you don't love me, you don't love anybody. I just don't think you're capable. I thought you loved me, but that was self-delusion, something like that. I'll ask my shrink. I imagine your name will be cropping up from time to time."

"Where are you going, Cresta?"

"Where? Back to the discos, the theater and the nightclubs. That's where I belong, not here in the sticks."

"How do you intend to get to Jericho Falls?"

"The same way you did. I'll ask Orin to lend me his horse, and I'll pay some yokel to bring it back to him. Then I'll take a bus to wherever there's a plane back to the Big, rotten Apple."

Josh stood up, and Cresta saw the marks on his chest. "I see you've graduated from hickies." He stepped toward her, his arms outstretched. She slammed the case against him. "Don't, Josh. Don't demean yourself any more than you already have." He sat back down, holding his head in his hands. Cresta left.

Josh went to the door and watched as she made her way toward the village. He kept hoping she would turn around, but she didn't.

Cresta couldn't face Avarilla. Let Josh explain her absence, using whatever lies he wished. It didn't matter. Nothing mattered except getting back to home ground. When she got to Jericho Falls, she'd call Jason. He would be pleased that she was coming back early. Perhaps he could still arrange that European deal for her. All that money plus side trips to St. Tropez and Monaco could erase a lot of pain.

Who was she fooling? She wasn't going to get over Josh as easily as a cold. He'd infected her. It would be a long time before she would be able to get him out of her system. Anguish overtook her with its full and brutal force. She sat down on the wicker suitcase and sobs wracked her body. "Oh Josh, I love you so. I'll never love anyone else." When she was cried out, Cresta dried her tears and blew her nose. She smiled thinly to herself. "I can't go to Orin looking like this. He'll never loan me the horse."

She fixed her makeup and realized that she didn't know exactly where Orin lived. She followed the road until she came to a house. In the front yard a child was playing in a swing made from an old rubber tire. Cresta realized that it was the little girl who had given her a flower the day they had arrived. "Why, hello," she called.

Marinda rearranged her face into a beatific smile and came to lean against the tumbledown fence.

"I used to have a swing just like that," said Cresta.

"Did you?" replied Marinda noncommittally. "What are you doin' carryin' a suitcase?"

"I'm going on a trip."

"Really."

"I'm going back to New York City."

"Why?"

"Well, I—have to go back to work."

"What do you do?"

"I'm a model."

"I'd like to be a model." Framing her oddly pretty face with her grotesque hands, she asked, "Don't you think I'd make a good model?"

Cresta swallowed. "Well, yes, I think you'd be very photogenic."

"You don't think my hands would get in the way?"

"Well you don't always see the model's hands. I remember once when I was a bride, the bouquet I was holding covered them." Cresta hoped she was convincing.

"Then," Marinda went on, "I should only appear in pictures with bouquets." She looked at Cresta sharply. "What do you want?"

"I was looking for Orin's house," Cresta said. "Is it near here?"

Marinda's smile returned, meanly. "Orin's house?" she repeated, making it sound dirty. "You got to cross the covered bridge, then after a stretch of cornfield there's a branch in the road off to the left. You can't see his house though." She grinned. "It's hidden by a bouquet of trees, but it's there all right."

"Thank you."

"You're welcome . . . Cresta," Marinda replied and waved goodbye with both of her hands.

Cresta walked on, feeling guilty that she didn't like the little girl. But it wasn't because of her deformity, but rather her acerbic personality. Cresta felt she had been mocked. She thought that Marinda must have given her the wrong directions when suddenly she saw the house appear behind the trees. Cresta was surprised to find it so plain and unassuming. Not like Orin at all. But what did she expect? A mountain version of a sultan's love palace?

She was out of breath when she reached the porch. She knocked on the door. No answer. Then she called, "Orin? Orin?" He didn't appear. Cresta opened the door and entered the parlor. It was like stepping into a surrealistic dream.

The room was completely empty. There was no furniture, no rug, no curtains, not even a lamp, and nothing of a personal nature. Sunlight filtered through the dirt-streaked windowpanes, capturing dust motes in its piercing shafts. Cresta felt a cold breeze stir around her ankles. One of the windows was broken. Leaves and pine needles had drifted in and filled the corners of the room. It was empty, and yet there was a life force here, an unmistakable odor of habitation. A pungent, human aroma of sweat and desire.

The walls, plain wood planking bereft of paint or varnish, were scarred with deep scratches. Fingerprints tarnished the window panes. They resembled a strange breed of insects which were attempting to escape to the outside world. Parts of the floor were more worn than others, and there were stains, dark and wine-colored like giant birthmarks.

Cresta, standing in the center of the room, had the unsavory feeling that she was standing at the bottom of an open grave. An acute wave of nausea swept over her, causing the entire room to shimmer and pulse. She was suddenly aware of movement behind her. She turned her head. Orin was standing in the doorway, wearing tight leather pants.

"Orin," she gasped weakly.

"Yes, Cresta." He smiled. "I'm here."

Part Three

Be sober, be vigilant;
because your adversary the devil . . .
walketh about, seeking whom he may devour.

2 PETER, 5:8

19

September arrived and the mountains under-
went a subtle metamorphosis. Mornings came
later, wearing a cloak of crisp, invigorating air.
The ground was laced with spiderwebs spun
overnight and decorated with dewdrops, like mis-
placed strands of pearls. Pigments of fall paint
began to dapple the trees with blazing color.
Creeks flowed faster, and the water bubbling
against the rocks created a distinct musical
message for the inhabitants of Chestnut Ridge. It
said that autumn was coming early and would
only have a brief stay. Winter would make its
appearance sooner than usual and, like a thought-
less guest, it would wear out its welcome.

The message was understood by all, and preparations were begun for Summer's End.

It was ten days since Cresta's abrupt departure.

Josh had spent every night with Roma, as well
as most of each day. With her as guide, Josh ex-
plored his own sexuality as completely as a
zealous explorer might investigate a newly discovered territory. When he happened to encounter
one of Cresta's left-behind possessions—a scarf, a
pair of panties, her unplayed guitar—he gave her
nothing more than a passing thought. He was

utterly preoccupied with Roma. He did not even reflect upon his purpose in coming to Chestnut Ridge. The mountain road had been cleared, but it did not occur to Josh to leave the community, even to inquire about the safety of Harry Evers and company.

A series of sharp raps on the camper door stirred Josh. He got out of bed and slipped into a pair of shorts. While passing through the kitchen, he noticed the time and groaned. It was ten till eight. He and Roma had been awake till past four.

Avarilla, accompanied by a gust of chill air, stepped inside. "Go put on somethin' heavier, Josh, while I make coffee. Roma's here, I take it?" Josh was surprised by Avarilla's question.

"Yes, she's here."

"Then wake her up. I don't want her lingerin' about. I want to talk to you."

Josh scanned the old woman's face. "You sound serious."

She returned his gaze without blinking. "I am," she replied. "Very serious."

After putting on jeans and a flannel shirt, Josh sat down on the edge of the bed and pressed his lips against Roma's cheek. "Roma, Roma, wake up."

She opened her eyes and yawned. Her yawn turned into a frown. "Oh, Josh, I'm still so sleepy."

"Aunt Avvie's here."

Roma stretched. "She's probably angry with me. I was supposed to help finish the quilt for Summer's End."

"She wants to talk to me. I'm going to chase you out after you've had your coffee."

When they entered the kitchen Avarilla was

pouring freshly perked coffee into cups. There
was a note of disapproval in her voice as she
spoke: "I was expectin' you last night, Roma. We
won't get the quilt finished unless you help out."

"I'll come by today, Aunt Avvie. An' this evenin'
too." The old woman nodded.

"Hey, Aunt Avvie," said Josh. "What about this
Summer's End Fair? I thought you didn't approve
of tourists swarming all over the Ridge?"

Avarilla eyed the young man. "There's lots of
things I don't approve of," she replied. "The fair is
necessary. By sellin' our goods we make enough
money to buy those supplies which we need to
keep us through the winter."

"I see," grinned Josh. "Double standards."

Avarilla nudged Roma. "Drink your coffee,
Roma. I want to speak to Josh alone."

Roma hurriedly drank her coffee and left.

"Pour us another cup, Josh, an' sit down here
next to me." Avarilla stroked her forehead and
began. "Josh, there are things that need tellin'."

"I don't understand . . . ."

"Why did you really come to the Ridge, Josh?
I'm nobody's fool. You told me you came to join
your friends at the Indian burial mound. You
made a brief trip down there an' that was that.
Your friends are gone an' you've stayed."

Josh looked sheepish. "I should have confided in
you, Aunt Avvie, but I didn't want to alarm you."

"You'd better explain yourself."

Josh told her of Harry Evers' discovery. The
testing of the skull and bones for authenticity. His
assignment to investigate. When he finished, he
tried to read the expression on her face. He had expected surprise, even shock. Instead, her face was
filled with a terrible sadness. "I must ask you to

keep my confidence."

"Yes, I will," she replied dully.

"You don't seem surprised by my story."

"Josh, I'm an old woman. Nothin' surprises me anymore. I've seen many, many things which I can't explain or understand. But I accept them. There's nothin' else to do." She touched Josh's cheek. "I'm concerned about you an' Roma. It seems to have gone pretty far."

"Yes, it has."

"I should have known. I should have heeded the signs. Even when Cresta left, I was sure that the two of you would make your peace, but now I know why she left. It was because of Roma, wasn't it?" Josh nodded. "Josh, you must give up Roma." She looked at him sadly. "An' I'm goin' to tell you why."

"Please do," said Josh, barely controlling his anger.

Avarilla spread out her hands in a helpless gesture. "I've lied to you, Josh."

"Lied? How?"

"You're not my nephew. I'm not your aunt." She touched his hand. "You are my grandson. You an' Orin are brothers, not cousins."

"We're twins, then?"

"Yes. Twins."

Josh shook his head. "If . . . if we're twins, then Sissy is my mother. Jesus, you're saying that idiot down there is my mother?"

Avarilla slapped Josh hard across the mouth. Her voice was level, but there was no mistaking her rage. "Don't you ever call Sissy an idiot. She wasn't born that way. I told you that. Her affliction came later. That has nothin' to do with you. *Nothin'!*"

Josh rubbed his mouth. "I'm sorry. That wasn't right, what I said. I—I didn't mean it."

"Then don't say what you don't mean."

"But my parents . . ."

"Kind people, my brother an' his wife."

"But why?"

"Because of Sissy. She couldn't care for both of you. She had no husband, an' I was a middle-aged woman at the time. So I made a very painful decision. I gave one of the twins, you, to Harley an' Leoma to raise. You see, they had just lost their baby, an' oh, they loved you on sight."

"You gave me away," he muttered, shaking his head.

"I had to Josh. It was hard. I still don't know if it was right. But I knew that that child would have a better opportunity for education an' a better opportunity for life. An' I selected you, the first-born."

Josh held his head in his hands and mumbled, "Sissy . . . my mother." He looked at Avarilla sharply. "Does Orin know?"

Avarilla shook her head. "I don't think so. I think he believes what I told him."

"Just as I did," Josh replied bitterly. "Who else knows?"

"Just myself an' Sissy, but she hasn't quite put it all together yet, even with your comin' back to the Ridge. An' the granny women, Jewell an' poor Faye, they assisted in the birthings. An' Reverend Hooper."

Josh managed a grin. "Well, I guess the secret's pretty safe. Sissy's not all there, Faye's dead, and Roma tells me the preacher's only rowing with one oar. Do you plan to tell Orin?"

"I don't know."

"What do you want me to do? How am I supposed to react?"

"I want you to promise to say nothin' of what I've told you."

"Not acknowledge my own brother, my own mother?" Josh was incredulous. "and who, may I ask, was my—our father? Or is that a secret too?"

"That is even a secret from me, Josh. I don't know. Sissy's husband, Ben, did not give her children. He was drafted into the army an' was killed overseas." She measured her words. "He was already dead when Sissy conceived."

"Wait a minute. This is too much for me to follow. You mean you haven't any idea who fathered Orin and myself?"

Avarilla bowed her head. "None. An' Sissy denied bein' with another man." She lowered her voice. "I suspect that she was raped an' the poor thing could only live with it by forgettin' it."

"Jesus, what next?" groaned Josh. He looked up. "But what has this got to do with Roma and me?"

The old woman licked her dry lips. "I don't know how to say it except to say it plain, Josh." Then the words tumbled out. "Orin is Roma's father."

Josh sat back. The flesh beneath his tan paled. "Then that makes me Roma's uncle." He slammed his fist down on the table again and again until Avarilla got up to comfort him.

"Josh, I'm sorry. I don't know what to tell you."

"Then tell me this. Isn't it true that Roma has been . . . intimate with Orin?"

"Yes, that's true."

"Jesus! Are they aware of their relationship to one another?"

"Roma wasn't, at the beginnin'. But Orin has always known."

"What happened to Roma's mother? Who was she?"

"Martha died givin' birth to Roma."

"Then who raised her?"

"Why, Josh, we all did. I've explained how things are here on the Ridge."

"Then why didn't somebody explain to Roma . . . about incest?" Avarilla flinched at the word. "Or do we call it something different up here in the mountains? 'We take care of our own.' Isn't that what you said? Hah! Some care you took of Roma!"

Avarilla touched Josh's shoulder, but he pulled away. "Sometimes, Josh, there's no stoppin' somebody from gettin' what they want."

"You mean Orin?"

She nodded. "I don't know what makes Orin the wild thing that he is. It seems like I could never control him. He always took what he wanted. God forgive me for sayin' it, 'cause he's my own flesh an' blood, but sometimes I—I don't like Orin."

Josh looked at his grandmother with suspicion.

"You know what I mean, Josh? I love Orin, but I don't like him." The old woman's eyes were glazed with tears. "Don't pull away from me, Josh. Don't you think I repent for what I did? Perhaps Orin needed to have his brother beside him. Perhaps he would have turned out different."

"What makes you think I'm so perfect?" Josh asked sadly.

"There's good in you, Josh. An' you're strong, stronger than you realize."

"Maybe you should have given Orin away and kept me."

Avarilla turned away. "Maybe I should have. We sometimes live to regret our decisions, Josh. But now you've come back to the Ridge—to me."

"And do you think that's going to make a difference?" asked Josh. "Jesus God! You gave me away, your own flesh and blood. How in the hell do you think that makes me feel? Do you think I should be jubilant now that you're telling me what I needed to know all my life? I guess deep in my heart of hearts I knew that things weren't as they should be with Mom and Dad. We didn't really seem to belong to one another. Do you know what I mean? In a way, it comes as no surprise that we didn't."

"They were good people, Josh. They loved you an' they provided for your schoolin'. Orin's had none."

"The city mouse versus the country mouse, eh? Let me tell you, *Grandma,* for all my education, I've never felt at home in the city—any city. What's that old saying? You can take the boy out of the country, but you can't take the country out of the boy." He sat down. "I guess I've always been waiting to return. So what good is all that education now?"

Avarilla's expression was hopeful. "Then you will—stay on?"

"Stay on," he repeated. "You make it sound so simple. Already the complications are far greater than anything I could have imagined. What do I do to make a living. Dig up arrowheads and sell them to tourists? Plant corn? Raise hogs? How do I live in the same community as my twin brother without acknowledging him? And how, in God's name, can I give up Roma?"

"But you must. It's not—natural."

"Oh yes, everything must be according to nature's plan. Well, I can't give Roma up. I'm in love with her."

"Are you sure it's love, Josh, or somethin' else? I'm not so old that I don't remember passion. I know how strong it can be."

"Oh yes, there's passion. That's for sure. But it goes much deeper than that. Maybe it's because we're related, I don't know. But we're on the same wavelength. We know what the other's thinking without speaking it. There's a comfort in being with Roma that I've never had with any other woman. She's like me, and I'm like her. Aunt Avvie, you've seen us together—caring, touching, talking. Can you honestly say that our attraction is just sex?"

She shook her head. "No, I can't honestly say that, Josh. But it can't continue. It's against nature."

"Against nature! Since when is love against nature?"

They looked at one another for a long time. Then Josh pressed his head against his grandmother's breast and Avarilla kissed the top of his head. "Josh, I'm sorry. I'm sorry for everythin'. But I couldn't keep the truth from you any longer. It's been my cross to bear. I feel that my burden has been lifted. I know you will think things out an' will do what is right—for all of us."

Avarilla was gone. But the echo of her words remained. Josh sat, a stunned expression frozen on his face. His entire world was turned upside down, and he was slow to react. The full impact was yet to come.

He flung out his arm and knocked the cups and saucers to the floor. The sound of the breaking china routed the spell which had been cast over him. "Now that was Goddamn smart. Now I have to clean up the Goddamn stuff."

After sweeping up the broken cups and saucers and wiping the floor, Josh stripped and took a shower. He dried, donned fresh clothes and left the camper. He needed to take a walk. He needed to sort out everything Avarilla had told him.

20

Although the sun was bright, the morning air was sharp with autumn. Josh avoided the pathway to the Thicket and the house beyond. He didn't want to see Sissy; he wasn't prepared for that yet. As he turned toward the village, he glanced over his shoulder at the covered bridge and recalled the night he had been frightened by Jewell Runion. His memory was fuzzy. He hadn't paid much attention to her insane ramblings, but now what she had said seemed important. She'd babbled something about twins and the preacher lying. But what would the preacher have to lie about? Josh believed Avarilla, but his instincts told him that she had withheld something. She hadn't revealed all of the facts concerning the circumstances of his and Orin's birth. Did she, in fact, know the identity of his father? Did the preacher? And if he knew, then Faye and Jewell must have also been privy to the information. Josh decided that he had to ask a few careful questions. According to Roma, the preacher was insane. He wouldn't be of much help. But perhaps Jewell could be.

In the village Josh was surprised by the activity which greeted him. The young men were hastily assembling various booths for the fair, attended

by the young women, who kept them in
sandwiches and cold drinks. Josh stopped to
watch them work. It was ludicrous, he thought.
Who was going to come to a small mountain fair,
and for what reason? To buy a jar of homemade
preserves? A doll made of cornhusk? His eyes fell
upon a youngster hammering a board into place.
The tool was tightly held by a deformed hand.
Near him a girl of twelve, her forehead shadowed
by facial hair, poured drinks into tin cups. A
robust boy of fourteen concentrated on the nail he
was driving, his thick eyebrows growing together
so they appeared to be one. A child of ten was
struggling with a paintbrush clamped between
paw-like hands.

That's what the tourists would be coming for—
the freak show. Not to buy preserves, cornhusk
dolls or handmade quilts, but to view the odd band
of youngsters who lived on the Ridge. Josh suddenly felt ashamed. Whether that feeling was
brought on by his own thoughts or the thoughts he
had projected upon others, he did not know. He
turned away.

The sun had grown warmer now and he was beginning to perspire. He removed his sweater and
tied it around his waist as he approached Sophie's
General Merchandise Store. Sophie liked him and
she might have some information to impart. Josh
took the steps two by two, and took the door
handle. The door was locked. He knocked, and the
inside bell tinkled. Through the window he saw a
shadow moving toward him.

Sophie was in her bathrobe. Her face was pale,
and her hair fell about it in limp, untidy curls.
"Oh, my," she stammered. "I must look a sight, uh
huh, a sight. I just this minute got up."

"You're sleeping late, Sophie."

"I haven't been sleeping well at night. I've been trying to catch up in the mornings. Come in, Josh, and have a cup of coffee." She stopped him at the doorway to her living quarters. "If you'll just give me a minute."

A lone kerosene lamp burned on the counter. Josh wondered idly if she kept it burning all night. Within a few minutes Sophie, her hair brushed and her face washed, motioned him through the curtains. "I thought you'd be getting ready for the fair," Josh said.

"The fair?" Sophie replied vaguely. "Oh yes, Summer's End. That always sounds so sad to me. I hate to see summer end. Everything begins dying then, uh huh, dying. Sit, Josh, sit. I'll pour you a cup of coffee. You're right, uh huh, absolutely right. I must prepare the store. It's the best time of the year for business." She emitted a hard laugh. "It's the only time for business anymore."

"I don't understand, Sophie. Except for you, everyone seems to disapprove of tourists. Why the fair?"

"It only lasts one day," she sighed. "And I suppose that will eventually stop like everything else."

Josh wondered how he was going to ease her into the subject he wanted to talk about. He asked brightly, 'How long have the fairs been taking place, Sophie?"

"Ever since I've lived here. It used to be real lively, with dancing and kegs of beer and so many, many nice, friendly people, uh huh, friendly. They came from all around. But over the years they've stopped coming, uh huh, stopped. Only stray tourists make it up to the Ridge anymore." She spat out the words. "Backpackers, hippie kids, those with no money to spend." She offered a quick smile. "Of course I think we could get them all back. People forget . . . things."

"What do you mean, Sophie?"

Sophie jumped up from the chair. "I forgot. I made some cinnamon rolls. I like something sweet in the mornings, don't you, Josh? It sort of helps you wake up, uh huh, it sort of helps."

Josh was determined not to let the subject drop. "You mean the disappearances, Sophie?"

Her hands flew to her throat. "How did you . . . ah, yes, the disappearances." She puckered her lips. "It sounds so mysterious, doesn't it? Just like Amelia Earhart, uh huh, just like. Well, of course, it's common knowledge. But the plain fact is, it hasn't helped business, not at all." She cocked her head to one side. "My husband was one of the first to disappear." She cupped her hand to her mouth and whispered. "I've always suspected foul play."

"Why is that, Sophie?"

"He wouldn't leave me on purpose," she replied defiantly. "We were too much in love, uh huh, too much."

"When did this happen, Sophie?"

"It was in the autumn of 1949. I suppose that's why I dislike the autumns. Of course, there were disappearances before that."

"A bunch of college kids from Wesley," ventured Josh.

"Why, yes, I think so. We hadn't lived here for more than a season when word came that they'd got themselves drowned."

"Perhaps your husband was drowned, Sophie."

"Oh, no, not Kalem. He was a wonderful swimmer. What a figure he cut in his swimming trunks. Wait, I'll show you. I have a picture of him."

"Oh, don't bother yourself."

"It's no bother. The album's right by my bed." Josh frowned. He wondered how he was going to get her around to talking about Sissy's pregnancy.

Sophie returned, pushed the plate of cinnamon buns aside, and opened the flaking leather album. "Here, here he is. A fine figure of a man. The suit was knitted. Maroon, as I recall."

Josh glanced at the picture and stopped chewing. He held the album up to the sunlight. The camera had caught Kalem Balock admirably. Twenty-four and aware of his imposing physique, Balock had flexed his muscles as he posed. The sun was in his face, and his deep-set eyes were nearly shut. They were additionally shaded by the thick black hair which fell over his forehead. He was smiling, but it was a manufactured smile. His teeth were large and very white.

"He had the most wonderful hair and best set of teeth I ever saw on a man. Uh huh, in my entire life."

"He looks familiar . . . ." Josh began.

Sophie slipped the album from his grasp. "You're forgetting your cinnamon buns, Josh."

"Where was this taken?"

"That was from our honeymoon on Maryland Beach."

"But isn't there one of you, Sophie?"

"I'm afraid not. Kalem forgot to take one of me. Have another cinnamon bun. I thought I'd make up some for the fair. Sell coffee and buns at an outrageous price." She twisted her mouth. "That is, if anyone comes this year."

Josh casually asked, "Do you happen to

remember when Orin was born?" Sophie looked at him oddly.

"In the fall. November, I think. Why would you want to know that?"

Josh shrugged. "Just curious. After all, he's my cousin, and no one seems to acknowledge the father."

Sophie's face darkened. She jerked her head away from Josh's gaze. "I don't know anything about that." She stood up. "I've got to get to work. If you'll be kind enough to excuse me, uh huh, excuse me."

Josh persisted. "You weren't around, then, when Orin was born?"

"No, no, I never—I wouldn't want to see *that!* I have a weak stomach, uh huh, a weak stomach."

"Then who attended Sissy?"

Sophie looked confused. "The granny women, uh huh. Avarilla, Faye and Jewell."

"What about the preacher?"

"The preacher?"

The bell in the front rang sharp and clear. Sophie stuck her head through the flowered drapes. There was no one there, but the bell was still shaking. She looked at Josh sternly. "Why do you want to know these things?" She gathered her robe about her. "They got nothing to do with you. Uh uh, nothing."

"Has Jewell come back from visiting her family?"

"I don't know."

"But you do know where she lives."

Sophie was breathing heavily now. "Down, down the road, opposite the Thicket. The house needs painting. Weeds all over the place." She stood next to the drapes, nervously twisting them in her hands.

Josh softened. "Well thanks, Sophie. I'll leave you alone now so that you can get ready for the fair."

"Yes, yes," Sophie muttered. "I must do that. I must—get ready."

As Josh was walking past a booth advertising "Apple Cider," he saw Alex.

"Hello, Alex," he greeted. Alex smiled broadly. "Are you in business yet?"

"I just got the sign up. Cider doesn't come in until tomorrow. You be coming to the fair?"

"I wouldn't miss it," lied Josh and continued on.

A country fair was the last thing on Josh's mind. He was trying to decide what approach to use on Jewell Runion. Josh stopped and pressed his forehead against a tree. Roma, Roma, why did everything have to get so mixed up? There's no way I'll give you up, no way.

The house was as shabby as Sophie had said. It needed a man's hard muscle to set it right. Josh let himself through the front gate. On the porch he knocked and called Jewell's name. When there was no answer, he entered the house. In the front hall he looked into the mirror, straightened his hair and called Jewell's name once again. He wandered into the parlor and then into the kitchen. The kitchen was cluttered with undone dishes and spoiling foodstuffs which had not been put away. Thinking that perhaps Jewell might be working in the yard, Josh pushed open the screen door leading to the back porch. The area was littered with a cracked whetting stone, unused tools, and a collection of flowerpots.

Josh sat down on the step and wiped the perspiration from his forehead. The day had grown even warmer and he was thirsty. The stone well beckoned; he licked his lips at the thought of a drink of cool well water. "Just what the doctor ordered."

He got up and walked through the weeds to the well site. After spitting on his hands, Josh began to turn the crank. The weight surprised Josh. He suspected that the bucket might be caught on something. He dug his heels into the earth, ground his teeth together and continued turning. As the thick rope wrapped itself around the wooden cylinder he could hear water streaming from whatever he was raising from the well below. The sweet odor of decay began to permeate the air and, as it grew more intense, black-winged blowflies, drawn by the smell, began buzzing maniacally around the well opening.

Josh saw the top of Jewell's head first. Her hair resembled unbraided hemp. The body turned, and her eyes, protruding and opaque like the eyes of a beached fish, stared inquiringly at him from a gray and bloated face. Then he saw the rope which was wrapped around her broken neck, cutting into her rotting flesh. "Jee-sus!" Josh looked away but continued turning the handle. When he could turn no more, he secured the handle and brushed away the flies which were now attacking his sweating face.

Josh had seen dead people before, but not like this. His father had looked relaxed in his coffin. Someone had said, "He looks like he's just about ready to sit up, doesn't he?"

His mother, carefully made up, appeared to be

sleeping. *"She never looked so good."*

Once, in New York, he had walked by a man who had been hit by a car and had suffered a heart attack. There had been no blood. The man's eyes were closed and he was peaceful. "Move on. Come on, buddy, take a walk."

Josh forced himself to turn. He grasped his throat as his eyes flooded with tears and he began gagging.

The body held but half its flesh.

The top half of Jewell Runion was still intact. The flesh was spongy and close to falling from the bones, but still whole. Josh staggered backward in horror. Except for the white and thoroughly picked bones, the bottom half of her body did not exist at all. The crawfish had done their work.

21

Josh could not look at Orin's face. Instead he concentrated on his brother's hands, watching them while Orin worked. They were large and capable, clearly the hands of a person who had spent most of his time out of doors. A network of veins covered the backs and stood out in harsh relief. And as Orin reached for the hammer, Josh saw that his palm was as tough and calloused as the paw of an animal. He became self-conscious of his own soft-blistered hands.

"You do nice work, Orin." Josh leaned against the sawhorse while his brother put the finishing touches on Jewell's casket.

Orin took a long time to answer. "I do better work when I have more time."

"You mean when the body doesn't have to be buried in a hurry?"

Orin turned to look at Josh. "That's right," he replied evenly. "When the body doesn't stink."

Josh had already decided he didn't like Orin. The fact that they were brothers—twins—didn't alter that. And the knowledge that he had slept with Roma increased his dislike. "Do you ever think about dying, Orin?"

Orin grinned crookedly. "At thirty-two? That's a

little early to be thinkin' about such things."

"Not so early. People die all the time. From the cradle on."

"Not up here. They mostly die of old age."

"Jewell Runion didn't die of old age."

"She sure as hell smells like she did."

"I thought you liked Jewell."

"I did . . . when she was alive."

"I guess you don't have many suicides up here." Orin shook his head.

"An ugly way to do it."

"Well I guess it isn't as easy here as in the big city. There you got gas, you got pills, you got high buildings." Orin laughed and continued working. "Jewell, she had her well."

Josh persisted. "Being so close to death sort of makes you feel vulnerable."

"I never thought about it," replied Orin.

"You expect to live forever?"

"I'm livin' now. That's what counts."

"But at our age, we begin to experience death. It comes to friends, relatives," he paused, "parents."

Orin stopped work, pondered the meaning of Josh's words but said nothing. Josh went on. "Don't you ever think about your parents dying?"

Orin spat onto the sawdust which covered the floor. "I only got one parent."

"That's right. You never met your father."

"I'm a bastard," Orin said evenly, then he grinned. "You knew that, Josh. What are you fishin' after?"

"Nothing. I just wondered if you were ever curious about . . . your father."

"Why should I be? I'm here, he's not."

"How do you know he's not here?"

"If he were here, I'd know it," Orin replied

softly. "An' I'd kill him."

"Yeah," admitted Josh. "I guess I'd feel the same way." He looked back to the casket. "Nobody makes out a report, anything like that?"

"Not up here."

"Just bury them as quickly as possible?"

"When they smell, yes. If you want to be useful, you can help me load the coffin onto the cart."

"There's to be no wake, no service?"

"Got to get her in the ground as quickly as possible."

"Are you going to take her to the graveyard?"

Orin nodded.

"I'll come with you."

"Don't need no help," Orin replied quickly.

"I'll come anyway."

A tuft of dry grass moved in front of a stained headstone. A fieldmouse, brown and sleek, emerged and scurried toward a berry bush several graves away. The snake, a copperhead, tracked the rodent's movements. Slowly it unwound its sinewy body and slid through the grass until it, too, reached the berry bush. The fieldmouse was standing on its hind legs, reaching for a low-hanging treat. The copperhead hissed and struck. The mouse squealed, but it was too late. The snake dove forward and swallowed it whole.

Reverend Hooper turned his head away. He should have shouted to warn the fieldmouse. The preacher railed at himself. The incident reminded him all too clearly of his impotence in other matters. As he was returning to the church, he saw two figures approaching in the distance, a horse-drawn cart between them. He ran up the front steps of the church and disappeared inside. He kept the doors open a crack and watched.

The cart transported a casket. But there had been no funeral, no wake. Why had he not been called in? And who had died?

As the procession neared, Reverend Hooper identified the first man—Orin Chastain. Hooper shuddered. A stormy night in November so many years ago. A young woman's agonized cries. The first birth, and then the infernal deliverance of a second child, the spawn of the devil, and praise be to God, its ultimate destruction.

The preacher's eyes widened as the second figure walked into the sunlight. His eyes shot back to the first man and then back again. He was filled with horror. Rubbing his eyes in shock, he muttered a prayer.

"What hath God wrought?" he whispered. "*They live!* Both of them live. The devil has dug his way out of the grave an' survived. *Survived.*"

Orin set aside his shovel. "That deep enough?" questioned Josh. The hole was no more than three feet in depth.

"It's deep enough," replied Orin. "Now give me a hand an' we'll slip it in as easy as a finger in . . . ."

The coffin fell into place with a dull thump. Orin started to shovel dirt into the hole when Josh caught his arm. "Shouldn't we say something?"

"I got nothin' to say. If you got somethin' to say, say it."

Josh knelt, picked up a handful of dirt, and sprinkled it on top of the casket. "Rest in peace, Jewell Runion," he whispered.

They filled in the hole and patted the mound smooth. Then Orin erected a small wooden marker on which he had carved Jewell's name, hammering it into the ground with the flat side of the shovel. Then he looked at Josh. "Come on, we'll ride back." They climbed into the cart and sat down side by side. Orin cracked the whip over the horse and the wagon moved away, slowly disappearing in the rising dust.

Reverend Hooper, his frightened eyes on the dissipating dust, made his way to the fresh grave. When he saw the marker he burst into tears. "Jewell, sweet Jewell. So this evil has also caused your death." He fell upon the mound of earth and embraced the grave. "God help me to stop this blasphemy!"

Orin pulled up in front of Roma's house. He cast a sidelong glance at Josh. "Isn't this where you're wantin' to go, cousin?"

The mocking tone of Orin's voice infuriated Josh. He drew back his fist and swung around to stare into his brother's face—his own face. Disconcerted, he unballed his fist and dusted off his pants. "I'm obliged, Orin."

"You're a lot of things, Josh. Obliged is only one of them."

Roma wiped her hands on her apron and went to meet Josh. "I just got back from Aunt Avvie's. I thought you'd be here." He took her face in his hands and kissed her. It was an expressionless kiss, not the kind she was used to receiving. "Josh, are you all right?"

"Yes. Yes, I am now. Orin and I just buried Jewell. I need a bath."

"I'll put the water on."

"It still doesn't seem right to me . . . no funeral services of any kind."

"It wouldn't do anyone any good to have to go through all that."

Josh sat down at the table. "I know, I know. I guess I'm just a little shook up still. God! If she were going to commit suicide, why didn't she pick an easier way?"

"Like pills or gas?"

Josh looked at her.

Roma shrugged. "We don't have those things here on the Ridge."

"That's what Orin said."

Josh watched Roma's face for a reaction. There was none. She got up and began filling pans and buckets at the indoor pump. She said at last, "What made you go to see Jewell anyhow?"

"I just wanted to see that she was all right. She seemed to be so distraught over her friend's death. When she didn't answer I tried the door. It was unlocked. I went inside, but she wasn't there. I thought she might be working in the garden so I went out the back way." Josh frowned. "If I hadn't been thirsty, I might never had found her. I still think she deserved some kind of service."

"Aunt Avvie said that there's a time to be born an' a time to die," Roma added. "Jewell Runion just picked the wrong time."

"That's rather callous." Josh was quiet for a moment, then he asked, "Would you like me to stay on in the Ridge? Is that why you seduced me, Roma?"

Roma smiled. "That's one of the reasons."

"And what about Orin? I'm sorry. I had to ask."

Roma sat down opposite Josh. "Orin was my first. I was thirteen when we mated. But he didn't force me. I wanted him as much as he wanted me."

Josh winced, and the words were out of his mouth before he'd realized he'd spoken them. "And did you enjoy it?" he asked.

"It was satisfyin' for both of us," Roma replied matter-of-factly.

Josh couldn't hold back any longer. He stood up. "Goddamn it, Roma. You're so casual about the whole thing." She looked at him blankly. "I know Orin's your father." Roma shrugged her shoulders. He knelt in front of her and more gently said, "You don't seem to understand. That sort of thing has an ugly name attached to it. It's not right. It's not . . . normal."

Roma twisted her mouth, making it ugly. "It seemed normal enough to us," she replied sharply.

"Roma, I don't mean to hurt you."

She stood up. "Then don't—talk about the past." She went to check the water on the stove.

"But don't you understand? I . . . ." Josh caught himself. There was no point in explaining that he and Orin were twins, and that she was his niece. From all indications, the revelation wouldn't have bothered her. He decided to withhold the information a little while longer, if he ever told her at all.

The rising steam furnished an ethereal backdrop for Roma. "The water's startin' to boil. You get undressed an' I'll fill the tub."

Josh obeyed and, as he climbed into the tub, Roma knelt to wash him. "By the way, we finished the quilt."

Twilight quietly drifted over the mountains and the mauve sky became feathered with rose and violet. Josh awoke with a start. The image of Jewell Runion, hanging above the well shaft, had crept into his dreams. Looking around, Josh realized that he was in Roma's bed.

Next to him the cornhusk mattress was indented with her body and the sheets smelled of sex and Je Reviens.

"Roma?"

"In the kitchen," she called.

Josh threw aside the covers and rushed into the kitchen. Roma was standing next to the stove. He wrapped his arms around her and pressed his nude body against her back. "I thought I'd lost you," he whispered.

"You won't lose me, Josh."

"What are you doing?"

"Makin' caramel apples for the fair."

Josh clapped his hands together and laughed until tears came to his eyes. "That makes everything all right."

"Josh, don't make fun of me. It's the only thing I can make."

Josh swung Roma around. "With your looks and expertise in other departments," he inclined his head toward the bedroom, "you don't have to be Julia Child, too."

"Who's Julia Child?"

Josh began laughing again. "It doesn't matter, Roma."

"You hungry? You want some supper?"

"Do you have bacon and eggs?"

Roma nodded.

"Then let's have that. I'll fix them."

Josh cooked while Roma continued making caramel apples. While they were eating, Roma asked, "You'll help me take the apples to the village?"

"Do you think they'll be safe overnight?" asked

Josh in mock seriousness.

"Who'd want to steal caramel apples?" replied Roma. Then she realized that Josh was making a joke. "You can stop teasin' me."

Roma separated the caramel apples with wax paper and carefully packed them in baskets. Then she and Josh left for the village.

Josh was surprised by the transformation of Chestnut Ridge. The booths were finished and were stocked with homemade goods to sell. There were foodstuffs to be sold, native handicrafts as well as games of chance. As they walked, Josh asked Roma, "How many people do you expect?"

"We'll be lucky if fifty show up. Seems like there are less an' less each year."

"Is there any advertising?"

"What do you mean?"

"Posters, notices, ads in newspapers. Things like that."

She shook her head.

"You've got to advertise if you're going to sell the product, and the product in this case is Summer's End."

Roma looked at Josh. "Perhaps next year."

While the fiddles cried and the banjos thrummed, the tourists and their children—eyes bright, coins ready—wandered among the booths. The turnout from the neighboring towns was surprisingly large; at least a hundred people had traveled up the mountainside to enjoy Summer's End.

The residents of Chestnut Ridge were joyful. They were taking in more than enough money to see them through the winter months.

Josh turned away and melted into the crowd. He

tried his luck at the games of chance and bought snacks from the various food stalls. Avarilla's revelations still occupied his thoughts. She *had* to know who had fathered himself and Orin. Even if Sissy could not provide the answer herself, in a community as small as Chestnut Ridge, secrets were hard to keep.

Sissy! Josh could not come to terms with having Sissy as his mother. She was a defective human being, and he had always considered himself a perfect specimen, at least physically. This made him all the more curious about the identity of his father.

As he walked among the tourists, Josh overheard bits of their conversations. "Did you see those funny-lookin' hands?" "Get her to make change." It was just as he had suspected. Many had come out of curiosity, to see the "freaks" close up. "Do they all have eyes like that?" He was beginning to understand Avarilla's hostile feelings toward outsiders. Without realizing it, he had come to think of himself as a native of the Ridge.

Josh found himself in front of the booth where Marinda was selling fruit pies by the slice. He watched her cajole the tourists into buying. She appeared completely unaware of their whispers and glances. When the group had moved on, Josh sauntered up to the booth and placed a quarter on the counter. "I'll have a slice of rhubarb."

Marinda smiled sweetly. "It's the best. It's also the very last piece."

Josh bit into the pie and without really tasting it, commented, "Mmmm, it's delicious."

"Yes," agreed Marinda. "I'm good at pies." She looked toward the general store. "Not as good as Mrs. Balock, but still, they're right tasty."

"Do the tourists ever stay over here in the Ridge?" Josh asked.

Marinda shook her head. "No. They're afraid to." She seemed to enjoy this knowledge.

"Because of the disappearances?"

"That, an' other things."

"What other things?"

"We're . . . different up here. People are afraid of other people who are different."

Josh decided to take advantage of Marinda's willingness to talk. "I was curious about the preacher," he said smoothly. "Does he ever leave his church?"

Marinda busied herself with her pies. "I don't know."

"But you've seen him?"

"Oh, yes."

"I understand he's not quite right. Is he able to talk?"

"We're not supposed to talk to him."

"Has he always been . . . strange?"

"Ever since I can remember. You're not eatin' your pie."

"I'll take it with me."

When he was out of Marinda's sight, Josh chucked the remainder of the pie into a trash barrel. He visited Roma's stall. Her caramel apples were selling fast. "I ought to be able to close up early, Josh. You'll come back with me?"

Josh grinned and replied. "I'm afraid if I come along, love, you'll not be getting to your chores. Besides, I'm enjoying myself," he added with false enthusiasm. "I'll be by later on."

Avarilla's booth was larger and busier than the others. Josh stood behind the customers. There was a "sold" sign on the flying bird quilt. The other items were rapidly being depleted—corn-husk dolls, pickles and preserves, homemade soap and a variety of baskets. Josh figured that his grandmother had spent the entire year making these items. He admired her perseverance.

She was charming the visitors by giving them a demonstration of how cornhusk dolls were made. She saw Josh and waved. Josh waved in return.

Behind Avarilla's stall, Reuben was doing a brisk, if discreet, business selling his wares. He would more than make the two hundred dollars needed to get him through the months when it was too cold to manufacture liquor outdoors.

Josh bought a pint from him and finished it off behind a tree. He was hoping that the liquor would raise his spirits, but it had just the opposite effect. He became depressed, morose. He wanted to get away from the fair and be by himself.

Near the edge of the village Orin was using his horse and cart as a ride for the tourists' children. Josh stood in the tree's shadow. His brother was flirting outrageously with the mothers of the youngsters. Josh smiled to himself and contemplated joining Orin at his stand. That would be something to make the women take notice.

We should have gotten together a magic act, Josh mused bitterly. One of us could be nailed in a coffin and buried. Then the other could appear behind the audience to startle and amaze all. Maybe next year. Josh was surprised at how easily that thought had joined the others. *Maybe next year.* Was he going to stay in the Ridge? Give up his career and New York City and . . . but he almost forgot . . . he had already given up Cresta.

Ten yards away a flat section which had been covered with pine boards nailed together was

being used by the tourists for square dancing. Alex
was doing the calling, while the three young musicians played. Josh wondered idly what had happened to the three old men. Perhaps they had
retired themselves from their musical activities. A
few people began to dance. Josh thought sardoni-
cally that the scene was a real slice of Americana
. . . . unless one looked close.

Brandishing a torch, Reverend Hooper moved
through the Holiness Church of Jesus Savior. He
prayed in a loud, quavering voice as he drove the
serpents from their places of sanctuary. Starting
in the choir stalls and swinging the torch in a low
arc, he forced the snakes through the altar rails
and into the main part of the church.

"I cast thee out! Return to the wilderness
whence you came! I have set before thee an open
door!"

In the glow of the torchlight the preacher's skin
looked repulsive and artificial. Lack of exercise
and poor diet over the years had turned the robust
man into a ruin. "An' the Lord said, 'Behold, I give
you the power to tread upon serpents!'"

The snakes, repelled by the heat, wiggled and
slithered toward the open doors of the church.
Some, angered, struck at the preacher. Their
venom ran down his boots like spittle.

He worked his way along the pews, one arm
waving the torch, the other grabbing handfuls of
snakes and flinging them into the aisle, which was
now alive with writhing reptiles. His face was
suffused with blood, his eyes white, the pupils cast
up, as he raved his lunacies. "I shall take up
serpents an' they shall not hurt me, for I am
anointed!" He pulled at his hair and pitched

himself from side to side, emulating the pattern of the swinging torch. "I *am* the weapon of the Lord!"

When Josh returned to Roma's cabin he was silent and withdrawn.

"You're real quiet, Josh. Is anything the matter?"

Josh looked up from where he was sitting. He smiled at her astonishingly beautiful face. "No," he replied vaguely. "Nothing I can talk about."

"It's that woman, isn't it?"

"Her?" questioned Josh, but he knew who Roma meant. "Cresta? No, I wasn't thinking of her. Honestly, I wasn't."

Roma persisted. "Do you still love her?"

Josh gazed at Roma thoughtfully for a moment or two before answering. "I loved Cresta because she loved me. I think that can be rightly called a reaction and not true love."

"She was beautiful."

"So are you, but in a different way. And I might ask the same question. Do you still love Orin?"

"Love him? I never *loved* him." She sighed. "But he'll want me back."

Josh went to Roma. "I don't understand what you mean, Roma."

"Don't you? Can't you tell by the way he looks at us? He's just waitin' for you to leave an' then he'll have me again."

"And if I don't . . . leave?"

Roma looked directly at Josh; the pupils of her eyes were pinpoints. "Josh, I'm afraid. I almost hope you go. That way you'll be safe."

"But even if I go," said Josh evenly, "you don't have to do what Orin wants."

"You don't know him," Roma said. "You *don't*."

"Well, I'm not going any place, love. I want to stay here."

Roma turned. "You really mean that, don't you?"

"Yes."

"But Orin . . .?"

"Orin doesn't frighten me, Roma. I can take care of myself. Josh walked to the open window. "I feel different here. It's like I was never really myself before I came here." He sniffed the night air. "It's like the mountains have somehow transfused their power into my blood. I feel different and yet the same and I don't ever want to leave. Perhaps I cannot."

Roma joined him at the window. "Do you think you could be happy here, Josh? Happy with me an' this life?"

"I don't honestly know. I don't think I've ever experienced happiness." He slid his arm around her waist. "But there are things which must be reconciled."

"You mean your job?"

"No . . . other things."

"What other things?" Roma asked carefully.

Josh kissed Roma on the lips. "They don't seem important now," he whispered. "Don't be afraid."

Roma smiled at the moon, "I'm not afraid any more."

Night had come to Chestnut Ridge. Having driven the serpents into the woods, Reverend Hooper stood in the doorway of his church and breathed in the crisp air. The moon sliding across the heavens caused the yellow light to alter and change. The vibrant rays bleached out the lines in the preacher's face and added vibrant color to his hair, and in that moment he looked young again.

"I am filled with joy, sweet Jesus, an' with the Holy Ghost! An' if any man hears my voice an' opens the door, I will come to him."

Tears of happiness coursed down his rutted cheeks. He no longer feared the night.

22

Summer's End was over for another year. The following day the natives of Chestnut Ridge wasted no time in taking down the banners and dismantling the booths. They worked in haste and good humor. They were anxious to go home and prepare themselves for their Saturday social. Life had resumed its normal pattern in the mountain village.

Watching the residents at work in the fading light of the afternoon sun, Josh was reminded of Pieter Brueghel's medieval paintings of peasants. Nearby a group of youngsters were playing games. From what Josh remembered of his childhood, he assumed it was hide and seek. One little girl with a hairline extending nearly to her eyebrows leaned against the base of a red maple, covered her face and counted while the others, shrieking, ran away.

The screen door of the general store opened. Sophie Balock shuffled onto the porch and began gathering up empty boxes. In the failing sunlight, she didn't see Josh, who was sitting on her steps.

"Looks like you sold out, Sophie," he remarked.

Sophie straightened up. "Oh, Josh, you startled me."

"Here, let me help you."

"No, no, I can manage, uh huh, manage."

Josh, ignoring Sophie's protestations, took the boxes from her and carried them into the store. The place looked as though it had been ransacked. Barrels and boxes were empty of goods. The shelves had been stripped. Even the last piece of hard candy had been sold. With all the merchandise gone, the store looked drab and depressing.

"Looks as though you've been robbed," said Josh.

Sophie managed a half-smile. "Now I wonder who was robbing who?" She placed her hands on her hips and, standing in the center of the floor, made a complete turn. Her smiled became an expression of triumph and she drew herself up to her full height. "Well, that's that, uh huh, it sure is."

Josh inclined his head toward Sophie and offered her a questioning look.

"Selling all this junk is gonna get me out of here."

"You're leaving Chestnut Ridge?"

"That's right. I'm leaving. Uh huh, leaving."

"You're going away? When?"

"As quickly as possible," Sophie sang out. "Tomorrow at the latest. Uh huh, the very latest."

The lines of tension had disappeared from her face, for the first time since he had known her. She looked truly happy.

Beneath the floor, not four feet below where Sophie and Josh stood, two people lay facing one another on the ground, their bodies touching, their deformed hands entwined, listening to the conversation above.

Marinda moved closer to Alex, pressing her

narrow adolescent body against his. In response Alex grinned and crookedly slid his hand downward. He undid the buttons of his pants and withdrew his formidable penis. Marinda, still listening, wrapped her fingers around Alex and massaged him while she worked her dress up over her hips. Then she guided Alex into her. He moaned. She touched his lips with her hand, signaling him to remain quiet so that she could listen to Sophie and Josh's conversation.

"So you're leaving the Ridge, Sophie. Not many do that."

"I've been planning it for years. Now that I have the money, nobody's going to stop me." She moved around the store as she continued speaking. "I never belonged here. I was never liked. You shouldn't have to be somewhere where you're not liked."

"Where are you going to go, Sophie?"

She looked surprised. "Go? I haven't given it much thought. The main thing is to get off this damn mountain. But wherever I go, there's going to be people who are friendly, uh huh, friendly and nice to me. And there's got to be a beauty parlor." She primped before an imaginary mirror. "I've let myself go, uh huh. I surely have. But a good perm and a color rinse should set things right."

"When are you leaving, Sophie?"

"Tomorrow morning," she announced. "I got myself a ride. Uh huh, down to Jericho Falls."

Josh smiled. "You don't waste any time."

"Not any more," replied Sophie. "I've been wasting time for years."

Alex dug his fingers into Marinda's buttocks as he rode his climax to its conclusion. Marinda, ahead of him, bit down on her lower lip to keep from crying out. Her sharp teeth penetrated the soft flesh, and blood began to flow from her mouth into Alex's. Shuddering and twisting, they held onto one another tightly until their throes had subsided. At last they broke apart and gave their full attention to the conversation taking place above them.

Josh took Sophie's hands and turned her around to face him. "Before you go, Sophie, I need to know some things."

"What things?" Sophie asked guardedly.

"I think you know." Sophie shook her head and tried to pull away, but Josh held her fast. "Who made Sissy pregnant, Sophie? Was it your husband? Was it Kalem Balock?"

"I never knew for sure," wailed Sophie. "How could I? I certainly wasn't there when it happened. I do know this, Kalem had an eye for every pretty thing that lived here. Sissy was only one of them. Uh huh, only one." Her face became ugly and bitter. "I went there that night, you know."

"Where? Where did you go?"

"I went out looking for Kalem, I heard from Jewell Runion that Sissy had gone into labor. When Kalem didn't come home that night, I thought he might be with her." Sophie shivered. "It took all the courage I had. It was a stormy night and I hate storms."

"Tell me what happened," Josh asked, scarcely controlling the excitement in his voice.

Sophie closed her eyes and began. "I'd started off two or three times, but the storm scared me back. But I was jealous, uh huh, and finally I just grabbed the lantern and left by the back door. I didn't want anyone to see me, to know what I was doing. I was wearing Kalem's black slicker. I don't know what I would have done if I'd found him there at Sissy's. Cried a lot, I suppose. I hid at the edge of the Thicket. The rain had stopped by then. I saw Avarilla arrive and heard Sissy screaming. Lord, how she screamed. The window to her bedroom was partway open, uh huh, and I saw a man pacing about. I was sure it was Kalem. So I snuck over to the window and looked inside. It wasn't Kalem after all, but Reverend Hooper. I looked in the other windows. Kalem wasn't there. I guess he was in somebody else's bedroom that night. So I come on home.''

"You didn't see anything unusual?"

"No. There were a lot of other windows I could have looked in that night for Kalem Balock, but I didn't. Maybe I didn't really want to know. It was only the next day that Kalem didn't come back home at all.''

"Did he take anything with him? Clothes? A suitcase?''

"No, nothing. He just didn't come back." She added vehemently, "I hope to hell he was killed!''

"But you didn't . . . hear anything concerning Sissy and that night?''

"Well there has been talk. Uh huh, gossip. But I was never one for repeating . . . .''

"Repeat it, Sophie!" Josh demanded.

"I over . . . rather, I heard Faye and Jewell talking about that night. It didn't make sense to me. They said two babies were born, only something was wrong with one of them. Uh huh, and one died and was buried someplace.''

"Died? Buried? What do you mean?''

"I don't know what it means. It scared me. They

went on about evil and Satan and I didn't want to hear any more. I have to go now, uh huh. I have to pack."

Josh realized that he had gotten all the information out of Sophie that she had to give. "One more thing, Sophie. Would you have a spare snapshot of your husband that you could give me?"

Sophie looked at him. "You can have any of them. All of them. I'm not going to mourn Kalem Balock any more."

Josh selected the photograph of Kalem in a bathing suit, put it in the breast pocket of his shirt, and thanked Sophie. As a parting gesture, he kissed her on the cheek. "I hope you like your next home better than here. Good luck."

Sophie's eyes misted as he walked out of the store. Then her thoughts returned to her packing. "And I won't say goodbye to anyone."

Josh walked slowly through the village. He was more confused than ever. Faye and Jewell had said that one had died . . . but both he and Orin were alive and well. Perhaps Sophie didn't hear the conversation properly, since it was obvious that she had been eavesdropping.

He took out the photograph of Kalem Balock and held it up to the sunlight. The resemblance was remarkable. He hadn't seen it at first. But now the nose, the jawline, the deepset eyes, the texture of the hair, even the structure of the body were more than adequate testimony that he had fathered Sissy's babies. Damn it! And he had abandoned them all. Left his wife, Sissy, his children and the mountains. Jesus, didn't anyone in Chestnut Ridge know what happened to Kalem? If he was dead, then Josh wanted to know for sure.

If he wasn't, then somehow, some way, he would find his natural father.

Josh was heading for Roma's cabin. Suddenly he halted and changed his mind and his direction. He would go to the church. The preacher would know the truth about the night of his birth.

The day was quickly fading. Josh stopped by the camper and picked up a flashlight. He climbed the path leading to the church and started as something on the ground twisted and moved away. It was a copperhead. Gingerly he walked in a wide arc around it and hurried on his way. The church, bathed in an eerie green-gold glow, loomed before him. The front doors were open. He called out the preacher's name.

Josh stopped to listen. He could hear nothing except the echo of his own voice fading into nothingness. The coming night pressed around him like a physical weight. It was as if the air had thickened. Josh reached the bottom step and flashed the beam about. A black snake uncurled and wiggled away, becoming lost against the night.

Josh investigated the rest of the steps thoroughly with the light before stepping onto them. He stood before the open doors, straining his eyes against the blackness inside. "Reverend Hooper, are you there?" There was no response. Josh stepped inside and aimed the beam around the interior of the church. He saw the pews, the pulpit and the Good Shepherd window. He started down the aisle, keeping the beam close to the floor in case there were any more serpents.

Josh heard someone breathing. He swung the beam around and cried out in horror. The round circle of light illuminated Reverend Hooper's cadaverous face. The preacher's eyes were unfocused and glazed, his mouth slack and a yellow froth edged his lips. "Who is it?" His voice, thin and agonized, sounded as if it were coming from somewhere very far away. Josh let the light fall. He turned the beam around so that the old man could see his face. The preacher staggered backwards as if he had been struck by a mighty force.

"You're—not—Orin!"

"No, I'm not," Josh answered. "I'm Joshua, Orin's twin."

Reverend Hooper's face became distorted with fear and his eyes became protuberant, as if two tiny animals were clawing to get out through his eyes. He thrust his arms in front of him, holding the palms flat, the fingers spread apart as if trying to block out Josh's image. "You came . . . back from the . . . grave! Avarilla killed you . . . we buried . . . *you* . . . under the willow tree!" Then suddenly his back arched like a bow, his mouth stretched open and a scream, horrendous in its power, issued from the depths of his own purgatory.

There was a sharp crack followed by a splintering sound and then a deafening roar like an explosion. Josh looked up. The stained-glass window had shattered. Shards of colored glass flew in all directions. He covered his face with his arms to protect himself, and when at last he looked back at the window, the remaining lead filling silhouetted against the sky resembled a web spun by a giant spider. Except for the face of Christ, there was not a pane of glass left. Then the lead holding that piece snapped. The pane dangled for a moment, turning slowly and distorting the features of Christ. Then it, too, fell, crashing to the floor. The glaring, evil light of the moon flooded into the church.

Josh, thinking the preacher might have been hurt, flashed the light on him. His eyes were tightly shut. He didn't appear to notice the phenomenon which had taken place. The preacher's eyes snapped open. He threw back his head and shrieked with hysteria. The yellow froth turned scarlet. "There is no God!" he screamed. "There is only the devil!"

Josh began to gag. He stumbled down the aisle, crashed into pews, fell, recovered and lurched forward again. The light pitched crazily in front of him. On the porch he leaned over the edge and retched. Still trembling, he closed the doors of the church. It was a symbolic act, as if closing the doors could forever seal away the ghastly image from his waking mind.

23

Sophie was sitting on the edge of her bed, counting her money. Her hair was tortured into rag curlers after having been freshly tinted with strong, black coffee. Her face was slathered with cream and she was wearing her favored nightgown, a confection of white eyelet lace and pink ribbons. She licked her fingertips and finished the stack of bills and the handkerchief full of silver. She pursed her lips and exclaimed, "Six hundred and twenty-six dollars and forty-five cents. Damn! It still comes out different. I'll just do it one more time. Uh huh, one more time."

Next to the bureau were the two suitcases Sophie had packed. One more night and then freedom. She'd arranged to ride with Reuben, who was taking a delivery down to Jericho Falls in his horsedrawn wagon. Sophie wasn't looking forward to the trip and Reuben with his smell and all, but it didn't matter. After all, she was getting out.

In the kitchen, a curved talon as sharp as a dagger neatly slit the wire screening of the door. Then a hand reached inside and flipped open the hook. The fingers of the hand were foreshortened and the thick thumb receded into fur-covered flesh.

Sophie stopped counting and turned her head toward the kitchen at the sound. She jumped up; the change in her lap fell clattering to the floor. She looked at the flowered drapes in the doorway leading to the kitchen. Why hadn't she taken them down? The curtains billowed slightly. A breeze, that was it! She had left the kitchen door open and the screen door latched. It was just a pesky breeze and nothing more. She bent down to pick up the coins, but she kept her eyes riveted to the ruffled drapes.

She would not feel truly secure until she investigated. She chided herself for being like a frightened child who couldn't sleep at night until it looked beneath the bed. She had nothing to fear now, Sophie reasoned. She was leaving that accursed community, going to start a bright new life.

She hurriedly swept the coins into the handkerchief and tied several knots to keep the silver from spilling again and set it on the nightstand. She smiled at her own foolishness and, barefoot, padded over to the drapes. She raised her arms to open them. The taloned hand slashed through the fabric and the nail of the longest digit cut neatly through the tip of Sophie's nose.

Sophie screamed and staggered backwards. The curtain was ripped to shreds by two pairs of grotesque hands. Sophie stared in horror at the visitors. The human identities of Alex and Marinda were still visible, but they were much changed. Marinda's cheeks were covered with hair, her flared nostrils larger, her eyes beneath now shaggy brows yellow and glowing. Her lips were stretched back over her teeth, which had become large and sharp. Alex's entire face was heavily furred. His ears were large, elongated and pointed at the tips. Four large incisors, two bottom and two top, distorted his mouth.

Sophie, bleeding, backed into the closet door. Alex and Marinda were changing. They threw back their heads and howled as the fur sprouted and grew. It was a painful yet sexual sound, as if they were experiencing some kind of masochistic climax.

Alex dropped to the floor and began moving toward Sophie. The shotgun! Her hand flew out and clutched the doorknob of the closet. Alex dove at her, his powerful teeth clamped around her narrow wrist. Sophie shrieked; he snapped it like a dead branch. Screams of agony shattered the night. His incisors worked through muscles, tendons, and arteries, until the hand was torn from the arm. Sophie's bulging eyes were riveted on the bleeding stub at the end of her sleeve. Sophie fell to her knees and rolled under the bed. Marinda's claws caught her bare feet and rent the bottoms like knives cutting through warm butter.

Despite her pain, Sophie had the presence of mind to tear a ruffle from her nightgown, and, using her teeth and her remaining hand, tied a tourniquet above her mangled wrist. Her hair and curlers became entangled in the springs of the bed. Sophie pulled and twisted but managed to leave several clumps of hair behind. She dragged herself to the head of the bed and pressed her body against the wall. Tears of fright and pain blurred her vision. She blinked them away as she tried to will her mind to function. Thinking as a process was impossible; Sophie could only act from the instinct of survival.

Sophie heard them breathing and saw them
crouching on either side of the bed, savoring her
whimpering fear. Marinda stood up. Sophie
watched as she walked on padded feet toward the
nightstand. The patterns of light began to shift.
Marinda had picked up the kerosene lamp. The
shadows began moving crazily, and Sophie
smelled the acrid odor of kerosene. There was a
loud whoosh; she knew with heart-rending certainty that Marinda had set fire to the bed.

The coverlet ignited first and fingers of smoke
began to drift toward the ceiling. As the flames
burned Sophie was shocked into a vital realiz-
ation. "My money!" she cried. "Oh, my money!"
Her escape was blocked by Alex and Marinda
standing on either side of the bed and her hope
chest at the foot. Sophie moved to the back wall,
shoved her arm up between the wall and the brass
headboard, and pushing, managed to make a space
large enough for herself. She grasped the headboard and pulled herself to her feet. The bed-
clothes were in flames. The paper money, curling
and burning like leaves, was turning into bits of
blackened soot which floated toward the ceiling.
Sophie, weak from loss of blood, knew she was
going to die. But with the money gone, she didn't
really care. Through the feverish flow of the fire
she saw the creatures positioned by the bed. They
were watching her. The pillows were burning now,
and the stench of burning feathers filled the air.

Sophie moved sideways, hoping to reach the
bedroom window. Suddenly the bed was brutally
slammed against her chest, breaking her ribs and
driving one of them into her spleen. Again and
again the heavy headboard crushed Sophie's body.

The brass was hot. The flames licked her night-dress and she heard a crackling sound. She realized her hair had caught fire, and mercifully Sophie slipped into unconsciousness.

Later Sophie's body was dragged away to a secret place. A feasting place.

Josh lay face down in the dry and brittle grass. How long he had lain there, he couldn't say. Time seemed to have stopped there on that lonesome hillock. Perhaps it was a moment or two, possibly half an hour. His hands were pressed against his head and he massaged his skull, as if the pressure would somehow alleviate all the horror he had seen. The past weeks blurred together and rushed through his tortured mind like a nonstop nightmare—seeing the strange skull, coming to Chestnut Ridge, meeting the deformed young people, the hideous cave in the coal mine, Avarilla's revelations, Jewell Runion's body, and finally the hideous ravings of Reverend Hooper.

He wanted to scream until his throat was raw and bleeding. But his larynx was tight and constricted, and even his sobs remained pulsating in his chest. Josh sat up and rubbed his temples. The throbbing pain in his head subsided, and he could breathe normally at last.

There *was* an answer to everything which had happened. That answer lay buried beneath the willow tree near Avarilla's house. He stood up.

A red glow and plumes of black smoke were coming from the village. The youngsters must have built a bonfire with the dismantled booths. He heard the nasal twang of a fiddle and the lively plunk-plunk of a banjo. The Saturday night social would be starting soon. Earlier, Avarilla had mentioned that she was taking Sissy with her that night as a special treat for her work on the quilt. Josh made plans to meet Roma there.

But he wasn't going to the social, not now. He began walking the path which would take him to the Thicket and, he hoped, his past.

24

Avarilla's house was dark and could not give testimony for what it was about to witness. Josh's footsteps were silent as he crossed the yard. When he was halfway between the willow tree and the house the countryside was suddenly lit up by a shard of lightning. The sky moaned, and the previously peaceful clouds began to churn. Josh blinked but did not stop. A violent gust of wind swept the silvery branches of the willow to one side, leaving the thirty-two-year-old gravesite open to the night. Josh froze. Silhouetted against the electric sky, a shovel was jammed into the earth. Waiting for him.

Josh moved toward the shovel. As he touched the handle, thunder blared from the heavens and lightning galvanized the countryside. He raised the shovel and plunged it deep into the earth. A piercing wind shrieked, and its cries were echoed and re-echoed throughout the Thicket.

As the hole grew deeper, the odor of the rich soil became mixed with something else—something long forgotten, long dead.

Josh knelt and looked into the shallow grave. Bits of rotting material were folded around something. It crumbled in his trembling hands and revealed a small skeleton inside. Josh was puzzled. A shadow appeared beside him and stretched across the grave.

"That was Reuben's pup. I told him it ran away."

Josh turned, and looked at Avarilla. The wind blew tendrils of her hair across her face. "Tell me the whole story this time."

She knelt beside him and spoke in a flat, emotionless voice. "I reckon it all began with Kalem Balock. After he moved here, things started changin' in the Ridge. Kalem was as evil as he was handsome. Oh, he could be charmin' as all get-out. An' I was fooled like everyone else. I didn't suspect a thing. None of us did. It was beyond our fancies. Even when our farm animals were found dead, their throats torn, their flesh eaten, we didn't suspect. A pack of wild dogs, we told ourselves. But then outsiders, tourists, began disappearin' an' I knew that an evil force was in our community." Avarilla's voice turned bitter. "Kalem ws a ladies' man. He caused every female heart in the Ridge to flutter. He bedded most of them. But that wasn't none of my business." She paused. "Till he turned his attentions on Sissy. Despite her . . . affliction, Sissy was real pretty. I warned Kalem to stay away from her. I warned him.

"Sissy got pregnant. I wasn't sure who the father was. But I was still foolish enough to think that Kalem had heeded me. Foolish, foolish old woman. Sissy got bigger an' bigger every day. But I didn't think it was twins. Big babies ran in the family. Her time came early. I was in Jericho Falls attendin' Leoma. Her baby was born dead, an' they were both brokenhearted. They wanted that baby so bad." She glanced up at the turbulent sky.

"There was a big storm that night, an' I almost didn't get back to the Ridge. When I got back home I found a note from Jewell. Jewell an' Faye were worried about complications an' had called in Rev'rend Hooper to do some prayin' over her." She laughed bitterly. "A lot of good that did.

"Reuben was only twelve then. He was upset by Sissy's cryin' out. So he took his pup an' went to sleep in the barn." Here she paused and ran her hands over the mound of soil as if drawing strength from the rich earth. "Toward midnight you were born. What a fine-lookin', healthy baby you were, Josh." Her voice began to break. "Then, a short time later, another baby came." Avarilla gasped, unable to keep the horror out of her voice. "An' that baby bore the mark of the beast. It was covered all over with hair, just like an animal. An' it had claws."

Josh looked at Avarilla. Her face, bleached white by the lightning, was unnaturally composed. And he knew that she was telling him the truth.

"The preacher swore Jewell an' Faye to secrecy an' sent them home. He an' I knew what we had to do. He went out to dig the grave, this grave. I took the baby an' laid it on the kitchen table an' went to get a knife. Then—then the baby changed before my very eyes. The hair an' claws disappeared an' he looked just as normal as the other one. How could I kill him? How? He had come from Sissy's body. He was my own flesh an' blood. Tell me, how could I end his life?

"I hid the baby an' I snuck out to the barn an' got Reuben's pup. I cut its throat, wrapped it in a piece of flannel an' then, the preacher an' me . . . we buried it.

"The next day I took you over to Harley an'

Leoma. I can't call it love at first sight, because I
saw you first. Oh, how they rejoiced. You were like
a miracle to them.'' She reached out and touched
Josh's cheek. "I gave you away because I loved you
the best." Her voice became hollow as if she were
speaking from a great distance. "I kept Orin here.
I thought that way I could watch him, find a
pattern to the changin', an' keep him out of
trouble. Then Kalem came to call. The very next
night he showed up at the house an' demanded to
see his child. He began laughin' an' asked if it
looked like him. An' as he laughed he began
changin'.''

"Changing?''

"Changin' into his beast form. Half-man, half-
wolf. It was a terrible sight. My blood runs cold
just to tell of it. He started to come up on the
porch, but I was prepared for him. I had a shotgun, an' I shot him an' I killed him. I carried his
body to the Lookout an' dropped it off the bridge.
It fell into the stream an' was carried down to the
river.''

"Oh, my God!" exclaimed Josh. "Then the skull,
the bones were . . .''

"Kalem Balock.''

"My father.''

"Even in death, Kalem reaches out to curse us
all.''

"You believe that Kalem Balock was a . . . a
werewolf?''

Avarilla nodded.

"How could such a thing happen? How did he
get that way?''

"I don't know, Joshua. I can't even imagine.''

"And where did he come from?''

Avarilla took a deep breath. "Somewhere in Europe."

"I just can't believe this."

"Joshua, believe what I tell you," Avarilla said gently. "You saw the remains of Kalem Balock. You can't explain away that." Avarilla cried out in aguish. "God help me, but I kept Kalem Balock alive in Orin! So many people have paid for my foolishness. So very many. You see, I believe Orin caused the mine accident that killed all those men. When he was still a teenager he had bedded every woman in the Ridge, married an' single, an' made each of them pregnant. Yes, he killed those men. He wanted their women all to himself."

"You're saying that the children are . . . ."

"All his. All like Orin. Like Kalem. Only to a lesser degree. They cannot change as fully as Orin, but they can change."

"That means Roma is one of them," Josh groaned.

Avarilla nodded slowly. "But it's Orin who makes them do evil things. He has power over them. They do everything he says. Orin wants Roma back. She has no choice but to go to him."

"No! I won't let that happen."

Avarilla quietly added, "Orin means to kill you."

Josh looked at his grandmother, hoping that she was exaggerating, but he knew that she was not. He suddenly thought of Cresta. "My God, Cresta. Do you suppose Orin let her leave?"

"I don't know. I liked her even though she was an outsider. I prayed for her safety."

"Who did you pray to? Surely not God?"

"I pray to the powers of nature, Josh. Look, look

around you. Can't you feel its power? Can't you smell it?" The air was charged with the over-whelming aroma of ozone, and the thunder was so powerful that it shook the earth on which they stood. She put an arm around his shoulders. "Don't you see you were meant to return? Now you must take your rightful place. After all, you were the first born."

"What are you saying?"

"The others, the ones who are only partially tainted with the strain of the wolf, can be tamed. But not as long as they follow Orin. This evil must be stopped. An' the evil is him . . . *him.*"

"You mean . . . kill him?" Josh's voice was hoarse with emotion.

"Yes."

"When?"

"Tonight. Now."

Josh stood up. "There's no other way?"

She shook her head sadly.

"Where do I meet him?"

"You'll find him." Avarilla embraced Josh. "Go with my blessin', Joshua."

A blessing or a curse, Josh wondered. He walked away into the darkness.

Josh moved like a sleepwalker down the Thicket, towards the covered bridge. He looked to his right; in the distance he could see the Lookout. There was a glow coming from it as if it were on fire. And he knew instinctively that that was where the ritual would take place. He hurried through the shivering woods and reached a pathway leading to the Lookout. The giant boulder was lit by scores of torches stuck in the earth and wedged in between rocks. It looked like a gigantic birthday cake, Josh mused.

Birthday. Birth Day.

Appropriate.

He braced himself as he stepped onto the swinging bridge. Gripping the rope rails, Josh willed himself not to look down. Though falling into the gorge would be an easier death than what he was to face.

Easy now. One foot in front of the other. A whipping wind caused the bridge to veer sharply to the left. Josh closed his eyes and went on.

As Josh stepped onto the boulder, a distant shaft of lightning charged the night sky.

Silhouetted against the brilliant backdrop, gathered singly and in groups, they were waiting to watch the spectacle.

The time of the beast had come.

Josh took off his boots. He preferred to be barefoot. A leather sole could slip on the smooth surface of the rock. Then he removed the rest of his clothes. He did not want the fibers of the cloth driven into the wounds. Josh sucked in the night air and waited. For the first time in his life he knew he was at a disadvantage. It was a sensation he had never before experienced, and it was very lonely. There was no way he could win. Orin was cruel and would want to savor his advantage, reducing him slowly, watching the life flow from him until the ultimate death.

Josh dragged his gaze around the "arena." The young people of the Ridge were in full attendance —Alex, Marinda, and all the others. They were in their human forms, their eyes glistening, their faces expectant and their mouths hung open in bloodthirsty grins. They were there to enjoy his destruction.

He didn't see Roma among them. He was glad.

From the other side of the boulder, Orin emerged. He, too, was nude. He offered Josh an arrogant smile. It was the smile the victor bestowed upon the vanquished. He moved forward on the balls of his feet toward the center of the boulder.

Josh felt sick and bloodless. Every nerve in his body was jumping, and he envied his brother his confidence, his power, his life. The only way he could bring honor to himself was to see how long he could stay alive. Josh went to meet his opponent, his twin, his brother, his executioner.

The two men faced one another, dropped into a crouch and began circling, looking for advantage, their nostrils flaring and their eyes blazing, their exhaled breath becoming plumes of white mist.

A woman's scream rent the air. Roma rushed from the bridge onto the boulder. She stumbled to the center and collapsed beside the two men. Wrapping her arms around Orin's legs, she cried, "Orin, don't do this. I'll stay with you. I promise. Let Josh go." He looked down at her with scorn, kicked out and sent Roma sprawling across the stone. Several of the others rushed to her side, not to aid her, but rather to restrain her. They dragged her to the edge of the rock and held her fast as the fight continued. Josh realized now that Roma was the winner's prize.

Josh swung a fist at Orin's face and, while the blow landed, it had no more effect than if it had struck a concrete wall. Orin threw back his head and laughed. Then, with the back of his hand, he struck Josh across the ear and sent him reeling to the ground. Roaring flashes of pain exploded inside his head.

Orin advanced and kicked Josh in the ribs. Josh

groaned in agony. Another powerful kick struck
him in the face. Orin's sharp toenails tore into his
cheek. Josh rolled away from his brother. Placing
his palms against the surface of the stone, he
pushed down hard and managed to get to his feet.
Orin was in no hurry. He stood sturdy against the
rising wind, a proud grin splitting his face. There
was a ripple of laughter among those who watched
and an anguished sob from Roma.

The two men circled again, poised to attack.
Josh moved in fast and appeared to slip. His feet
shot out from under him. He was on his back.
With a cry, Orin lunged forward. Josh rolled away,
jumped to his feet and was out of range. Orin
looked up from a prone position. His face had
turned ugly. Rolling fast, Orin got to his feet and
began forcing Josh toward the swinging bridge.
Josh, unaware of his position, continued backing
up. Suddenly, Josh felt the bridge post press
against his buttocks and knew he had been maneuvered. He started to break, but Orin blocked him
with a brutal kick in the stomach, knocking the
breath out of him and forcing him backwards.
Instinctively Josh reached out to grab the rope
handles for support and left himself completely
unprotected. Orin hit him full in the face with
both fists. Josh staggered blindly, a gagging sound
breaking from his throat. He fell against the rope,
causing the bridge to swing. Josh slipped from the
boards and dropped into space.

His hands, flailing wildly, caught hold of the
wooden slats. When he was sure he had a firm
grip, Josh started to pull himself back up. Before
he could complete the action Orin stepped onto
the bridge, his eyes gleaming, his teeth flashing.
Using the full weight of his body, Josh began

swinging himself back and forth, causing the
bridge to also move. Orin could not keep his
balance and was forced to jump back onto the
boulder. Josh used those few seconds to pull himself up onto the bridge and standing. Lowering his
head, he dove at Orin like a pile-driver. Josh's head
crashed into Orin's chest and it seemed as if the
huge rock itself quivered with the impact. Orin
was down. Roaring with anger, he clamored to his
feet and staggered toward Josh.

Then, with extraordinary speed and power, Josh
rushed at Orin, leading with the flat of his left
hand. The blow struck Orin's nose and caused jets
of blood to spurt from each of his splayed nostrils.
Orin fell backwards against a pile of large rocks
which supported a torch. The flames burned the
flesh of his shoulder, and a deep growl emitted
from Orin's throat. He wrenched the torch from
its holding place and advanced toward Josh,
swinging it in front of him in a bright arc of light.

The pain inflicted on their leader riled the
others. Several began to will themselves to
change. Josh stared in horrible fascination. One
young man's eyebrows began to grow straight
until his entire forehead was covered with bristly
hair. A female entwined her hands and held them
high in a prayerlike attitude. Her nails, growing
long and white, resembled candle tapers. Roma
spoke his name just once. It was borne on the wind
to the valley, where it grew in volume until it became a shout of desperation. Then Roma dropped
to her knees and elbows and began clawing at the
surface of the rock.

Orin slammed the torch down across Josh's left
shoulder, and Josh fell to one knee, grunting with
pain. He swung his left hand up, grabbed the stalk

of the torch and wrested it from Orin's grasp.
Then he plummeted it upwards, striking Orin
brutally in the stomach.

Josh's eyes widened in horror. For a moment he
had the distinct impression he had injured himself.

The hair covering Orin's abdomen began to
crackle and burn. Orin roared, lurching backwards. His heel caught on a loose stone, and he fell
onto his left shoulder. He lay still, regaining his
strength. The spectators sucked in their breaths
and waited.

Josh flung the torch over the edge of the
boulder. There was an eerie silence. Orin twisted
and turned upon the rock. And when he righted
himself he was no longer completely human.

Orin threw back his head and howled.

It appeared as if a shadow passed over Orin's
body. But it was not a shadow. Hair sprouted from
Orin's quivering flesh. He closed his eyes, and an
ecstatic expression transformed his face. His
upper lip began to quiver, then giant incisors shot
downwards to be joined by a row of equally sharp
bottom teeth. His nostrils opened and widened.
The hair on his head began to vibrate and move
downwards, joining that of his eyebrows. The eyes
seemed to recede into the head, and when he opened them they were lit by some inner fire.

Josh reeled, stupified. The surge of optimism
which he had felt just a few minutes earlier
evaporated. He knew that he was about to die. He
looked down at Orin's hands, if indeed they could
be called hands any more. They bristled with hair
and were distorted into near-paws. The thumbs
had receded; the remaining fingers were now
tipped with curved and deadly talons.

Orin lunged at him. The claws tore into Josh's flesh. He felt his blood begin to flow, and he knew that his death was going to be by sheer butchery. As he moved away from the half-natural who was his brother, Josh's fear gave way to something that was even stronger in the human spirit. He became angered at the injustice, the imbalance of the conflict. The sky suddenly filled with an unearthly glow, unlike anything Josh had ever seen. It was as if all the lightning from all the storms in the world had struck that night. He stretched his arms to the skies and drew strength from the electrically charged atmosphere. He felt the galvanic power enter his veins and he, too, began to metamorphose.

His bare flesh tingled as shafts of hair forced their way through his epidermis. His fingers and toes writhed as they began to alter and change shape. He felt his toenails elongate and curve downward, scratching the rock on which he stood. His nostrils suddenly opened, and he smelled things more acutely than ever before. His ears reformed themselves, and night sounds entered them which he now understood. His testicles tightened in his scrotum. His penis sheathed in its protective foreskin, changed shape and sent vital signals careening through his groin. His eyes gained a wider periphery of vision and came into true focus for the first time. He opened his mouth to cry out in pleasure. Instead, his jaws stretched forward, his teeth lengthened and sharpened in a bray of joy that became instead a howl of triumph.

Josh turned on Orin. Now they were truly twins. The beast looked out through his eyes, something previously leashed by his own hand, now summoned from the depths of his shoul. Fright flick-

ered briefly in Orin's eyes. Snarling, Josh sprang
and seized Orin's throat, sinking in his teeth to the
gums. He could smell Orin's fear as he tore open
his throat. The blood began to flow. And it was
good.

Orin crumpled to the ground. Before Josh could
continue, the others sprang to life. They fell upon
their vanquished leader and tore him to bits.

Josh loped toward his mate to claim her. Her
head was high, her eyes bright. His legs trembled
with excitement as he licked her.

Joshua Allen Holman had fulfilled his destiny.
He had taken his rightful place in the hierarchy of
man and beast.

He was, after all, the first born.

Epilogue

The Ospedale di Giacomo, an ugly, sprawling building of beige and umber stone, was located in the middle of Rome between the Via del Corso and the Via Ripetta. The hospital served the Italian film community as well as those employed in the other related arts, both national and international.

At 10:37 P.M., an ambulance, sirens shrieking, pulled up to the emergency entrance. The attendants sprang from the vehicle and eased the gurney across the concrete platform. The glass double doors opened automatically. The attendants expertly maneuvered the gurney past harried nurses, quarrelling doctors, and curious patients. And as they were passing the admittance desk one of them called to the head nurse, "Eight centimeters dilated."

The other added, "Says her doctor is Forcetti."

The efficient head nurse, unperturbed by emergencies, scanned the assignment sheets. "Take her to delivery. In the meantime, I'll page Dr. Forcetti."

A contraction attacked the young woman who lay on the gurney. Her face was bleached with pain and beads of perspiration clung to her body

like a cold, clammy mist. She pressed her fists
against her eyes and opened her mouth so wide
the pink of her lips blended in with her flesh.

"Hold on, little mama," said one attendant.

"We'll have you there in no time," said the
other.

Cresta fought back her tears, but she was un-
successful. She bit down on her lower lip and
clutched her swollen stomach. "No one told me it
was going to hurt this much," she said to no one in
particular. Her eyes overflowed with tears which
blurred her vision. She tried to concentrate on
something—anything but the pain. She watched
the ceiling, which was quickly moving above her.
Odd, she thought to herself, the ceiling made of
rough-hewn wood and vaulted like the apse of a
church, and yet the walls were white and shiny as
glass and the overhead lights were round
phosphorescent tubes, brutally bright. As the
lights rushed by her line of vision, scenes from the
past as disjointed as film clips assailed her mind
like hurrying nightmares. The suffering, the hurt,
the humiliation returned.

*The terrible empty room in Orin's house. His
perverse relish as he told her that it was he who
had slept with her that night she had mountain
fever. Sick with shame and revulsion, she fled from
the house. She encountered Reuben in a horse-
drawn cart and offered him fifty dollars to get her
away from Chestnut Ridge . . . away from Orin and
Josh.*

Another contraction tore through Cresta's body.
She cried out, both in pain and in protest of the
past. A nun, her face shiny and pink as if it had
been molded from marzipan, took her hand and
held it tightly as they waited for the elevator. The

nun's voice was filled with concern. "Soon, my dear miss."

Back to New York to a self-imposed quarantine in the apartment, weeping and cursing Josh and Orin. Then tired of depression, Cresta began, both emotionally and physically, cleaning house. She packed Josh's clothes and possessions and had them moved to the basement of the building. Screw him. He had treated her badly. She was going to keep the apartment.

The rising elevator gave Cresta the strange sensation that she was levitating. Any minute she would float up to the ceiling like a balloon. She closed her eyes. The sensation subsided but her stomach continued churning.

Jason was all too willing to arrange a European assignment for Cresta. He secured a very lucrative modelling deal for her in Rome. Cresta was intoxicated by the amazing city. Rome seemed to grow out of the ground, part and parcel of the rich and fertile earth around it. It was a city eroded by the weather and the sea, but it remained eternal. Cresta's ardor for Rome helped her to put aside her painful memories. She missed her period, but thought little about it, believing it a result of the recent upsets in her life. But when she missed her period a second time, Cresta made an appointment with a doctor.

The elevator doors opened and the overhead lights began again . . . glowing circles of brilliance . . . shimmering madonna's halos . . .luminous wedding rings.

The doctor confirmed Cresta's fear that she was pregnant. Since she had already informed him that she was unmarried, he delicately suggested that he could arrange for termination of her pregnancy. To her susprise, Cresta heard herself reply that she wanted to have her baby. It meant a loss of working time and, of course, the loss of a great deal of money. But she had plenty of money, stocks, investments, tax shelters, everything which accompanied the life of a successful model who had a smart business manager. Now she would have something more than money. She would have something to love.

The gurney was turned to abruptly to the left, and Cresta, clenching and unclenching her hands, cried out in agony. "Hurry." She pleaded, "Please hurry."

The modelling assignment led to a small part in a Fellini film. Cresta surprised everybody, including herself, with her natural acting ability, and there were promises of other roles. But as she neared her fifth month, she was simply too large. She contacted Dr. Anthony Forcetti, who was considered the best obstetrician in Rome. The doctor, concerned about Cresta's unusual weight gain, recommended a sonogram. Cresta was smeared with "jelly" and wired to the television-like computer. Soundwaves were projected through her body and they waited for the outline of the baby's form to appear on the screen.

"Just as I thought," the doctor exclaimed. "You're going to have twins."

Cresta was too shocked to say anything. She watched while the doctor outlined the babies' forms on the black-and-white screen. "You see, Cresta, they share a single outer membrance, the chorion. That means they are the same sex and will be identical." Then he pointed to the forms on the screen again. "And they're going to be boys."

The doors to the delivery room opened, and a

large, white-tiled space came into view. Cresta accepted a shot of Demerol and the nurses undressed and prepped her. She was placed on the delivery table and covered with sterile sheets. One nurse slipped the sterile leggings on her and, after Cresta was helped into the stirrups, another pair of hands sterilized her with Betadine, swabbing her with great gobs of cotton. "Don't push!" the nurse commanded.

Dr. Forcetti, a handsome Italian in his mid-thirties, loomed above her and offered her an encouraging smile. "You're a little early, Cresta. Three weeks early, in fact. Why did you wait? Why didn't you take a taxi to the hospital hours ago?"

"I wasn't sure," Cresta murmured. "And I was frightened."

"Didn't anyone come with you?"

"No," she replied harshly. "This is my project. Mine alone!" She began crying again. "I'm not going to die, am I, doctor?" Her voice was plaintive and reedy, like a little girl's.

He shook his head. "You're going to be fine. And the babies, too. They're just anxious to see the world." Dr. Forcetti hurriedly finished scrubbing and examined Cresta. "She's fully dilated," he announced. The drug began to take effect. Cresta smiled dreamily at Dr. Forcetti and said, "I'm glad I don't know which one it is. I'm glad. It makes them more mine."

The doctor didn't seem to hear her. "You can push now, Cresta!"

"Thank God." As another contraction overtook her, Cresta bore down, threw back her head and howled. The sound was so startling that one nurse crossed herself.

Cresta was sleepy when they wheeled her to a room on the ward. She was put into bed, given a sponge-bath by the nurse and dressed in a frothy pink nightgown her maid had brought to the hospital. Around one A.M. she awoke, unsure of where she was. Then she remembered. "My babies!" Cresta cried. "Where are my boys?" A nurse approached her bedside. Cresta demanded, "My twins. Are they all right?"

"Of course they are, my dear. Big, healthy boys, both of them.

"But where are they?"

"They're in the nursery. We'll bring them to you right away. Dr. Forcetti said you planned to nurse them."

Cresta waited anxiously for the twins to arrive. She only vaguely remembered seeing them after they were delivered. They were quite red and each had a full head of fine, black hair. Their eyes, exactly like Josh and Orin's, were light grey flecked with gold and reminded Cresta of mother of pearl.

The nurse, her face split in half by a giant grin, entered the room, carrying the infants. "You're going to literally have your arms full, Mrs. Farraday."

"It's Miss," corrected Cresta.

Without changing expression, the nurse presented Cresta's babies to her. Cresta was glowing as she kissed each of them and happiness streamed from her like sunshine.

"What are you going to name them, Miss Farraday?"

Cresta sighed, "I don't know. I've been making lists for months, but I haven't made up my mind."

Both infants began crying at once. The nurse smiled indulgently. "Here, let me help you." She undid Cresta's hospital gown and the babies eagerly seized Cresta's swollen nipples and began sucking.

Cresta leaned back against the pillows and gazed out the tall Gothic windows of the room. The gathering clouds parted to reveal a full moon, as thin and transparent as a communion wafer. One of the twins began to twitch his body and kick his feet as he tugged with more urgency at his mother's nipple. Cresta smiled. "They're so beautiful. Not just because they're mine, but they are beautiful."

"Yes, they are," agreed the nurse. "They're going to grow up to break every girl's heart in Rome."

"No, no," said Cresta quickly. "I'm going to be taking them back to New York City. That's where they're going to be brought up and they're going to have every Goddamned advantage I can give them. They'll be terribly spoiled and excruciatingly handsome, and they're going to have the best education money can buy. My boys are going to leave their mark on the world."